THE DARK ONE

"Gripping, intriguing, and sexy. Engaging characters and edge-of-the-seat action—this book has it all." —Christine Feehan

"*The Dark One* grabbed me and wouldn't let me go. Sensual and engaging." —Susan Squires

"This story hooked me from page one and never let me go. I can't wait for the next one!" —Amanda Ashley

"A deliciously dark world . . . with speckles of humor, great passion, and exceptional characters."
—*Romantic Times BOOKreviews*

"This well-written tale, complete with fascinating characters, utterly romantic love story, and divine sensuality, captivated me from the very beginning to the heart-stopping ending."
—*Paranormal Romance Writer*

"Completely, utterly, absolutely engaging. I was swept away by the story of Armond Wulf and Rosalind Rutherford. *The Dark One* is one of the most wonderful tales I've gotten my hands on in a long time. I'm so thankful Ms. Thompson decided to make this a series. The Wild Wulfs of London will definitely be on my 'must buy' list!" —*Romance Divas*

"Ronda Thompson delivers a fresh and everlasting Regency romance with a touch of magic and evil that will stand the test of time. Oh, and the smokin' hero helps!"
—*Romance Reader at Heart*

"I love paranormals, and this one is one of the best!"
—*Romance Junkies*

"Readers will believe in the existence of the werewolf . . . sub-genre fans will fully treasure the first Wild Wulfs of London thriller. 5 stars!" —Harriet Klausner

PRAISE FOR RONDA THOMPSON'S
WILD WULFS OF LONDON SERIES

THE CURSED ONE

"Chills will run up your spine as danger and passion rise, and Thompson works her magic. Succumb to the lure of the Wulf."
—*Romantic Times BOOKreviews* (4 ½ stars)

"Intense, sexy, and poignant." —*Fresh Fiction*

"Vivid description, wonderful characters, and a story line that holds you tight . . . destined for the keeper shelf."
—*Romance Divas* (5 kisses)

"Though I know I sound like a broken record, I make no excuse for it because the Wild Wulfs of London are Hot! Hot! Hot!"
—*Romance Reader at Heart*

"Thompson has written a story that will stay with me for a long time. She has put feelings and love into it and come out with a winner." —*Fallen Angels Reviews*, Recommended Read

THE UNTAMED ONE

"Thompson cleverly blends paranormal elements into a fine-tuned historical romance with well-crafted characters and a tender, blossoming romance."
—*Romantic Times BOOKreviews*

"*The Untamed One* is compelling and sexy. It's also smart and well written." —*Romance Reader at Heart*

More . . .

CONFESSIONS OF A WEREWOLF SUPERMODEL

RONDA THOMPSON

St. Martin's Paperbacks

This is a work of fiction. All of the characters, organizations, and events portrayed in this novel are either products of the author's imagination or are used fictitiously.

CONFESSIONS OF A WEREWOLF SUPERMODEL

ISBN: 0-312-94925-1
EAN: 978-0-312-94925-9

Printed in the United States of America

St. Martin's Paperbacks edition / October 2007

St. Martin's Paperbacks are published by St. Martin's Press, 175 Fifth Avenue, New York, NY 10010.

10 9 8 7 6 5 4 3 2 1

*To Linda Castillo. Thank you for always
being there for me, for believing in my talent
and for supporting me no matter what is going
on in my life. You're a true friend and
one hell of a talented author.*

CONFESSION NO. 1

Most women find the bloating, cramping, and bitchiness of PMS bothersome at worst. I turn into a monster a week before my period . . . literally.

Doing an underwear ad on a New York rooftop when it's blowing snow outside can get pretty hairy. And I'm not speaking figuratively. I like my job, but there are days when everything goes to hell. Today is one of them. The skimpy lace panties I wear ride up my crack. My bra is two sizes too small. I'm bloated and have a zit on my forehead that would make a Cyclops jealous. All these things have combined to make my day miserable, but now I've topped them all off with a fur outbreak.

"Lou! Are you coming out of there? The other girls have already gone up. We need to get moving!"

As I glance at the closed door, a growl rises in my throat. The photographer of the shoot, Stefan

O'Conner, thinks I'm in here primping. Sure I've been known to mess with my hair until I completely undo the stylist's work, but the hair I stare at now cannot be fixed. At least not without a good waxing product. My lip curls with disgust while studying the nasty patch of dark werewolf fur attached to my left shoulder. The wolf outbreaks during PMS started about six months ago.

I had almost convinced myself that what happened to me seven years ago on prom night was just a bad dream, like the nightmares that haunt me frequently. Now suddenly I'm prone to outbreaks that force me to face the reality that I am a werewolf. No ifs, ands, or buts about it. Speaking of butts, I turn my back to the mirror to make sure mine is normal. At least I haven't sprouted a tail . . . yet.

When I turn to face the mirror again, I hope I imagined the fur outbreak. No such luck. At least the past six months have prepared me. Slinging my beauty bag on the bathroom counter, I dig through it like a dog digs through a trash can.

My beauty bag is with me at all times now and represents my lifeline to normalcy. It weighs about ten pounds and is filled with every kind of beauty product available, plus my own tried-and-true concoctions, and what I like to call werewolf essentials. I'd start my own line, but as far as I know, I'm the only werewolf supermodel in the world.

How does one become a werewolf? you might ask. Good question. Now, more than ever, it's something

I need to find out. I have deduced the when and where. I am totally clueless about the how or why. But if I want to keep the life I've made for myself, it's pretty freakin' clear that I need these questions answered.

I manage to find the green goop I've been digging for in my beauty bag. While smearing it across my shoulder, I consider the only logical conclusion I've arrived at concerning my altered state. Werewolfism must be hereditary. The fact that I'm adopted makes the possibility even more likely. I'd pick up the phone and press my adoptive parents for information regarding my biological parents, but sometimes you really can't go home. Like after you've murdered the star high school football player on prom night.

"Lou Kinipski! I swear if you make me lose the good light and the good snow, I'm not working with you again!"

Stefan's threat doesn't faze me. He tries to be a badass when he's working, but I know he has a heart of gold. I also know he has a hot body that he doesn't mind sharing with all the other models. That thought makes me frown. My knight in shining armor can't seem to keep his sword under control. I'd be a hell of a lot more interested in his sword if he could. But the sword business aside, I owe Stefan.

He found me working in a small café on the East Side six and half years ago and launched my modeling career. He taught me to trust men again. He gave me confidence that I sorely lacked. He gave me a life when I thought mine was over. I'm a little in love with him, but it's that sword-sharing thing that keeps me from taking our relationship to the next level. That and the fact that I am a murderer. Oh, and that's on top of being a werewolf.

"Lou, please!" Stefan stoops to begging.

His tactics might work if my name were really Lou Kinipski. My agency urged me to change my name six and half years ago when I started modeling, but I refused. I had already changed it once. When I ran away from Haven on prom night seven years ago, I chose an ugly name as a reminder that I was once an ugly girl. I may be drop-dead gorgeous now, but that was not always the case.

As I stare at myself in the mirror, it's hard to remember that I was once butt ugly and a geek to boot. The night I turned into a werewolf, I woke up beautiful. It's as if there was a trade-off for what happened to me. Like I had an ugly disease and it suddenly went into remission. Now I have a werewolf disease and it suddenly is out of remission. I need to know how to send it back into hiding, and as quickly as possible.

Since I haven't done so well in the past six months finding answers on my own, I've made an appointment to see a private investigator this Thursday. It's probably not a smart move. A girl with as many secrets as I have is only asking for trouble when she pays someone to dig around in her life, but what else can I do? The answers must be out there somewhere.

"Lou! I'm counting to three and if you don't open that door I'm shooting without you! Got it?"

I might as well count with him.

"One . . ."

Holding my breath, I prepare for a great deal of pain.

"Two . . ."

This is going to sting like hell.

"Three!"

Ripping the waxing cloth away, I put a fist into my mouth to keep from screaming. I gag on the cuss words stuck in my throat.

"Lou, sweetheart, you aren't in there purging, are you?"

Sticking a finger down my throat and puking up calories would be preferable to the horrific sting going on in my shoulder, but I have no need to purge. Whatever happened to me seven years ago, it kicked my metabolism into high gear and kept it there. I can eat whatever I want and never gain weight. That happy thought is chased away by not only the sting going on in my shoulder, but the ache that erupts in my gums. I take my fist out of my mouth and take a look.

Great. Fangs. Just what I need. I close my eyes and breathe deeply in an effort to calm myself. It would be easier to relax if my panties weren't up my crack and Stefan weren't pounding on the door again. Even without those distractions, finding a happy place is difficult. There's more going on with me today than just PMS and werewolf outbreaks.

The nightmares that have haunted me for seven years are taking a toll. I had one last night. Behind my closed lids, flashes of the dream return to me. Him. Me. Sex. Then blood. Blood on the walls. Blood on the sheets. Blood everywhere. I shudder.

"Lou?"

Stephan's voice brings me back to my current dilemma. Upon opening my eyes, I'm relieved to see that the red place on my shoulder now minus the werewolf fur is already fading. I heal at an alarmingly fast rate, another gift of whatever curse has befallen me. Why do gifts always come with a trade-off? Why can't I be beautiful and not be a werewolf? And then there's the big question of how suddenly coming out of remission, or whatever I've been in, is now going to screw up my life.

Peeling back my lips, I see that the fangs I had a moment ago have retracted. Thank God. No fur. No "the better to eat you with" teeth. I'm ready to face the day. I flush the waxing cloth, adjust my two-sizes-too-small bra, dig my panties out of my crack, walk over and open the door. Stefan nearly falls inside.

"About time!" he growls. "I hope you feel good about throwing my schedule off and making the other girls turn into Popsicles on the roof so you can stand around and primp!"

"I do," I say, flouncing past him into a room that

looks like a war zone. Women's clothes are strewn everywhere. Blow-dryers, makeup bags, and shoes. A pair of giant lavender angel wings rests upon the bed. The wings are part of my outfit. I glance around for Cindy Emerson. Cindy does makeup and also serves as Stefan's assistant on shoots involving more than one model.

Stefan knows who I'm looking for. "I sent Cindy up with the rest of the crew. I'll help you into your wings. We need to hurry."

When he's working, Stefan is always in a hurry. He's full of nervous energy. I imagine it's because he's a Starbucks junkie and drinks about ten lattes a day. Rumor has it Stefan does not have the nervous-energy problem in bed. I hear he takes his time. Not exactly the kind of thing I like hearing about. I keep trying to put Stefan on a pedestal and he keeps screwing it up and falling off.

"Turn around, let me strap on your wings," he says.

Since the red place on my shoulder is still healing, I gladly give Stefan my back. The discoloration should be gone by the time we reach the roof and begin the shoot. His hands are warm against my skin. He smells good enough to eat. I don't know what cologne Stefan wears, but it always sets off a horny gene in me. Obviously, it sets off the same gene in all women.

"Pull your hair over one shoulder," Stefan says. "I don't want to get it caught in the Velcro attached to the wings."

After I do as instructed, Stefan's breath whispers across my skin. He touches me while he works. A delicious shiver races up my back. I try like hell to ignore it. If Stefan were just another handsome face with a hot body, I would have had him a long time ago. But our relationship goes deeper than mere sex. Or at least it does with me. I can't sleep with someone I care about. Not with all the lies attached to my past.

"Hurry up, will you?" I say, because my constitution is weak and I'm in a hotel room with a bald hottie. Stefan is bald because he shaves his head. He shaves his head because his father is bald and he knows he's going to end up that way one day, and he wants control over the situation. Did I mention that Stefan is a bit of a control freak?

"We're dealing with a little wind factor today," he says. "I need to make certain the wings are secure. Don't want you flying off the roof."

Wind, sleet, snow. I might as well work for the postal service. "You could have set this up inside," I complain. "Hot lights. Fake snow. Sounds good to me."

He makes a tsking sound. "It wouldn't look as original as this will. Turn around and let me have a look at you with the wings."

I turn around. Stefan's face is close to mine. We're nearly the same height, but I'm wearing three-inch heels and Stefan thankfully is not. He has big, dark puppy-dog eyes. They've been the downfall of many a model. I just can't be one on a list of many. Still, if the man had hair, I'd cave. I know I would.

"The wings are secure," Stefan says. "You look fantastic. Let's get to work."

When we're working, Stefan and I lower our guard and get nasty with one another. It's foreplay without the actual follow-through of sex, and it's as far as I'll go with him. I'm ready to get nasty with him today. More than ready.

'm not ready for conditions on the roof. The first thing I discover is that, like most men, Stefan lies. A little wind was an understatement. A little snow was an understatement. How about howling gales and a blizzard? How about goose bumps bigger than the zit on my forehead? I can't believe I'm thinking this, but I wish I had that werewolf hair back on my shoulder now. I wish I had it everywhere.

"Cindy!" Stefan shouts over the wind.

A petite blonde huddled inside a blanket hurries over. Her lips are blue and her teeth chatter. Cindy Emerson would rather wear a tool belt than carry a makeup kit, but she's too short and skinny to be a construction worker. Cindy is a lesbian. How do I know so much about her? Cindy's my best friend— has been since kindergarten. Every monster has its "Egore," and I guess Cindy is mine.

"Feeling okay, Lou?" Cindy shouts.

One word will clue her in. "PMS."

She cringes and steps closer. Cindy whips out a brush to powder my face. "You should have called in sick."

Cindy's right, but the dream had me spooked. I didn't want to stay home alone. While Cindy works on my face, Stefan instructs the crew to hit the lights. He pries blankets off the other girls and herds them toward the lovely fake ice castle he has set up. An ice castle about to collapse in the wind.

Once Cindy finishes with me, we move toward the rest of the crew. A sudden wind gust nearly has me airborne. Cindy grabs hold of me, which is a joke. She's such a weakling that if anything, I'd take her flying with me. Cindy might be a weakling, but I have a rather embarrassing amount of upper body strength. I hold on to her and we reach the crew.

"This sucks, Stefan!" Karen Sims, a leggy black girl from Queens, shouts at Stefan.

Adjusting his camera, he yells back, "It's going to be great. Just wait until you see the finished product!"

This is what Stefan always says when subjecting his models to the elements. He considers himself an artist. We all suffer for his art. I take up a position in the middle of the other models. The wind whips my midnight-black hair around my face. Once my hair was simply a nondescript brunette color. At one time my eyes were only hazel and now they are a vivid shade of jade green. I like the look but, good grief, I could have accomplished the same thing with hair dye and contacts, and not had to deal with the wolf stuff.

Stefan poses the other models. He stops before me and raises his camera. He lowers it a minute later and frowns. Stepping behind me, Stefan pulls my bra up, thus bringing my boobs beneath my chin. His hands are still warm and he's not wearing gloves. He returns to the front, stares at my breasts, glances up, and says, "Marvelous."

"I know," I assure him. "Hurry up before they freeze this way."

A smile tugs at the corners of his mouth. He leans close and whispers, "You are going to give it to me today. Right, Lou?"

We both know what he wants me to give him. My mind wanders to a place of tangled sheets and sweaty bodies. The thought warms me even though it's freezing in realityland. I smile at him, just a hint of one, the kind of smile that promises things I cannot deliver.

"That's what I want." He backs away and lifts his camera. "That sly smile. Like the cat that's just lapped up all the cream."

Stefan needs to suffer for his art like we do. Glancing at the other models, I say, "Let's go, girls," in my best Shania Twain imitation. Then we proceed to rock Stefan's world.

My hair is wet by the time Stefan calls for a wrap. More than my hair is damp. While Stefan shoots, he makes little sounds in the back of his throat. Sex sounds. My hearing is superior to that of a normal human being. The other girls can't hear the sex sounds, but I can. They bring out the beast in me. Which I wish were just a figure of speech.

Cindy rushes up and offers me a blanket. The blanket is damp and cold and I doubt I can get it over my giant wings. I brush her off and make a mad dash for the doors leading down to the service elevators. Reaching the door without busting my ass takes effort, but I manage. I'm about to open the door but it suddenly bursts open, banging with the wind.

A man steps out onto the roof. He's shrouded in black from head to toe. Black leather jacket. Black jeans. Black boots. Dark sunglasses. Sunglasses? I glance up at the cloudy sky.

"I'm looking for Lou Kinipski!" he shouts. "Her agency told me I could find her here!"

About the time that it registers that he's looking for me, it also dawns on me that his jacket has emblems on the sleeves. He's a cop.

"What's this about, Officer?" Stefan shouts.

"Private matter!" the cop shouts back. He points to the badge pinned on his jacket. "Official business!"

A sick feeling settles in my bloated gut. The officer stares at me and I know it's not just because I'm half naked and beautiful. It's hard to remain anonymous when my face is plastered on a ton of billboards all over New York City.

"Is there somewhere we can talk, Ms. Kinipski?" he asks me.

I can only think of three things a police officer might want to discuss with me. Texas. Seven years ago. Prom night . . .

CONFESSION NO. 2

Men in black are hot . . . unless they've
come to arrest you for murder.

I'm in the bathroom again. I managed to get the tattered angel wings off and put on a robe. The cop waits on the other side of the door. I'm sure Stefan, Cindy, and the other models are in the hallway speculating as to what's going on. Most of them, all except Cindy, probably think I have a bunch of unpaid traffic tickets.

I wish. I don't drive. Not in this city. I may sprout fur, fangs, and howl at the moon on occasion lately, but I'm not crazy. I'm thankful I haven't had another outbreak to deal with on top of a police officer wanting to speak with me, but my hair is still wet and it smells like a wet dog. I notice the cop sniffing in the elevator and hope he thinks it had something to do with the feathers on my wings.

Taking one of the hotel's fluffy towels, I wrap it around my head. I dig in my beauty bag and spray myself with perfume, hoping to mask the smell. My street clothes are in the other room so I'm stuck in the robe. I'm also stuck about what I'm going to say if the good-looking officer in the next room asks me about Texas, seven years ago, prom night.

Has someone finally dug up Tom Dawson's body? Have they connected the crime to me even though I look completely different now and I've changed my name? Cindy told me that everyone in Haven thinks Tom and I eloped on prom night, which is about as unlikely as me turning into a werewolf and killing him. I suppose someone could have dug him up. I don't get much news from Haven these days.

Cindy's lifeline to home has been cut off, as well. A girl doesn't tell her father she's a lesbian when he's the pastor of the Haven First Baptist Church. Or so Cindy learned when he kicked her out and told her not to come back.

A soft rap sounds on the door. "Miss Kinipski? Are you all right in there?"

"I'm fine!" I yell through the door. "I . . . I'm fixing my makeup."

Sounds plausible to me. I am a model and therefore assumed by most to be totally into my looks. Which reminds me, I should fix my face. I grab my beauty bag and get to work. While I smooth streaked makeup, cover the third eye on my forehead, and wipe away running mascara, I try to think of something to say if the officer does ask me about a past I thought I had left behind. I've tried to forget about that night for the last seven years, but it floats to the top of my suppressed memories.

I can almost smell the rich dirt of Mr. Riley's cornfield, almost hear the rock and roll playing on Tom's truck radio, feel the gentle caress of spring on the night air . . .

"Come on, Sherry, I just want a kiss. A kiss isn't going to hurt anything, right?"

Sherry Billington had never been kissed. Oh, okay, once in the third grade by a boy with buckteeth, glasses, and a nasal condition, but that didn't count. Tom Dawson was the kind of boy who counted. He was the star player of our high school football team and had already been offered countless college scholarships. I was no one. Not in the scheme of things in Haven, Texas, where nothing much went on anyway.

It was hard to believe that Tom had actually asked me to dance at the prom. Harder yet to believe when he drove up beside Cindy Emerson and me walking home afterward and offered me a ride. He hadn't offered Cindy one and that should have been my first clue that he had no intention of taking me home.

Now he wanted to kiss me. "Why" was the only question that came to mind. Tom had recently broken up with Abby Sinclair, head cheerleader and voted most likely to grace the centerfold of Playboy *at some point in the future. I'd heard the breakup had something to do with the fact that Tom would nail anything that moved if it stood still long enough. That thought brought me back to reality.*

"I'd really just like to go home," I'd said. "My parents will be worried about me." That wasn't true. Clive and Norma Billington went to bed every night at ten-thirty sharp, right after the news. The last thing either would be worried about was me in a truck with a boy parked beside a cornfield making out. I'd never given them any trouble. They'd never given me much of anything in return. They treated me okay, but neither were affectionate people.

"Just one kiss, then I promise to take you home," Tom had insisted, pouting his lips when he looked at me.

He was cute. I'd found myself thinking, why not? Maybe it was time I had a "real" kiss. Maybe Tom was tired of gorgeous, big-breasted girls and wanted someone a little more down to earth.

"One kiss," I had agreed. "Then I really need to get home."

Tom leaned in for the kiss. I shyly met him halfway. He had his tongue down my throat in a heartbeat. He nearly gagged me. I tried to pull back but he grabbed my shoulders and hauled me closer to him on the truck seat. His hand shot up my dress. My knees immediately knocked together. His breath smelled and

*tasted funny, like he'd drunk more than the sweet
punch being doled out to us in the gymnasium.*

*"Relax," he'd said against my bruised mouth.
"You'll like this. I promise."*

*Being unpopular hadn't made me stupid. That's
when I knew Tom Dawson had more on his mind
than a kiss.*

*"Stop it," I'd said firmly, trying to get away from
him. "I want to go home. Now!"*

*Tom's fingers cut deeper into my shoulders. "You're
not going anywhere!" he'd barked. "Not until I collect on a little bet I made with Phil Brewer. I told him
I'd bring your panties back with me. I bet him a hundred bucks."*

*A sick feeling had settled in my stomach. I should
have known Tom paying any attention to me had to
be some prank. A joke. It had been foolish to believe
for a second he might have been interested in me.
Tom had always been a bit of bully, but if he thought
I was too intimidated by him to do anything but roll
over and play dead, he had another think coming.*

"I hope you have a hundred bucks, asshole."

It had been the wrong thing to say.

"Miss Kinipski? I really need to talk to you. Will
you come out now, please?"

The rock and roll playing on the radio fades. The
biting feel of Tom's fingers digging into my tender
flesh fades. Haven, Texas, fades. I blink and look at
my face in the mirror. For a split second, I see Sherry
Billington staring back. I blink again and she's gone.

Where am I? Oh, yeah, New York. Hotel room. About to be arrested for murder. I take a deep breath, walk to the bathroom door, and open it.

The officer leans against the doorframe. He's removed the sunglasses and now I know why he wore them. The cop has the biggest, bluest eyes I have ever seen. The eyes don't match the rest of his hard body image. I suppose that's why he hides them behind the sunglasses.

"I'd like to ask you a few questions," he says.

Stalling seems like a good idea. "And you are?"

"Detective Terry Shay. NYPD."

Using another stalling tactic, I ask, "Really? Seems like most of the detective shows I see on television, the detectives don't wear the uniform. They wear nice suits or sometimes casual clothes—"

"What detectives wear is not what I'm here to talk to you about, Ms. Kinipski," the officer interrupts. "We're not exactly into fashion at the precinct."

I asked about the dress code because Cindy and I watch cop shows all the time. Cindy likes them. She enjoys watching them in my apartment on my big screen, even though she lives next door and could just as easily watch them on her television.

Stalling is not working. Shay doesn't seem distracted by the fact that I'm considered famous in certain circles or that I'm barely dressed and we're in a hotel room together. I'm not used to that. Have I actually met a man who doesn't think with the front of his pants? If I have, he'll be the first.

Now that I think about it, maybe jail wouldn't be so bad if he was my warden. He could bring his handcuffs to my cell . . . damn this PMS, bitch-in-heat stuff. I do not look good in orange. Jumpsuits went out of style in the eighties. I can't go to jail. They probably wouldn't let me keep my beauty bag on hand to fight the werewolf outbreaks. The inevitable can't be put off any longer, however, so I ask, "What do you want to talk to me about, Detective?"

Shay reaches into his jacket pocket, pulls out a photograph, and extends it toward me. "Have you seen this woman before?"

It takes a minute to realize he didn't ask me about Haven, Texas. Or prom night. Or Tom Dawson. I take the photo. At first glance, I think the picture is of me, which doesn't make sense. Then I realize the girl just happens to bear a striking resemblance to me.

"No, I don't know her." I hand the photo back to him. "But I see the resemblance between us. Why are you asking me about her?"

Shay stuffs the picture into his pocket. "She liked to tell people she was you. Use the resemblance to her advantage to get past the lines at clubs and restaurants."

I laugh, though I sound nervous. My knees are weak with relief that he's not here to arrest me. "I didn't know impersonating a supermodel was a crime," I say.

The detective never cracks a smile. "It's not, Ms. Kinipski, but Sally Preston used your name to get into a club called the Pink Palace last night, and now she's dead. I'm just following up on any possible connection between the two of you."

The word "dead" always has a sobering effect on people. Apparently even on werewolves. "Dead?" I repeat dumbly. "What does that have to do with me?"

"Maybe nothing," he answers. Shay takes a notepad and pen from his pocket. "Unless whoever killed her thought she was you. Do you have any enemies?"

The words "whoever killed her" are as unpleasant as the word "dead." "Enemies?" If I keep repeating everything he says he'll think I'm an idiot. "No. None that I know of."

He scribbles something in his notebook. "How about crazed fans? Stalkers? Pissed-off ex-boyfriends? Have you recently received any threatening letters or gotten any strange phone calls?"

Most models have a crazed fan or two, but I'm discreet about giving out personal information. The apartment building I live in has good security. My cell is unlisted. "No," I answer. "I'm sorry this woman is dead, but whatever happened to her has nothing to do with me."

Shay glances up from his notepad. His gaze slides up and down me before returning to my face. "You're sure?"

At least now I know RoboCop is human. He just checked me out. "Positive," I answer.

He replaces the notebook and pen inside his jacket, reaches into another pocket, and withdraws a dog-eared card. "If anything occurs to you, if you suddenly feel as if you're being followed or you receive any strange phone calls or threatening letters, give me a call."

Reluctantly, I take the card he extends. "I'll call if I think of anything." I almost add that I *won't* think of anything, but then I'm sure Shay already has that preconceived notion about me. Unfortunately, the world seems to associate smart with unattractive and attractive with "NASA is not going to call her for a job interview" when it comes to women.

Now that he has concluded his business, Shay removes his sunglasses from his jacket pocket. How many damn pockets does that jacket have? I might not have to carry my beauty bag if I had a jacket with that many pockets. He slides the glasses back on, nods and heads toward the door. "Sorry to interrupt your—"

"Shoot," I provide. "Hey, we both have shoots in our line of work." Oh, my God. Now I've had a Sherry Billington outbreak.

"That's funny," he says in a flat tone that lets me know it isn't.

Since I'm not being hauled off to jail, I'd like to send Shay away with more than a glance at my cleavage and the certainty I have shit for brains. "Cause of death?" I blurt out.

He pauses, his hand already on the doorknob. When he turns to face me, he removes the sunglasses again. I guess there's something in the cop handbook about not wearing sunglasses during official business.

"Blood loss," he answers.

"Blood loss" seems like an odd term to use as a cause of death. But then, maybe not. "Do you mean she was stabbed or shot to death?"

He sighs and slips the glasses back on. "I shouldn't discuss details with you. The case is still open. Leaks could give whoever is responsible an advantage."

A geekish snort slips past my defenses. "Do you think I'll be talking to this guy?"

"I hope not."

Shay is perfectly serious. I hope not, too. He reaches for the door again but now he has me curious. "I think you owe it to me to tell me what kind of psycho we're dealing with . . . if you think I really could be in danger."

"You said you weren't," he turns back to remind me.

"I could be wrong." But of course I'm not wrong. I'm just curious.

The glasses come off again. "Blood loss from a bite wound. Sally Preston's jugular vein was severed by a vicious bite to the neck while she was having sex, we're assuming with the murderer."

A flash of the dream explodes inside my head. Blood flecking the ceiling . . . pooling on the sheets. I have that woozy feeling people get right before they faint. I stumble back a step. Shay moves fast for a tall, built man. He takes my shoulders between his hands and steers me toward the bed.

"Your face is white. You need to sit down."

I do sit . . . on someone's shoe, but I'm too numb to care. It's nice to know that the sight of blood still sickens me, considering all the weird things going on with me lately.

"Sorry about that," Shay says. "I forget that most people don't have to deal with this day in and day out. I'm a little hardened to it all. I should have been more considerate."

His baby blues are leveled on me. Damn, his lashes are so long, if he were a woman, Revlon would be all over him. "Someone being bitten to death is everyday?"

Shay shakes his head. His hair is good, too. Longer than he's probably supposed to wear it, and thick. "No. This is not everyday. Sorry I had to bother you with it. Now, I should be going." He stands and moves toward the door again. "Call me if you need anything, I mean, if you think of anything that might help the case."

"I will," I say, still dazed. I won't call Shay. The poor woman's murder has nothing to do with me. I'm certain of it. The dream flashes in my head again as if to mock me. Across the room, Shay opens the door and comes face-to-face with four frozen angels, Cindy and Stefan. He nods to the models.

"Ladies."

The girls watch him walk away. When they glance back at me, it occurs to me that I might look like I've just had sex and a shower. A big grin breaks out on Karen Sims's face. She rushes into the room.

"Don't tell me. He's a rent-a-cop, right? Did a little striptease for you? Hey, is it your birthday?"

I wish. I mean about the striptease. Birthdays are a model's enemy. "No, he's the real deal," I assure Karen.

Now the girls hover over me, I'd say like mother hens due to the feathers, but that would be a stretch of the imagination.

"What did he want, Lou?" Stefan asks. "Unpaid parking tickets or something? Are you in trouble?"

Stefan is adoringly protective of me. If I tell him a detective is worried that a recent murder might be a case of mistaken identity, meaning I was the murderer's real target, I really will have a stalker problem. Him. "Identity theft," I answer, which is in a way the truth.

"Sheeeit," Karen draws out. "You been shopping online, girl?"

I shrug, which can be taken as a yes.

"Let's get this room cleaned up," Stefan instructs everyone. "I need a Starbucks."

Something stronger sounds good to me. It's been a hell of day. Karen eyeballs the card still clutched between my fingers.

"Nice ass on that man," she says. "Is that his number?"

I should give her the card and hope she hooks up with Shay. Someone should get some of that. Instead, I open my robe and slide the card into my two-sizes-too-small bra.

CONFESSION NO. 3

I obviously do not understand the old adage
"let sleeping dogs lie."

Shay's card still rests on my bedside table three days later. While I dress for my appointment with the private investigator, my gaze darts toward the card. I should have trashed it. Our business is over. It's only the "heat cycle" thing that makes me think about him. Messing with a cop would be like playing Russian roulette. I'm sure as soon as my hormones calm down, I'll be able to forget Terry Shay and his baby blues. Racket from the kitchen breaks into my thoughts.

Cindy is banging things around in there because she's mad about my appointment with the investigator. What she doesn't understand is that in my case, the need for truth outweighs the consequences of

someone else finding out the truth right along with
me. Cindy is aware of what happened seven years
ago. She's also aware of the recent outbreaks. She
thinks I'm panicking unnecessarily. In other words,
she's in denial.

When I'm bent on doing something Cindy considers self-destructive, she reminds me that a full-
blown transformation only took place once. She's
certain I just have a werewolf bug or something and
it will go away soon. I can't be as certain. Thus the
need for a private investigator.

"Lou, I can't get this jar open!" Cindy yells.

Due to my wicked past, Cindy has trained herself
to call me Lou. It's a matter of survival and she takes
her position as my best friend and confidante seriously. At times, we both forget who we once were
and where we came from. We like our lives now.
What Cindy seems unwilling to realize is that if I go
wolfy again, I won't have the job that helps pay half
her rent in this overpriced building. I won't have
anything but a real fur coat.

I go to the kitchen. Cindy hands me a jar of orange marmalade. She's made us toast and hot chocolate. I take the jar from her, give the lid one good
twist, and it pops off.

Frowning, she says, "I hate that you can do that and
I can't. If I was as strong as you are, I could work construction. Maybe you should work construction, Lou."

"Your dream, not mine," I remind her, moving
around to perch on a bar stool. "I don't know why

you don't like your job, Cindy. You're great with makeup and you get to be around beautiful girls all day. I'd think that would be a lesbian's dream job."

Opening a drawer, Cindy digs through my silverware and comes up with a butter knife. She points it at me. "It's rude to refer to me in that manner and you know it."

"What?" I ask. "Calling you a lesbian? That's the name it's called. They gave it a name so gay women don't have to say, I'm a girl who likes girls, you know, versus a girl who likes boys. That is to say, not that I like every girl—"

"Okay, wiseass," Cindy cuts me off. She smears a piece of toast with marmalade and tosses it on my plate. "As far as having any advantage with women because of my job, that's where you're wrong. All the models talk about is men or shoes. Who's sleeping with who. Who wants to sleep with who and what pair of heels they want to wear while doing it."

I take a bite of toast. "I'm sure there are closet lesbians among us. You just have to flush them out. In fact, that Russian model, Natasha Somethingorother, she looks pretty masculine to me."

Cindy comes around and sits beside me. "Natasha Svetbroun is not gay," she informs me. "She's athletic. In fact, I worked a Nike shoot with her yesterday. I didn't want to tell you, but the reason I know she's straight is because she was talking about a certain photographer's athletic ability in bed. I'm sure you know which photographer she was talking about."

A bite of toast goes down the wrong pipe. Cindy thumps me on the back.

"Thought that would get to you," she says.

Once I finish hacking, I take deep breaths and say calmly, "Stefan's sex life is none of my business." If I repeat that to myself a hundred times a day, maybe at some point I'll believe it.

Cindy takes a sip of her hot chocolate. "Aren't you even curious about what she said about him?"

"No," I assure her.

When she shrugs and takes a bite of toast, I want to take a bite of her. She knows me well enough to know I'm lying. Finally, I say, "Okay, tell me what she said."

"Are you sure you want to know?" Cindy tortures me further. "It could just make the situation between you worse."

I think about it for a minute. "How could it be any worse?"

"Suspecting a man is good in bed and hearing he can make a woman yell like Tarzan are two different things."

"Ugh." I bury my hands in my hair. "I knew he was good."

"Hung, too, or that's what Natasha said," she adds cheerfully.

Peeking at Cindy through my fingers, I say, "If you were any kind of friend, you would have kept this to yourself."

Cindy brushes toast crumbs off her chin. "I just don't understand why you don't have him and be done with it. I know you're half in love with him. Why not take the next step in the relationship? Why let everyone else have what should belong to you?"

"Because everyone else has already had it," I answer dryly. "And there is the little problem of being a murderer and, in recent months, howling at the moon and scratching for fleas."

This is not a normal conversation, and I have to give Cindy credit for keeping her cool. I, in contrast, am in freak-out mode and have been since the outbreaks started six months ago. Cindy shrugs.

"You killed someone who deserved to be killed and a few fur-and-fang outbreaks aren't like a full-blown transformation. That only happened once and I don't believe it will happen again."

"Thank you, Dr. Phil." I sip my chocolate. I wish I could be as sure as Cindy, but Cindy isn't the one who smells like a wet dog after a shower. I glance at my watch.

"I've got to get going."

"I really think this is a bad decision, Lou," Cindy grumbles. "This guy is going to snoop around in your life. What if he finds out more than you want him to know?"

One last sip of chocolate and I climb off my stool. "The adoption file is sealed; I've learned that much on my own. The Billingtons wouldn't tell me anything when they told me I was adopted; I doubt they will tell me anything now. Besides, it would be foolish for me to go back to Haven and try again with them. How do I explain this?" I make a sweep with my hand of my gorgeous self. "I'm never going back to Haven, Cindy. Ever. This is the best way to find my birth parents."

My beauty bag is on the table. I've given up carrying a purse. I go over, retrieve a scarf, and tie it around my head.

"What if you do find your biological parents?" Cindy swivels around on her bar stool to ask. "What if they are just as normal as the next person? That isn't going to tell you why you sprout fur and fangs a week before your period lately and want to hump everyone. It might not solve anything, Lou. It might just cause trouble."

Cindy might be right, but it's the possibility that she's wrong that keeps me on course. I move toward the door. "I need to find them. If they have answers for me, then I might be able to reverse what's been happening for the past six months."

"What if it reverses everything?" Cindy asks. "Look around you, Lou. Look in the mirror. Can you ever really go back to being Sherry Billington now? Sometimes it is really better to let sleeping dogs lie."

I'm tempted to cave—agree with Cindy and spend the rest of the day pigging out and watching cop shows with her. What if I did manage to reverse whatever happened to me seven years ago? It wouldn't reverse the fact I murdered someone. It might reverse the good looks it gave me. One thing is for certain. Men like Stefan O'Conner and Terry Shay would have never given me a second glance as Sherry Billington. I haven't come clean with Cindy about my motivations for finding my birth parents. Not all of them.

Deep down, I want to know why. Why they gave me up. Why I couldn't have been raised by two people who loved me. I was a normal baby . . . wasn't I? Would I have stayed normal if I'd been raised somewhere other than Haven, Texas? If I hadn't met Tom Dawson? There are too many unanswered questions. There are too many things at stake to simply ignore what's been happening for the past six months. Why is it happening now? I have to do all I can to find out, even if it means a risk of exposure.

"Let yourself out," I tell Cindy.

Twenty minutes later my cab pulls up in front of a building that should have a condemned sign on the front door. I check the address again. I'm in the right place and I get the first suspicious inkling that I might be making a mistake. As usual, when I'm being stubborn about something, I ignore it. I pay the cabbie an extra fifty to wait for me.

The inside of the building is even less impressive than the outside. The lobby is empty, the floors scuffed. There's about two inches of dust on the vinyl furniture and the scarred sofa tables. My allergies immediately flare up. Through watery eyes, I glance at the directory on the wall beside the elevator.

Morgan Kane, PI, Floor 2.

After I push the button, the elevator fires up and heads down. The way it creaks and groans, I'm guessing it hasn't been serviced in about a hundred years. The doors open, emitting a musty smell that reminds me of the Billingtons' basement. I step inside and push floor two. The doors close, the thing lurches, and I'm on my way to where? The nearest freak show if I'm not careful.

The second floor is dark and eerie. I hear music and glance down the long hallway. There's a light shining through a door nearly at the end. I head that way. Once I reach the door, I knock, but the music blares so loudly I doubt Morgan Kane can hear me. I test the knob. It's unlocked. The door swings open.

Inside, a man stands before streaked floor-to-ceiling windows. He faces the uninspiring view of yet another dilapidated building across the street, but the man is inspired nonetheless. His fingers move over an electric air guitar, head swinging wildly to the hard rock of Led Zeppelin. His hair is shoulder length and dirty blond. He wears skintight black leather pants and snakeskin cowboy boots. Beneath his unbuttoned wrinkled shirt, flashes of skin peek at me and a ring through his left nipple catches the flimsy light streaming through the windows.

I don't know who he is, but he is not what I expected Morgan Kane to look like, so I assume I'm in the wrong place, which is a better dilemma than this guy's. He's in the wrong decade.

"Excuse me!" I yell, trying to be heard over the music.

He jumps in the air, goes down on one knee, and plays the shit out of his air guitar. I jump in the air when he suddenly breaks into song. Something about mamas sweating and grooving. More air guitar playing. Now some head butting with a few hip thrusts thrown in. I'm repulsed and mesmerized at the same time. I would shout out again, but I'm still hoarse from shouting over the wind during the underwear shoot. I spot the stereo, walk over, and switch it off.

The pounding music thankfully stops, but the rock god parties on. He continues to play and leap about in odd fashion for a good five minutes. Suddenly he stops, cocks his head, and turns to face me. His eyes are red rimmed and muddy brown.

"You my ten o'clock?" he asks without missing a beat.

"That would depend on whether or not you're Morgan Kane," I answer without missing one, either.

"In the flesh." He lays the air guitar aside and moves toward a desk on the other side of the room. "Step into my office," he calls behind him.

I don't step anywhere. I'm freaked out by the fact he laid an imaginary guitar aside. That's when I have an epiphany. There are people in the world way weirder than I am.

Across the room, Kane digs around the top of his desk, comes up with a pack of Marlboro reds, shoves one between his lips, and lights it up. I don't remember the last time I saw someone smoke inside a public building. My eyes immediately water. I sneeze.

"Bless you, cupcake," Kane calls in a smooth Southern drawl. "Now bring it on over here and let's talk business."

Cupcake? As Cindy often points out, I am freakishly strong. I could probably swing Kane around the room by his nipple ring. I'm disappointed that he doesn't look professional. I can't believe I actually got a reference on this guy. Last year one of the models I know asked him to find her little sister, who'd gone underground with some type of porn ring. Kane had found her. He's supposed to be good at finding people, but Meagan hadn't said anything about the nipple ring, the air guitar, or the cowboy boots.

"I'm allergic to cigarette smoke," I tell him.

He waves the smoke floating around his head away and snuffs the cigarette out in an overflowing ashtray. "You should have said so." When he flashes me a grin, I see that he has dimples hidden beneath the three days' growth of dark whiskers on his face. "You coming?"

I glance around. "I'm allergic to dust, too."

Kane moves around his desk and sits in a chair with stuffing dangling from several rips. "Sorry, cupcake, my cleaning lady comes later today." He leans back in his chair and props his boots on the desk. "Now, unless you're allergic to snakeskin, come over and sit down so we can talk."

Against my better judgment, I move toward him. "I'm not sure about snakeskin. But I'm sure I'm allergic to being called 'cupcake.' "

Kane flashes the dimples again, which would be a better charm tactic if he shaved. "Sheathe the claws, kitten. I'm here to help you."

I fight the urge to glance at my hands and see if I actually do have claws and take a seat on a cold metal chair across from him. Kane smiles again and I almost expect him to reach across the desk, pat me on the head, and say, "Good girl." Which would make him lose a hand.

Instead of reaching for me, he reaches into a desk drawer and pulls out a bottle of Wild Turkey. "A little hair of the dog," he says, then unscrews the cap, takes a swig, and offers it to me. It's a challenge of sorts so I take the bottle and actually drink after him.

"Tell me what you need, cup . . . ah, Ms. Smith, is it?"

I try not to cough from the liquor burning my throat, not to mention the dust and the cigarette smoke. I nod, a little embarrassed that I couldn't come up with a better fake name when I made the appointment. So I'm beautiful but not creative. Sue me. I didn't want this guy looking me up if I didn't show. Not to mention jacking up his prices when he found out who I am.

"That's my name for now," I say when I can finally speak again. "We'll discuss that more if I decide to hire you."

Kane leans farther back in his chair and I think it would be great if it tipped over and he fell. "Of course you're going to hire me, cupcake." He sighs. "Oops, I forgot again. What do you need me to do for you, Ms. Kinipski?"

The liquor seems to come right back up. I cough and choke while he smiles calmly at me from across his desk. Cindy would at least pat me on the back, not that I want this guy touching me. "How do you know my name?" I finally wheeze. "Did you trace my phone or something?"

His smile stretches. "Didn't have to. I know your face, even with the scarf and the sunglasses." He turns his squeaky chair around and motions to the streaked floor-to-ceiling windows. There's a giant billboard across the street with my face on it, lips puckered up to advertise "won't wear off until you're dead and buried" lipstick.

"I'm guessing Meagan referred me," he continues, turning to face me again. "If you want the best, you want me. Bottom line."

This guy's picture must illustrate the word "cocky" in the dictionary. I'm sure it's in there again under "slimeball." Something about him, besides the obvious, immediately rubs me the wrong way. But I've come this far. I may as well tell him what I want. "If I hire you, I'd want you to look for someone for me."

Kane shakes his dirty-blond head. "No, you'd want me to *find* someone for you. And I will. Just tell me who."

For the first time in six months, I really believe there is a chance of finding my birth parents. Of finding possible answers about my condition. Like most people confronted with actually getting what they wish for . . . Cindy's warning keeps sounding in my head. Morgan Kane might be able to find my biological parents, but what else is he going to find out in the process?

"How about I think about it for a couple more days and get back to you?" Even if I decide to proceed, it doesn't mean I have to hire Morgan Kane. Surely I can find someone who doesn't wear snakeskin boots or call me "cupcake."

Kane takes another swig of Wild Turkey. "Looks are often deceiving, Ms. Kinipski. If and when you decide you want the best, I charge fifteen grand to find someone. If it's more than one person, fifteen a head. I expect half up front."

At least he's not cheap. "Good to know you crack cases as well as you play air guitar," I say sarcastically.

The cocky grin that seems permanently attached to his face fades. He leans forward in his squeaky chair. "For the record, I don't play air guitar. I play real guitar in a band that has a running gig every weekend at Freddie Z's. I consider investigating a part-time job but I take it seriously. Ever been to the club?"

I've heard of Freddie Z's. Some of the girls like to go there, but I've never tagged along. Lots of noise. Big meat market. "No." I rise from my chair. "Not my kind of place." Turning, I head for the door. "I'll be in touch," I lie.

Kane blocks my exit a second later. "You sure you haven't been to the club? I feel certain I've seen you there, in the crowd."

Does Kane think I've been to the club, or is that a line? How many women walking the streets of New York resemble me? Sally Preston did. She's dead. No connection, I tell myself for the hundredth time since Terry Shay shoved her photo at me.

"I've never been there," I assure Kane. Shoving past him, I walk out into the hallway . . . and keep walking.

"Be seeing you, cupcake," Kane calls after me.

I'm one hundred percent certain Kane will not be seeing me again. He gets on my last nerve. There's a sleaze factor to him I'd rather avoid. The factor comes into play when I feel him watching me. Or rather, more probably, he's watching my ass as I walk down the hallway. He can take a good long look. This is the last he'll see of me.

CONFESSION NO. 4

*Cindy always tells me not to go borrowing trouble.
I tell her some people don't have to borrow
trouble. There are those like me who get all the
trouble they can handle for free.*

My face is pale in the neon blink of a light outside the window. There is a man on top of me.
We're having sex, although I can't feel him inside of me. I'm an observer—like in a dream where
you hover overhead, watching. I must like what he's
doing, even if I can't feel it. My head tosses back and
forth on the pillow. My mouth opens and closes,
moving in a way that looks as if I'm moaning.

I see myself, but not the man. Only the back of his
head—long dark hair, a glimpse of broad shoulders,
and a word tattooed on his left shoulder that I can't
read due to the strobe light effect.

The man's head and shoulders bob up and down,
he's really pumping. My head arches back and my

mouth opens wider. I'm climaxing. I'm looking at him, but I don't see him . . . only I must see something. My eyes suddenly widen. My mouth is moving again, but I don't think I'm moaning now. I'm screaming. The man's hands twist into my hair . . . but they are not hands. Not human hands. Covered with fur, claws jut from his fingertips. Then he bites me on the neck where the jugular is located.

Blood spurts on the ceiling, on the sheets, on my T-shirt lying on the floor, the word EROTICA scrawled across the front.

I sit up in bed, gasping for breath. Tears stream down my face and my heart hammers inside of my chest. It's the dream again, I tell myself. It's only a dream. The numbers on my alarm clock read two A.M. My hand shakes as I reach across the nightstand and switch on the bedroom lamp. Soft light floods my room, chasing away the monsters. All but the one in my bed. Me.

Someone knocks on my door. I know who it is. Cindy. This may sound weird—weirder than normal weird—but Cindy and I now have baby monitors set up in our apartments. The monitors were Cindy's idea, in case she heard me in here getting all wolfy or something.

I told Cindy six months ago that a whimper or two, a howl on occasion, even a full-out bark will be tolerated, but if she ever catches me peeing on my furniture, she is to find a gun and shoot me. I climb out of bed and pad through the apartment.

After unlocking my door, I swing it wide. The hallways stay lit at all times. Cindy's face is etched with concern. It's good to see her, but then I notice what she's wearing. A leather halter top and leather short shorts with fishnet hose.

"Gee, where are your knee-high boots and your whip?" I ask.

Rolling her eyes, Cindy shoves her way inside and closes the door. "Are you all right, Lou? I heard you moaning, and then it sounded like you were choking."

I'm glad the monitors only work one way. I'd hate to think what I might have heard coming from her side. Cindy obviously has company . . . or I hope she does. "Tell me that is not your regular sleeping attire?"

She ignores the question and moves through the apartment switching on lights. "You were having the nightmare again, weren't you?"

I rub my arms. January nights are cold in New York, but I know that's not the reason I'm chilled. "Yes."

"Same scenario?"

"Same," I answer. "Different location."

"I'll fix you some herbal tea. The kind that helps you relax."

"I'm okay," I call to her back. "You can return to . . . whatever it was you were doing."

"No trouble," she insists. "Sit down and relax while I fix the tea."

Walking to my couch, I plop down. I'm wearing, in contrast to Cindy, flannel pajamas and socks. I tuck my legs beneath me, lean my head back against the soft couch cushions, and close my eyes. I open them again quickly, afraid of what visions might haunt me.

Sounds of Cindy puttering around my kitchen soothe me. I hate to admit this, but I'm glad Cindy's dad freaked out when she told him she was gay. I'm glad he kicked her out. I'm glad she's here with me, especially now. I'm even glad I told her about prom night, and what I did—what I became.

Prom night is scarier to think about than the dream. Tom Dawson had brutally attacked me. He'd turned into a rage-filled monster because I had dared to reject his advances and he'd beaten me within an inch of my life. Then he had planned to rape me on top of everything else. I remember lying there, bruised, stunned, and bleeding while he told me what he would do to me next, and how much I would enjoy it. The rage had begun to build inside of me. I'd felt it coursing through my veins, giving me strength.

Tom had positioned himself over me. He was a football player and all muscle. He'd forced my legs apart, reached beneath my ruined prom dress, and ripped my panties off. The rage kept building and I had let it come. Suddenly, I reached out and raked his face. My arm had been covered in fur, claws jutting from my fingertips. Tom, the football player, a bully, and a would-be rapist, had screamed like a girl. He kept screaming. I don't want to remember anything else.

"Here's your tea."

Cindy sets the cup and saucer in front of me on the sofa table and settles beside me. "Feeling better?"

"A little," I lie. Reaching for my tea, I take the steaming cup between my shaking hands. "Cindy, do you think I should feel more guilt about killing Tom? I keep thinking because I don't, maybe is the reason I keep having these nightmares. Maybe it's why I've had these recent outbreaks. Something has triggered it."

She makes a snorting noise. "That asshole had it coming for what he did to you and what he planned to do. He could have easily killed you, Lou. You said you were so bruised, you didn't even realize you had transformed into someone beautiful until the bruises healed. He's not worth feeling guilty over, and he's not worth losing sleep over, either. You need to put it behind you. Only then will the nightmares go away. I bet the outbreaks stop, too."

Cindy moonlights as my therapist. I thought I had put the ordeal behind me. The nightmares keep bringing it back. Is the man in my dreams really me? A reminder that I can't ignore what happened seven years ago, or what I became, what I still might become? I reach over and pat Cindy's hand.

"Thanks for being here for me. I'm okay now. You can go back to your guest." I glance toward the wall separating her apartment from mine. "You did turn off the monitor, right?"

Cindy nods, her forehead wrinkled as if she's in deep concentration. "Yeah, I switched it off before

I came over," she says. I have a cream for those forehead wrinkles. But her brows are so thick, if they were dark she'd have a unibrow. "But something has just occurred to me. Do you think these dreams you have might simply be an unconscious need to be punished for what you've done?"

I eye her outfit. "Don't get any ideas, girlfriend."

Cindy laughs then swats me playfully. "You know I don't think about you in a sexual way. Kissing you would be like kissing my sister, if I had one."

She's like the sister I never had, too. "I think I've been punished enough for what I did in Haven," I say. "Really, Cindy, go home. One of us should have normal relationships."

Shrugging, Cindy says, "I imagine my friend has either left or has fallen asleep." Glancing down at herself, she adds, "And is this really normal? I'm not sure it would have worked out anyway. I'm not into the whole leather-and-whips thing."

For some reason, I had once thought having a relationship with another woman would be easier than having one with a man. Cindy has proven me wrong. Time and time again. I sigh. "Want to sleep on my couch?"

She smiles gratefully. "If you're sure you don't mind."

I'm thankful for the company tonight. I rise to get Cindy sheets and a blanket. "What'd you tell your guest about the monitor?"

"I told her that you're epileptic and I have to keep tabs on you," Cindy answers.

"Good one."

After I bring in the linens, Cindy helps me make up the couch. "You didn't throw out those tea bags, did you?" I ask. "I have a shoot in five hours and I need them to reduce the puffiness I'm sure to have around my eyes."

"I never throw anything of yours out," she assures me. "You and your strange concoctions. That orange peel and yogurt dish you whipped up for me last week was really tasty, though."

She's jerking me around. Cindy knows it was a facial, and not to eat. "Very funny," I remark.

"Who are you working with tomorrow? Your boyfriend?"

Stefan is on my shit list at the moment. I know he screws around with models. Hearing about it always puts me in a bad mood. Like he's cheated on me, which I know is ridiculous. "Yeah. I hope I don't bite his head off." And I do mean that literally as well as figuratively. "But I'm glad for the work; it will take my mind off things."

Fluffing her pillow, Cindy says, "Lou, if it pisses you off so much about Stefan, do something about it. You know you want to. You know he wants to, too. Everyone knows that. It's not a big secret."

I grab my teacup off the sofa table and finish it off, carrying the cup to the kitchen. "We've covered this ground before," I call to her. "It was bad enough when I was just a murderer, but now I'm having these outbreaks. That's not the kind of thing a girl wants to tell a man she hopes to have a serious relationship with. Besides, I'm not too sure most of my appeal for Stefan isn't the fact he hasn't slept with me."

"You've never given yourself enough credit, Lou," Cindy calls. "You're one of the most beautiful women in the world, and you still have crap for confidence."

In the kitchen, I grab the tea bags to put on my eyes when I go back to bed. Cindy's right. Old habits die hard. When I was a kid, awkward looking, too skinny, and all teeth and legs, I'd pore over fashion magazines and dream I would someday be beautiful like the women in the ads. The dream was hard to keep when the kids at school reminded me on a daily basis that I was not beautiful, that I would never be beautiful. I guess the problem is, I still know what's on the inside. And what's on the inside is totally screwed up at the moment.

Cindy has climbed beneath the covers when I return to the living room. "You know I've tried to have a few relationships with men in the past. They never seem to work out."

"That's because you choose men who don't care about you, Lou," Cindy says. "They only care about being seen with you. You're the one who never returns their phone calls. There's not an emotional connection there for you. That makes all the difference in the world. You just need to figure that out and give a guy you actually care about a chance. A guy like Stefan who so clearly adores you."

I've told Cindy a hundred times that I can't do that. I have trust issues. Now I have werewolf issues. I have all kinds of issues. "Maybe I can when I figure out exactly what happened to me, and why it's happening again."

"I hope so," she responds sleepily. "And I hope you're not just digging yourself in deeper by involving a private investigator and searching for answers that might not be out there."

Walking over, I stand above her. She looks so small and helpless beneath the covers. "Why aren't you afraid of me?" I ask her. "I'm afraid for you. I'm not even sure you should be here with me anymore."

Her eyes had drifted closed. Now she opens them. "You'd never hurt me, Lou. I know that and you should know it, too. What you did before, that was self-defense. It's not in your nature to go around killing people for the hell of it. Now, lighten up and go to bed. You need to look stunning for your boyfriend in the morning."

Cindy has been giving me advice since kindergarten. I love her. Deep down, I know I could never hurt her, but I guess the trust issues I have aren't just with other people. They include myself. I want to believe Cindy. I want to believe it desperately. As far as looking stunning for my boyfriend . . . I have a bone to pick with Stefan. He might not find me quite so chummy tomorrow.

've nearly forgotten about the dream by the time I finish the shoot the next day. It was a good day because I got to work with Karen again and I really like her. It was a bad day because I had to work with Stefan's new lover. I actually growled at Natasha when I stepped into the studio and saw her. I also growled when I saw the shoot setup. Stefan had the studio decorated like a hayloft. We had to wear designer jeans and cowboy boots.

I didn't want to think about Morgan Kane today. Or Terry Shay, or Sally Preston. I sure as hell didn't want to think about Stefan having sex with Natasha Somethingorother. Whenever Stefan asked me to give it to him today, I gave him the cold shoulder instead.

Besides cheating on me, he's had on a stocking cap all morning. I know his bald head gets cold sometimes and he wears a cap, but I might be able to envision him with hair if the cap weren't bright orange. Even Bozo doesn't look good in orange hair. Everyone is ready to call it a day and I head toward the dressing room with the other models.

"Do you need a ride home, Lou?" Stefan calls.

When Cindy and I don't share a cab, Stefan always offers me a ride home. He'd offer both of us one when Cindy does work with me, but he has a two-seater. I usually accept but today I'm thinking it's not a good idea to be around him. I might break the bonds of our supposed friendship and ask him point-blank about Natasha.

"No, thanks," I call back. "I'll get a cab."

He frowns. He's not stupid. Stefan knows something is up with me today. "Fine," he says. "I'm going for coffee. I'll be back in a few if you change your mind."

I shrug. "Whatever."

The girls eye me oddly when I reach the dressing room. Stefan isn't the only who has noticed my chilly attitude toward him today.

"You should have taken the ride," Natasha comments in her thick Russian accent. "He's a good driver, if you know what I mean."

About now is when all the girls would normally giggle over her obvious insinuation. No one does. Natasha hasn't been in the business long, at least not in New York. I heard she did some modeling in California before moving to New York. She isn't chummy enough with everyone to be talking about her sex life.

Karen pulls off her pointed cowboy boots and gives Natasha a dirty look. "He might drive around with you, girl, but we all know he's crazy in love with Lou."

Karen's statement sends a little shock through me. I figured everyone thought we had slept together; it never occurred to me anyone thought Stefan was in love with me. The statement obviously shocks Natasha, as well. She plants her hands on her hips and glares at me.

"He said the two of you are only friends."

Karen walks over in thong underwear and a silk halter. She pats Natasha on the shoulder. "Here's a lesson about American men. They'll say anything to get a woman into bed."

"Amen," Leslie Fields echoes.

Natasha puffs up like a toad. "Stefan is from Ireland," she announces, as if that is somehow relevant.

Karen laughs. "Men are men no matter where they come from. They're all pigs. You'd do better to get you a sweet girl like Cindy Emerson. I could see you two together."

When Karen glances at me and winks, I almost burst out laughing.

"I do not like girls," Natasha sputters. "People think because I have an athletic build, I am a lesbian. Not true."

Grabbing Natasha's wrist, Karen lifts it in the air. "Then why do you wear this big ol' sports watch? That's the first clue, you know. The big ol' sports watch."

I nearly burst out laughing again. Natasha wrenches her wrist from Karen. "I run," she explains. "I need stopwatch!"

"Uh-huh," Karen mumbles.

Now Natasha's face is blotched with red spots. I feel a little sorry for her. I know what it's like not to be part of the "in" crowd. "Lay off, Karen," I say quietly.

Natasha stomps to the back of the room.

"You're wicked," I tell Karen.

Her catty smile confirms it. "Truth is, if you're not going to take him, I want him for myself. If I have to convince old broad shoulders that she's gay to get her to back off, then so be it."

I imagine if Karen wanted Stefan, she could have him. She's exotically beautiful. Her skin is the color of hot chocolate. She's six feet two inches of legs. Men go crazy over her.

"I don't know why you'd want a skinny white boy like him, anyway," I tease her back, undressing along with everyone else.

"Hey, Lou, you should have come out with us last night," Leslie calls. "Freddie Z's was really rocking."

Mention of the club makes me think of Morgan Kane. "Was the band any good?"

"Oh, yeah," she answers. "Lots of loud rock and roll."

Which is the reason I never go there. Loud music hurts my ears. After recent events, I'm afraid I'd start that howling some dogs do when they listen to music. Besides, I don't remember being asked, but I don't point that out.

"Lou, if you're calling a cab, better do it," Karen says. "We're all leaving in a minute and it'll take one a little while to get here. I want to make sure you have a ride."

I've finished dressing and grab up my beauty bag. I fish out my cell. It rings. I jump. My phone doesn't ring that often. Only a few people have my number.

Stefan is one of them. I figure he's caught in a line at Starbucks and is double-checking on whether I need a ride. I flip my phone open.

"No, I don't need a ride," I say.

Silence. Finally a voice with a smooth Southern drawl asks, "Sherry? Sherry Billington?"

My throat has a big lump in it. I can't respond.

"Hey, talk to me, Sherry," Kane says. "At least I didn't call you 'cupcake.'"

I hang up. How did Morgan Kane find out my real name? How did he trace my cell number and what the hell else does he already know about me?

"Hey, girl, you okay?" Karen pauses before me. "You look like you just saw a ghost."

In a way, I have. I knew if I decided to hire Kane to find my biological parents, I would have to give him my adopted name, but so far, that information was still a secret.

"I'm fine," I say to Karen.

The other models start leaving. Karen asks, "Sure you don't need a ride? If you don't want to go with Stefan, you can go with me and Leslie."

What I need is a few minutes to collect myself. No one has called me Sherry for seven years. "Thanks, but no. Really, I'm fine. I have a cab on the way."

"How about we meet for lunch on Thursday?" Karen asks. "Maybe do a little shoe shopping?"

"Sounds good." I love to shop for shoes and Cindy never wants to go anywhere but Red Wing.

"Okay, see you later."

I'm suddenly left alone in the dressing room. I turn to face the ceiling-to-floor mirrors, a must-have for women who model everything from makeup to shoes. Again, I catch a flash of Sherry Billington in the mirror. My face shape is the same, but that's about it as far as the resemblance goes. My eyes are more slanted. My lips are fuller, my nose shorter. I'm taller now, stronger. And yet at times, I still feel vulnerable.

The door swings open. I jump.

"Sorry," Stefan says, latte in hand. "Just came in to make an inventory and see that everything that needs to be sent back gets sent back."

I haven't called a cab. "Does that ride offer still stand?" I ask.

He smiles. I try not to melt. "Sure. Just let me wrap up here."

I help Stefan because I'd like to hurry him along. I need to go home and think about what I'm going to do regarding Morgan Kane. I guess if he's gone this far, I need to hire him. If I don't, he might snoop around more in my life just for spite. At least I have the name of the adoption agency. Kane should be able to get past the sealed records . . . I hope. What he's done is basically blackmail me into hiring him. Very clever.

A few minutes later Stefan and I speed along in his little Porsche. We haven't said much to each other. It's awkward because we're usually chatty.

"It was one night, one time, I haven't called her since," he finally says.

My first reaction is a little jolt of joy. My second is more rational. "Guess you get a prize for acting like every other asshole out there, then," I respond.

"I'm not bragging," he says. "But I don't want what happened between her and me affecting our relationship . . . our friendship," he clarifies.

I do my geek snort. "You don't want it affecting our working relationship," I correct him. I'm not in the mood for this now. Not after having Morgan Kane blackmail me. "I'm over it," I say. "Let's just both forget about it. I thought you had higher standards, is all."

Stefan pulls up before the curb of my building. He puts the car in park and turns toward me. "I do have higher standards, but we can't always have what we want, can we, Lou?"

This is not my day. I'm not up to a serious discussion about our relationship and the fact we are both more attracted to one another than friends should be. Since I can't be honest with Stefan about everything going on in my life, I'll be honest with him about what I can. "No, we can't always have what we want," I answer. "Sometimes the timing isn't right. Sometimes other issues get in the way."

He stares at me and I'd like to pull that ridiculous orange cap off his head. "Tell me the truth. Is because of Cindy? Are you two more than friends?"

I didn't see that one coming. Stefan thinks I'm gay simply because my best friend is. It's funny . . . for about a split second. Does Stefan make that assumption just because I'm not all over him? The fault cannot lie with him; therefore it must lie with me, right? He's so typically male, sometimes I wonder why I like him at all. His question doesn't justify an answer. I open the door and climb out.

"Bozo," I say before slamming the door.

Marching toward my building, I wonder why Gus hasn't rushed to get the door for me. He usually does so to keep me from having to punch in my security code. I punch in the code and walk into the building lobby. Gus stands a few feet away, talking to a man in black. The doorman glances up, sees me, and calls, "Sorry, Ms. Lou. He flashed a badge and I had to let him in."

Terry Shay looks as good as I remember. Even though at the moment I'm in complete agreement with Karen that all men are pigs, I have to admit if I had a tail it would be wagging about now. Shay walks toward me. By his serious expression, I'm thinking this is no social call.

He pulls a photograph from his pocket. The girl in the photo resembles me. She smiles for the camera while perched on a bench. Her jeans are too tight. So is her T-shirt. The word EROTICA is scrawled across the front.

CONFESSION NO. 5

*Honesty may be the best policy, but I say when
confronted with a truth that may lead someone to
discover that I'm stranger than your average Joe, lie
like a son, or daughter, or whatever, of a bitch.*

recognize the shirt in the picture. Now I understand why I seem detached from my nightmares.
When I dream, I'm not dreaming about myself,
I'm dreaming about other women . . . and how they
are murdered. My hand shakes when I hand the
photo back to Terry.

"You found her in a sleazy motel." It's not information I intend to speak out loud, but I'm dazed and
the words slip past my defenses. I glance up at Shay.
His brow furrows.

"How'd you know that?" he asks.

The neon sign flashes in my head. I can't tell
Terry that I dream about the murders. He'll think
I'm crazy. I shrug. "A wild guess."

Shay's baby blues narrow on me. "Pretty damn good guess," he says. "Why do I get the feeling you know more about these murders than you're telling me, Ms Kinipski?"

Some type of explanation is in order. A lie. Something a little odd, but not as odd as the truth. This is where watching too much *Court TV* pays off. "I'm psychic," I blurt.

Shay blinks at me. "What?"

I've stepped in it now, I have to follow through. "I got that she was murdered in a hotel from touching the photo. I sometimes have visions from touching an object related to an individual, or seeing a photo."

Terry opens his mouth to respond, but Gus interrupts.

"Miss Lou, Detective, do you mind taking your business elsewhere?" When I glance at Gus he blushes. "The residents get nervous when they walk into my building and see a police officer talking to another resident," he explains.

My building is very upscale. Gus takes his position seriously. No funny business goes on in the lobby. He leaves me little choice but to invite Terry up to my apartment. I never have men in my place. It's my sanctuary.

"I guess we can go up to my apartment," I say.

"Either that or the station," Shay offers.

No, thank you. "This way." I move toward the elevator. The building is a high-rise. I live on the tenth floor and never realized how slow the ride up is until

I'm stuck in the elevator with a good-looking man . . . a detective, to top it off. Shay has a particular scent. Axle grease mixed with Brut aftershave. It's a complete turn-on. The situation, however, is a complete turnoff.

"So, how long have you been psychic?" I don't have to be clairvoyant to detect sarcasm in his voice. Shay is obviously a nonbeliever.

"For a few years." I immediately wish I could modify my answer. I think those people are born with "the gift." The elevator doors open and I step off. "I mean, I really only came to understand what was happening to me in the last few years," I add, fumbling for my keys.

Shay makes a grunting nonbeliever sound. After I unlock my dead bolt, I open the door and stick my head inside, looking for signs that a werewolf lives in my apartment. I don't see any clumps of fur on the furniture or rawhide bones scattered around on the floor . . . or bones of any kind.

"All clear," I announce and open the door. Shay follows me inside. His masculine presence immediately invades my space. I'm not sure I like it.

"All clear of what exactly?" he asks.

It's a good thing I have a fast brain to go with my lame mouth. "The girl next door sometimes hangs out here watching my television. I have a bigger screen."

"Ah," he comments. "I thought you meant ghosts or something."

I give him a "very funny" look and set my beauty bag on the entry table. "Would you like me to make coffee? Tea?"

"Coffee would be nice."

Even as Shay says this, his eyes move around the room, scoping everything out. They land on my home theater system and light up. "Nice," he comments. "Love to watch a game on that thing."

I'm not psychic, but I do have a vivid imagination. I picture Terry reclining on my couch, watching a game and getting peanuts or popcorn or whatever guys eat while watching sports all over my imported rug. It's not a pretty picture. My imagination plants me next to him, maybe playing with his big gun while we watch TV, and I warm to the idea.

"This way," I instruct, assuming Shay will follow me to the kitchen. My kitchen is spacious and airy. The appliances are all stainless steel, the countertops black marble. Shay slides onto one of my dainty bar stools. He looks about as at home as a rabbit would in a fox's den.

"Okay, tell me what else you 'sense' about Lisa Keller's murder."

He's not one for small talk. Now that I know what's really going on in my nightmares, I see no reason not to share the information. "The man who murdered her has a tattoo on the back of his left shoulder." I close my eyes as if seeking a vision. A moment later I open them and sigh. "I can't make it out in my head. It says something."

Shay lifts a skeptical brow. "I thought you had to be touching the photo to get your 'visions.'"

Oops. "I only have to touch it once . . . the karma stays with me after that." What a load.

Terry glances around and I figure he's looking for a shovel to get through the bullshit. His gaze travels back to me. "Where were you last night?"

"Home," I automatically answer.

"Alone?"

While I scoop coffee into a filter, it dawns on me that Terry is not just chatting me up. He's suspicious of me. And I guess he has every right to be. "Some of the time," I answer. After filling the pot with water and starting the coffee, I turn toward him. "A friend dropped in later and spent the night."

"Oh." Shay frowns. He takes out his notepad and pen. "What time did he drop by?"

Why did Shay automatically assume it was a he? And why do I get the feeling he's not happy to hear I have late-night male visitors? Or is he just disappointed that I have someone to vouch for me for part of the night?

"Around two," I answer. "And it wasn't a he, it was a she."

My answer receives another brow lift. "Any chance I can verify that with your friend?"

Not until I get my story straight with Cindy. "I can give you her cell number," I offer. Cindy's probably next door napping after spending the night on my couch. I'll have a chance to clue her in before Shay talks to her.

"Name and number?"

"Cindy Emerson," I answer then rattle off her cell number.

"And you say she arrived around two in the morning?"

This sounds strange. A woman coming over at two in the morning and spending the night. About now is when I should explain that Cindy lives next door. Of course if I do, Shay will probably want to see if she's home so he can question her. I have to tell Cindy that I've suddenly become psychic on top of being a werewolf before he speaks to her. It would be just my luck for her to pop in about now.

"Lou! You here?"

Oh, my God. I *am* psychic! Leaving the coffee perking, I make a beeline for the living room. I groan upon seeing Cindy. She hasn't bothered to change from her outfit last night.

She draws up short upon seeing me. "What's with the face?" she asks. "You look guilty. You got a man in here or something?"

At about that time Cindy's gaze strays past me and widens. I'm sure Shay now stands behind me. "Cindy Emerson, Detective Terry Shay. Detective, Cindy Emerson."

This is a bad situation. Cindy showing up in leather and a cop in my apartment who is suspicious of me for somehow being involved in murders I should know nothing about, but that I unfortunately do.

Shay steps around me. "Ms. Emerson, can you tell me where you were last night?"

He's clever, indicating that he doesn't already know where she supposedly was last night, at least from two in the morning on. Cindy blinks at him.

"And why is that your business?"

I inwardly groan again. Cindy's watched enough police shows to know you don't get cocky with the law.

"I'm investigating a crime," Shay answers. "I'd like to know your whereabouts last night, say around two in the morning. And for the record, it has nothing to do with you, Ms. Emerson, but it does involve Ms. Kinipski."

"Oh." Cindy visibly relaxes. What a friend. She's relieved I'm the one in trouble, not her. "I was here at two this morning, spent the night in fact."

"Cindy lives next door," I feel moved to add. "We're, ah, friends."

Shay takes a moment to appreciate Cindy's outfit. He continues, "Did it appear that Ms. Kinipski had been home all evening?"

Cindy considers his question. "It appeared that way to me. She was wearing her favorite flannel pajamas, wasn't wearing makeup, and she had been sleeping. I came over because—"

I frantically shake my head while Shay's focused on Cindy. I don't want her talking about the nightmares.

"Because she had a falling-out with her friend," I answer for her. "Cindy was upset. She wanted someone to talk to."

Damn. Cindy is an open book. Now she has this "I did?" look on her face. Fortunately, she's a quick study. "Yeah, that's right," she agrees. "Hey, let me ask you something. This 'friend' I had over last night took some of my stuff. I want to know if she's psychotic."

Now would be a good time for Shay to tell Cindy he has no further use for her and she can go. "Depends on what she took," he says instead.

Please do not answer something weird.

"My knee-high boots, my little black whip, and all my underwear," Cindy provides, as if there isn't anything odd about having knee-high boots and a black whip.

"Definitely psychotic," Shay says, and I'm impressed that he can keep a straight face. "I'd steer clear of her."

"Stupid dyke," Cindy mutters. She glances between the two of us. "Why is Lou in trouble? I can vouch for her. She's a good citizen, a supermodel, you know?"

"I'm aware of Ms. Kinipski's profession," Shay assures her. He takes in Cindy's outfit again. "And what profession are you in, Ms. Emerson?"

If Cindy hadn't already made it perfectly clear that she's gay, I'm sure Shay would think she must be a prostitute.

"Makeup specialist," she answers. "I was there that day you came to see Lou on the roof, remember? Someday I hope to become a construction worker."

Too much information. "Are you finished questioning Cindy?" I ask Shay. "I'm sure she has other things to do." I give Cindy a look that tells her she'd better find something else to do if she doesn't.

Shay snaps his notebook closed and places it back in his inside pocket. "That's all for now. I have your cell phone number if I need anything else from you."

"Right," Cindy says. She turns and heads for the door. Upon reaching it she says, "You should come watch *COPS* with us sometime. You can tell us what's real and what's just a load of crap."

Shay doesn't respond. "Coffee should be done," I say to distract him. I head back into the kitchen. Shay slides back onto his bar stool a moment later. I pour coffee in two floral-decorated cups and place one in front of him. "Sugar or cream?"

"No. Just black."

His coffee preference doesn't surprise me. Maybe I am psychic. Maybe it's because I was a waitress before I became a supermodel. I can always tell the just-black type guys. No nonsense. No frills. Just give them the caffeine and don't try to dress it up. Manly men. I wonder what it means that Stefan likes lattes . . . and girls with broad shoulders?

"Your *friend* is interesting."

Sipping my coffee, I consider the use of his emphasis on the word "friend." Does Terry now think I'm gay? Maybe it's best to let Shay draw his stereotyped conclusions. I detect a hint of interest toward me from the detective. Not just the business between us, but the fact that he's seen me mostly naked and has possibly thought about that a time or two. As hot as he is, I don't want him sniffing around me any more than necessary.

"She's a little out there," I agree. "I've known her since kindergarten." That's all I'm giving him concerning Cindy. "Shouldn't we get back to business so you can leave?"

Shay nods, easily switching back to business. "The murder took place shortly before two A.M. It happened across town. You couldn't have been there and gotten back home, removed your makeup, and changed your clothes before Cindy Emerson came over. That is, if she's telling the truth."

I suppose it's his job to be suspicious. I let the remark about Cindy's credibility slide. "And it was a sex crime, right? I also couldn't have had sex with her before I ripped her throat out."

Coffee cup raised halfway to his mouth, Shay suddenly sets it back down. "I never told you that."

Oops again. "I'm assuming it was the same as Sally Preston's murder. Am I right?"

Eyeing me with the baby blues, he nods. "Yeah, it was the same guy. No semen samples to confirm it, but everything else was the same. I just find it odd that you automatically assumed that."

Shay has worn out his welcome. "Is it your normal first reaction to mistrust everyone you meet, or is it just models or women in general you have a problem with?"

"Yes," he answers. He rises. "Look, I don't believe in psychics. If you want to convince me you have special abilities, tell me something we don't already know about this guy."

I'm not falling for any tricks. "I need to touch the photo again because the karma has faded."

He stops himself before he can do a complete eye roll and removes the photo. I don't want to look at it, at her, not knowing what I now know. I close my eyes and hold the photo in my hands.

There is something I know that no one else knows. Something I should not mention. Something that will send Terry Shay running, never to darken my door again. I open my eyes and look at him. "The man who killed both women is a werewolf."

I get nothing from him. No widening of the baby blues. No frown. No laugh. Nothing. Shay takes the photo and stuffs it back into his pocket. All delicious six feet two of him turns and walks away. I hear the door close a moment later. He thinks I am totally whacked. Well, that's one way to end a forbidden relationship before it gets started.

C all me a glutton for punishment because the next day I make the short ride downtown to the dilapidated building housing one Morgan Kane. I don't hear music blaring from behind his closed door. All is quiet. I test the knob. I know most people would simply knock, but if the door's open and Kane isn't around, I might do some snooping of my own.

The office is not empty. Kane sits in the chair behind his messy desk, head leaned back, eyes closed, cowboy boots propped up on his desktop . . . sleeping. I'd say he looks innocent in sleep, but he doesn't. I stalk across the room, surprised I can be quiet in high heels—surprised I'm stalking, period.

I'm pretty good at it. I come up behind Kane and stare down at him. At least he doesn't snore. I get close . . . real close. His breath smells like peppermint. I had expected tobacco and liquor. He still needs a shave. He does shave his neck, I note. He's groomed to look like he needs to be groomed.

Having Kane's neck so close puts thoughts in my head. If I can will the fangs to come, maybe I can just kill him instead of being forced to hire him. As tempting as the idea is, I know that, deep down, like Cindy believes, I am not a killer. Or at least I sincerely hope not.

"Either kiss me or slit my throat, cupcake." His eyes open. They aren't as bloodshot today.

"I didn't plan to kiss you," I assure him, not bothering to say that I didn't plan to kill him, either.

He smiles at that. "What can I do for you, Sherry?"

Kane purposely baits me. He must assume if I changed my name, there's a reason. Lou Kinipski isn't exactly a name anyone would choose to flatter their celebrity image, so he probably finds it curious. "First, you can tell me how you found out my name."

After removing his boots from his desk, he straightens in his chair. I stare at the back of his head. My first impression concerning his hair was that it's dirty. Not so. The color is dirty blond; the hair itself is not dirty.

"You could use highlights," I decide, walking around him to sit in the cold metal chair.

"I'll discuss that with my hairdresser next time I'm in the salon," Kane says sarcastically. "Now, what is it that you wish to discuss with me, cupcake?" He cringes. "I mean, Sherry, or do you prefer Ms. Billington? Ms. Kinipski? I get so confused."

"I'd prefer that you go to hell. But Ms. Kinipski is fine. Now, answer my question."

Kane leans forward, places his elbows on the desk, and steeples his fingers beneath his chin. "First, I deduced that you were from Texas. You've almost lost the accent, but not quite. Second, I suspected that you don't have a good relationship with your adoptive parents, or they would have given you more information than you have concerning your biological parents. By tracing your modeling career, I know that you've lived in New York for at least six years, probably a little longer. By my guesstimations, that would have made you fairly young when you left your Texas roots to seek fame and fortune in the big city."

Kane opens a drawer and takes out the whiskey. I guess he needs to wet his whistle after trying to impress me with his gift for deduction. I am a little impressed, but I'm not going to tell him that.

"Young women flock to the city every day to do just that," I point out.

"True," he agrees. "Your name bothered me. I can see you taking a more glamorous name to further your modeling career. Lou Kinipski is not a glamorous name. Yet it reeks of falseness. So if you didn't change your name for professional reasons, then why? The natural conclusion is because you didn't want anyone from Texas to find you. Why? Runaway, of course."

I reach across his desk, lift the Wild Turkey bottle, and take a drink. "And that's why I became a famous model and had my picture plastered in magazines, on billboards, and so on. I didn't want anyone to know who I am."

"That also bothered me," he admits. "Just on a hunch, I looked through the reports on missing girls who would have been about your age when you left Texas. I ran across an interesting article about a couple eloping on prom night, never to be heard from again."

My heart lurches. Were there pictures along with the article? There couldn't have been or Kane wouldn't believe for one moment that I am the same girl who disappeared.

"And?" I prod him.

"The article was very small. The snapshot was poor quality. Even so." He shakes his head. "How much plastic surgery did you have and who the hell paid for it? Good ol' Tom? Where is he now? Did you ditch him after you got what you wanted and decided you were too good for a Texas farm boy?"

I'm sickened that Kane actually knows what I once looked like. More so that he knows there is a connection between me and Tom Dawson. Of course he would assume I had plastic surgery. That is the only logical explanation. I need to get him off any connection between Tom and me or no telling what else he might dig up.

"I didn't run away with Tom Dawson," I say. "I have no idea where he is. He was the star football player for our high school team. As you saw by the picture, he wouldn't have been interested in a girl like me."

While I lie like a son, or daughter, or whatever, of a bitch to Kane, I hope I've developed enough facial reaction skills during my modeling career to look truthful.

"Then where did you get the money to have the plastic surgery, and why did you run away to begin with?"

I'm not on trial. At least not yet. "None of this is really any of your business," I remind him. "All I want is for you to find my birth parents. I had a little work done. It wasn't that expensive." More lying. "I was a late bloomer, also. It's not that I don't want anyone from Texas to know who I am; it's that I don't have a good relationship with my adoptive parents and we parted on bad terms. I changed my name before I started modeling. I wanted a fresh start. Can we drop this now and get back to the real issue?"

Kane stares at me from across the desk. His eyes are not actually muddy brown. They're more the color of whiskey. Which is ironic. This whole situation is my fault. I had responded when he called me Sherry on the phone. I should have played dumb instead of hanging up in a panic like I did.

"Okay," he finally says. "What information will you give me that I don't have to go digging to find?"

I'd sigh in relief if Kane wouldn't pounce on that reaction, as well. "I have the name of the agency I was adopted through. The agency claims all their files are sealed. They also say they would have to have written permission from the birth mother to release the information. They supposedly have no known location for her."

"Typical response," Kane says. "And that is why people hire private investigators."

As much as it irks me, I came prepared. Lifting my beauty bag, I remove fifteen thousand dollars in cash. I place it on his desk. "That should get you started. One rule. Don't contact my adoptive parents. Like I said, we parted on bad terms and neither of us wants anything to do with the other. Got that?"

"Makes my job harder, but yeah, I got it." He slides the money across the desk and into the same drawer where he keeps his whiskey. He looks at me and shakes his head again.

"What?" I ask tersely.

"I just wonder how much of what I see is what I get with you."

I rise. "Stop wondering. You're not getting any of me."

He laughs as I walk toward the door.

"I'll be in touch."

Not a comforting thought. I have a feeling I just opened a can of worms I'd be better off to have left buried.

CONFESSION NO. 6

*Forrest Gump's mother had a lot of catchy
sayings. I never really understood any of them.
Life is not like a box of chocolates. Life is more
like a wad of gum stuck to the bottom of your
favorite pair of shoes. The more you try to
clean up the mess, the stickier it becomes.*

Manolo Blahnik on Fifty-fourth is heaven on
earth. Just the smell of fine leather footwear
soothes my battered soul. I'm living in the
moment, leaving everything behind. No worries
about werewolf outbreaks. No pictures of murder
victims being thrust at me. No nightmares. No Morgan Kane sniffing around in places he shouldn't
sniff. Just shoes. Mules. Pumps. Sandals. Like I
said. Heaven.

"What do you think of these, Lou?"

Karen models a pair of red Mary Jane pumps with
three-inch heels. The heels make her look about six
eight. Karen is six two and proud of it. Height is not
an issue with her. She dates tall men, short men, fat

men, skinny men, it doesn't matter. I've even seen her dancing with men who appear to be suckling at her breasts because of the height issue. I admire her for not giving a damn. I, in contrast, give too much of one.

"Wicked bad," I assure her.

"Cindy, what do you think?"

In a surprise move, Cindy decided to come shoe shopping in normal shoe stores with us today. Since she's a little starstruck by Karen, I think I know why she agreed to tag along.

"They look good," is about all she can manage around the slobber in her mouth.

"I think I'll get them," Karen decides. She frowns at me. "You're not into the spirit of the shoes, Lou. You've only tried on one pair."

Even shoes can't take my mind off my troubles. I'm a bit distracted. "Just enjoying new shoe smell," I tell her. "It's almost as good as new car smell."

Karen sniffs. "I never fully appreciated the new shoe smell before."

"It's really strong at Red Wing," Cindy offers. "Lots of leather in those stores."

"We're not going," I mutter to her. "And stop drooling. It's embarrassing."

Runway style, Karen flounces over in the killer red pumps. "Leave her be, Lou. She can drool if she wants. I don't mind. I'm used to it."

Have I mentioned that Karen doesn't have a humble bone in her body? She was born beautiful. I've seen baby pictures of her. She carries them with her. Karen has no conception of what it's like to be unattractive. Or even normal looking.

"I'm starving," I say. "Let's go have lunch."

Even frowning, Karen is nothing short of stunning. "But I've only decided on this one pair. I've never gone home with only one pair of shoes."

"We can always stop back on our way home," Cindy suggests. "Truth is, I'm starving, too."

Karen shrugs. "Okay, but only on one condition. You buy these shoes, Lou. You'd look great in them."

The shoes aren't made for walking. They're sex shoes. The kind of shoes a woman wears with a strapless corset, garter belt, and thigh-high hose. Due to current circumstances, they'd go wasted in my closet. On the other hand, the shoes might get a reaction from Terry Shay should our paths ever cross again. Those shoes would get a second look from a priest.

"Okay." I cave. "But only because I'm hungry."

I leave the shop wearing the shoes. I'm nearly as tall as Karen in them. Poor Cindy looks like a midget as we stroll down Fifty-fourth toward a little café the models frequent. The place has wonderful soups and salads. As we walk, Karen whips out her cell and makes a call. She says she's headed to the café and hangs up. I lift a brow.

"Just letting my service know where I'll be," she explains.

That's odd. Wouldn't her service just call her if they need her? Would her agency actually grab a cab

and come running to the café if they had to discuss
business? Mine wouldn't. Maybe I should switch.

It's a lovely day for winter in New York. The
Christmas lights still twinkle in the trees. It's chilly,
but not freezing. I'm envisioning the Cobb salad
smothered in blue cheese I'll have, when it happens.

The unthinkable.

I step in gum.

Gum!

On my brand-new pair of four-hundred-and-
seventy-five-dollar shoes!

Rarely do I say the F word. Where I come from,
the F word is not like saying "oh, shoot" like it is in
New York. I say it now.

Karen's head swings toward me. We had this
rhythm going, the three of us walking down the
street like Charlie's Angels. I've thrown the whole
line out of sync. Cindy stumbles. She actually trips
over the F word. She *never* heard that word growing
up in her house.

Karen repeats the F word. "He must have been at
the Starbucks on the corner to have gotten here
so fast."

He? Starbucks? What's Karen talking about? I
slide my shoe along the pavement as we walk, hoping to dislodge the wad stuck to the bottom. Then I
see him. Stefan stands outside the café, looking sus-
piciously like he's waiting for us to join him.

We haven't spoken since I called him a bozo and
slammed the car door in his face. Guiltily, I realize I

haven't thought about him for a couple of days. I've been too busy thinking about Shay, and the fact he's written me off as a total loony bird. I've also been thinking about Morgan Kane, and what kind of information he's digging up now.

"You just called him." I frown at Karen. "This is a setup."

She doesn't bother to deny it. "I thought you two should kiss and make up. He's been hell to work with the past couple of days."

Due to murders and mayhem, I haven't worked since the cowboy boots shoot. I'm not scheduled to work again until Friday. I have yet to convince myself that Stefan's grimy one-night stands are none of my business. I'm not sure if I'm ready to forgive and forget. At least he's not wearing the orange stocking cap I despise.

He smiles as I gimp along, dragging the bottom of one of my sex shoes on the pavement. When Stefan smiles, it's hard to stay mad. He has this naughty-little-boy thing going for him that women find impossible to resist. And therein lies the problem.

"Hi, Lou," he says when we reach him.

"Hi," I say back.

Stefan glances down at my feet. He laughs. This is not the four-hundred-and-seventy-five-dollar response I had hoped to get while wearing the shoes.

"You have paper stuck to the bottom of your shoe."

Glancing down, I'm tempted to cuss again. A Snickers bar wrapper is now stuck to my shoe. I place a hand on Stefan's shoulder, lean down, and pull it off. There's a waste receptacle in front of the café. I walk over and try to throw the candy wrapper in the trash. It sticks to my fingers. I say the F word again.

When I turn around, Karen, Stefan, and Cindy all grin back at me like village idiots. Grumbling, I march past them into the café. The burst of warm air improves my mood. Beneath my jacket, I wear a short-sleeved blouse. Shopping often leads to sweating, depending on how serious a woman is about it. I dressed to layer down.

The café is seat yourself. I spot a cozy booth in the back and head that way. I don't wait for the others. I'm focused on the fact I have gum on the bottom of my shoe and I'm careful where I walk. A discarded napkin isn't getting a free ride from me.

Once I reach the booth, I plop down and immediately lift my shoe to assess the damage. With luck, I might be able to scrape off the mess with a knife. Karen, Stefan, and Cindy scoot in from the other side. Cindy sits beside me, then Karen and Stefan take the outside across from me.

"I need a knife," I mutter. "Stupid gum."

"If you put ice on it first and freeze it, I've heard it's easier to get off," Karen suggests. "Or, you could just throw them away. That's what I do."

Okay. I'm a little tight with my money. I'm not trashing these sex shoes even if I'm never going to wear them again. They can sit in my closet, a little red ray of hope that at some future date, I can have a normal sex life again. Or an abnormal one. I'll take anything.

As soon as our perky waitress sets water glasses in front of us, I dig a piece of ice from the glass. I slide the ice along the bottom of my sticky shoe. The street cleaners must be on strike because in one short walk I have enough grime stuck to the bottom of my shoe to make mud, which of course gets all over my fingers. I pause long enough to grab a napkin.

"Lou, honey, I'll buy you a new pair of shoes if you'll stop flashing your panties at everyone sitting across the room from us. You are wearing panties, right?"

I glance up and across at Stefan. His words register a moment later and my head swivels toward the other side of the room. There are a number of people staring at me. One of them is Detective Terry Shay. Or I think it is. He's not looking directly at me. He's looking up my skirt. I uncross my legs and bang my knees together. My face is on fire. I know a million men have seen me in my underwear, but this is different. I'm not sure how exactly it's different. It just is.

"What are you doing here anyway?" I ask Stefan, totally unglued by seeing Shay looking up my skirt. By seeing Shay period. "I don't remember inviting you."

Stefan smiles despite my bad mood. "Karen invited me."

His admission warrants another glare at Karen. She picks up the menu and looks at it. "I can bring a friend," she informs me. "You brought one."

I would argue that Cindy is a mutual friend, but then, she would just argue back that Stefan is also a mutual friend. But enough about Stefan. What in the hell is Terry Shay doing here? I can't picture the café as one of his usual haunts. He doesn't look like a soup and salad kind of guy. He's meat and potatoes all the way.

Is he following me? But wait, he was already here before I walked in. In a city this size, it's hard to believe this is a coincidence.

Karen wears a rather sly smile she tries to hide behind her menu.

"You didn't," I say.

She shrugs and places her menu aside. "He contacted me through my service. Said something about checking your credibility. To me, sounded like a lame excuse to get information about you. I said he should meet me here today during lunchtime if he wanted to talk to me."

"What and who are you talking about?" Stefan looks around the room. He zeros in on Shay. "What's that cop doing here?" He turns the puppy-dog eyes on me. "You said he talked to you about identity theft, Lou. Why would he check your credibility with Karen?"

This situation is as sticky as the gum on the bottom of my shoe. I like having friends, but only Cindy is allowed into the personal side of my life.

"I get the impression Detective Shay thinks I stole my own identity. You know, charged my cards up and cried foul to get out of paying them. I'm sure that happens all the time with supposed identity theft problems." This lying stuff is getting too easy for me.

"Takes his job a little seriously, doesn't he?" Stefan grumbles. He charges to the rescue. "I can set him straight if you want me to."

What I want is for everyone to stay out of my business. And I certainly don't want Terry strolling over to talk murder in front of my friends. Where does he get off contacting Karen to ask questions about me anyway? I glance across the room to give him a dirty look. I come face-to-face with his crotch. It's a nice crotch.

"Mind if I join you?" he asks.

Now that's a loaded question. Before I can assure him that I do mind, Karen pipes up. "No, there's plenty of room. Just scoot in next to Lou."

If she were closer, I'd snatch Karen bald. Terry scoots in beside me. Too many bodies crammed together makes wearing a coat unbearable. I shrug out of mine. Cindy suddenly puts an arm around me and slaps her hand against the top of my arm. I glance at her. She leans in close to whisper, "You have some fur on the top of your arm."

Oh, great. I'm having another outbreak. I can do one of two things. Run from the café screaming, or howling, whichever the case may be, or act as if there's nothing odd about my best friend suddenly getting too chummy with me. I decide on the latter.

"I'd prefer you not to discuss my business with my friends," I tell Terry. "It's between you and me and I'd like to keep it that way."

Terry stares at Cindy's hand pressed against my arm, as if he didn't hear my comment. Finally he glances up at me. "Checking credibility is standard procedure."

"Well, I can vouch for Lou's credibility," Stefan says. He hardens his puppy-dog eyes on Terry. "I've known her for a long time. A very long time."

I guess that's supposed to mean something, the added "very long time." If Stefan is suggesting we're lovers, he can take a number. Cindy is obviously my lover in the minds of all present. Even Karen looks a little surprised.

"Maybe this isn't a good idea." Terry directs the comment to Karen. "I'll leave you all to enjoy your lunch."

Karen reaches forward and slaps his hand with a menu. "Don't be silly," she croons. "You have to eat, right? Stay so we can get better acquainted."

Recalling Karen's comment about Shay's ass, I know why she'd want to get to know him. Since I sit with another woman's arm draped around me, Karen feels she's been given the go-ahead to pursue Terry Shay sexually. That thought does not improve my mood.

"Maybe just some pie and coffee," Shay agrees.

The waitress appears and takes our orders. The moment she leaves is awkward, to say the least. Everyone keeps glancing at Cindy's hand plastered to my shoulder.

"So, Detective Shay, since this isn't business, can we call you Terry?" Karen attempts to save an awkward moment.

"I guess that would all right."

"Let me introduce you to everyone," she says, batting her lashes.

Shay's thigh is pressed against mine. I wonder if he's as aware of the contact as I am. Probably not, since Karen is vying for his undivided attention. "I already know Ms. Kinipski and Ms. Emerson," he says. "And I remember you and the photographer from before."

"Stefan O'Conner," Stefan says. He glances at me, at Cindy's hand, and raises a brow.

I rub my arms to signify "I'm cold," as if that were some type of explanation. Karen asks Shay about himself. She manages to pry information from him, although I get the feeling he'd as soon eat his pie, drink his coffee, and be on his way. I learn that Shay was born and raised in the city.

His father was a cop and his father before him. At one point Cindy rather loudly announces, "You feel cold, honey," and she helps me into my coat. At least I can move again. We finish our salads, and when the waitress brings the check, Stefan gallantly picks up the tab.

Shopping will have to be cut short. I can't shop during a fur outbreak. My apartment building is within walking distance. Cindy and Karen can proceed without me. We all climb from the booth.

"I'd like to talk to you," Shay says to me. "Alone, since you want our business to remain private."

There's a little of Morgan Kane in Terry Shay. I'm curious about what he wants to discuss with me. "I guess you can walk me home. Or at least partway."

Once we file out of the café, Shay hangs back as I make my excuses to the rest of the group. Cindy offers to continue the hunt for expensive shoes with Karen. I wonder if Cindy will end up dragging her into a Red Wing like she always does me. Stefan doesn't look pleased by the development.

"I thought I might give you a lift home," he says. "I wanted to apologize for what I said to you last time we were together. I think we should kiss and make up like Karen wants us to do."

Kissing and making up isn't an objectionable thought. Even if I had guilt feelings for not thinking much about Stefan the last few days, I realize that I miss him. He does care about me, and I care deeply about him. I value his friendship, regardless of whatever else goes on between us. Stepping forward, I place a hand on his arm.

"Some other time, okay? How about Friday after the shoot? You can give me a lift home then."

His gaze strays past me to Shay. "Are you in some kind of trouble, Lou? If you are, I want to help."

I'm beginning to understand other people can't always fight my battles for me. Stefan helped me out tremendously seven years ago. Cindy helps me out all the time. What's happening now is something I have to do myself.

"I know you want to help," I say. "And I appreciate that, but I'm a big girl. I'll handle this."

He glances away and then back at me. "I just like to look out for you. I care about you, Lou. You know that, right?"

Terry may send my hormones into overdrive, but Stefan touches me on a deeper level. I wish I could share what is happening to me with him. I wish I could tell him about my past and what I was running from when he found me. But I prefer that he only sees the surface. There's nothing wrong now with the outside of me . . . well, besides the fact I have fur on my shoulder.

"Sure I do," I answer. Giving him my best cover-girl smile, I squeeze his arm and walk away. "I'll see you Friday," I call over my shoulder.

Shay waits a short distance from me. Karen and Cindy walk arm in arm toward the expensive row of shops that line Fifty-fourth. I'm sure Karen's intentions were good when she got Terry and me together, even if she later decided she might want him for herself. Thanks a lot, girlfriend.

CONFESSION NO. 7

There's nothing worse than having an itch you can't scratch. Okay, that may be a little melodramatic. There are worse things, a lot worse. But I'm still living in the moment. And this moment is damn uncomfortable.

I itch like the devil as Shay and I start toward the general direction of my apartment building. My shoulder area seems particularly vulnerable to the recent outbreaks. Kind of like a stress zit that pops up in the same place when a normal woman's life gets crazy. I'll take the zit any day.

My jacket is too heavy to allow deep scratch penetration. I'm forced to deal with the discomfort. Both the shoulder fur and Shay walking beside me as if we're a normal couple out for an afternoon stroll in the city. I'm anything but normal, and Shay is . . . well, I'm not sure what he is besides hunkalicious. Maybe it's time to find out if he's more than a pretty face.

"You said your father was a cop," I say. "Do your parents live in the city?"

"Brooklyn," he answers. "Been there all their married lives."

"So that's where you grew up?"

As we stroll, it doesn't escape my notice that Terry's eyes constantly search the area. "Yeah. Me and my three brothers, and my sister. The house has only three bedrooms so Sis got the one room and the four of us boys were crammed into the other one. That'll make you tough."

I smile. It's hard to imagine not being an only child. "Are you close to everyone?"

"Yeah, we're all tight," he answers, his eyes still roaming the streets. "Got a couple of nephews and a niece, too. Kids are the best."

Before I get too many warm fuzzies, I remember Terry has dragged my friends into my business. "Let's clear something up. Leave my friends out of this. I'm not involved in the murders you're investigating. You had no right to contact Karen."

Suddenly Terry takes my arm and steers me into an alleyway. He glances around the corner as if checking to make sure we aren't being followed. I think Stefan is right. Shay takes his job too seriously.

"Here's the deal. Something interesting came up during DNA testing, and again when the profiler talked to the detectives on this case. I needed to know about your credibility. Psychics are a hard pill for me to swallow. I don't believe in the supernatural. I don't want to share information with someone trying to put something over on me."

I wish I didn't believe in the supernatural. I'm walking, talking proof that most people are blessedly ignorant about the monsters roaming their cities. Wait a minute; did Shay just say he wants to share information with me?

"What kind of information?"

He glances around the corner again. "Private information regarding these two cases. Information we wouldn't want leaked."

I wait until I have his undivided attention again before asking, "Why would you share information with me? I told you that I'm not involved in these murders. They have nothing to do with me."

I've never noticed how long and slender his fingers are until he runs them through his hair. He doesn't have detective hands. He has musician hands. "I'm still not convinced you might not be a target," he says. "It's conceivable that the killer might only be fulfilling his fantasies about you with women who resemble you and are easier to get to."

"Oh, that makes me feel better," I say sarcastically. "Is this what you wanted to tell me? Stuff that will make me paranoid?"

"No." He shakes his head. "That's not what I wanted to discuss with you. What you told me the other day in your apartment. I thought it was crazy. But because of the bite marks and furlike hair found beneath the victims' nails, the profiler on these cases suspects the murderer suffers from lycanthropy. You know, that disease where someone believes they're a werewolf?"

If anybody knows what lycanthropy is, it's me. I've done a ton of research on the condition. I've even tried to make myself believe I suffer from it. But like the murderer, I don't think that's the case. I wish now I'd never told Terry what I did. I've connected myself to the case, and I don't want to be connected. It's bad enough that I dream about the creep, and about his victims.

"So, why are you sharing this information with me?" I ask. "Just because my psychic abilities allowed me to pick up information on the killer doesn't mean I can actually pick him out in a crowd. Why drag me into it when I assure you I have no desire to be dragged into it?"

Shay looks away. He appears to be measuring his words before he glances back at me. "I've never believed in psychics. I do know how killers operate, and this guy isn't finished. I want to contact you and get your thoughts when and if he kills again. I also want to warn you to be vigilant. I think he might come after you."

He's totally creeping me out. And that's a hard thing to do to a girl who, at the moment, has an unnatural fur growth on her shoulder. Thinking about it only makes the itch worse. Thinking about it also reminds me that regardless of what I am, or what I

seem to be becoming, I have a human duty to my fel-
low man . . . and woman.

"I'll help if I can," I grudgingly agree. "And I'll
be vigilant when I'm out and about, but I really don't
think these attacks are aimed at me personally."

Shay guides me back toward the street. "You still
have my number, right?" he asks.

I'm not about to tell him his card still rests on my
nightstand, as if I'd actually get up the nerve to call
him some lonely night. "I think I have it somewhere."

Digging into his back jeans pocket, Shay removes
his wallet, slips out another card, and hands it to me.
"Just in case."

I drop the card into my beauty bag as we walk.
"All right, business concluded. You don't have to
walk me the rest of the way." I need to scratch. I can
barely suppress the urge.

"You're real good for my ego, Kinipski," he says
flatly. "You're always trying to get rid of me."

If it weren't for the itching, I'd be enjoying myself a little too much. I like the fact that Shay comes
from a big boisterous family. I've always fantasized
about being part of a big family. He likes kids, too.
That always wins a man points with a woman. That
thought makes me frown. I'm not sure if I can have
kids. What kind of children would I produce? And
would it just be one kid at a time or a whole litter?
That thought makes me shudder.

Shay stops me and pulls my collar up around my

neck. His hands are cold. "Sure you don't want me to walk you the rest of the way?"

It's tempting. Even with the itch driving me nuts. Which is exactly why I need to send him on his way. "I'm a big girl. I think I can handle walking two more blocks home. You'll have to go make someone else's day."

That gets me a smile. He has white, straight teeth. His hands still grasp my collar. His smile fades as he stares down at me. I'm thinking now might be a good time for him to kiss me. He's obviously thinking something else.

"Well, take care, Ms. Kinipski." He releases me and steps back.

I might be blushing. Like I expected something and didn't get it. I brush my hair off my cheek and try to act casual. "Since we're almost working together, I think it would be all right if you call me 'Lou.'"

He smiles that killer smile again. "All right," he agrees. "Lou it is."

About now I wish I hadn't chosen an ugly name to remind myself that I was once an ugly girl. Even Shay can't make it sound good. There's nothing else to say or do but leave. "See you around."

"Call me if you get any weird vibes, or whatever it is you do. And watch your back. Be alert to your surroundings."

I give him a little salute, which makes him smile again. He finds me amusing. Then I remember he also finds me gay. Is that the reason he didn't kiss me? Maybe he didn't kiss me because he's not attracted to me. That's a hard pill to swallow.

Turning away, I move on. As I walk along the street, sharing my energy with others, I feel Shay's eyes follow me. I feel them for a long time. Too long. Suddenly, the hair on the back of my neck stands on end. A feeling of unease settles over me. It's not a feeling a person gets from having the object of that person's desire staring after her. It's a creepy feeling.

Nonchalantly, I glance over my itchy shoulder. I don't see Shay. I do see a man stopped at a corner a block down, staring in my direction. He wears a hooded sweatshirt, hands stuffed inside his jacket pockets. Maybe he isn't staring at me. I can't see his face. There's only a black hole inside the hood of his sweatshirt. But he is staring, I know this instinctively. My senses sharpen in a heartbeat.

There's a peculiar scent in the air. In a sea of human bodies, human smells, his is different. A growl rises in my throat. Surprised, I suppress it. My gums suddenly ache. My fingertips sting. What the hell is going on? I'm in danger. I sense, smell, and taste it. Whatever is happening to me, it has to do with the hooded man on the corner.

Running away is a natural response in every creature, human or otherwise. Fight or flight. I turn away, prepared to get the hell out of Dodge, then something dawns on me. I'm not the weakling I was when Tom Dawson attacked me. I'm not helpless. I've got fur, dammit! I wheel around to confront the man, but he's gone. My gaze darts frantically among the people on the street. I don't see him. Sniffing the air, I realize I don't smell him, either. Was he ever there to begin with?

Shaken and worried I might sprout fangs or some other abnormality, I start for home. I fight the urge to keep looking over my shoulder. Did I see and sense what I thought I did? Or has Shay managed to flood my subconscious with paranormal delusions? I desperately want to believe the latter. Every human and inhuman instinct I have tells me that would be a lie.

A hot shower and a good shoulder waxing usually calm my nerves. I search the kitchen for something to eat. My fridge needs stocking and I settle for yogurt and pretzel sticks. No matter how calm I pretend to be, inside I still quake. I can't forget the feeling of his eyes on me—of his scent or my reaction to it. I realize the sense of control I thought I had over my life during the past seven years is a false one. For a split second today, I was transported back to prom night. I lost control.

A few pretzel sticks dipped in yogurt later, I still shake. My snack has absolutely zero calming effect. A girl needs chocolate and lots of it for immediate stress relief. Maybe a big fat cheeseburger and fries. A milk shake or two. My stomach growls and I take consolation in the fact that it's a normal response to hunger. Growling from the throat is not normal.

Placing the food aside, I move into the bedroom and stare at Shay's card. I'm tempted to call him, but for all I know, he's part of the problem. He could have messed with my mind today. Either that, or maybe he's the one who's psychic. The light blinks on my answering machine. I'm hesitant to push the button. What if I hear heavy breathing? I realize I'm being ridiculous and reach out and push the button.

Kane's voice blares back at me. "Hey, cupcake, got a lead on something. Meet me at the club tonight around nine and we'll talk about it."

Beep.

End of messages.

My excitement level rises a notch to know that Kane has information for me. Enthusiasm fades when I realize he just told me to meet him at the club. I'm not in the mood to go out; then again, maybe it would be good for me. I'm still not sure if I really saw what I think I saw today—if the man on the corner was stalking me, if the danger was real or imagined. I do know that once a person allows fear to take control of her life, it's hard to break free. I'm not going to cower in my apartment. I'm not going to cower ever again.

While I decide what to wear, I admit I'm not as brave as I often like to believe. I'll ask Cindy to go with me. She's the logical choice since she knows all of my secrets. Maybe we'll grab that cheeseburger and fries before we meet Kane. Just the thought of grease has a calming effect on me. I find my beauty bag, dig out my phone, and call Cindy's cell.

"Hello?" she answers.

"What's up?" I ask.

"Karen and I are in Red Wing smelling new work-boot smell."

Cindy can't see me roll my eyes. "At least you're not somewhere smelling old work-boot smell. Hey, I want you to go to Freddie Z's with me tonight. Kane has information for me."

A pause on the other end of the line. "You sure you want to mess with this guy? What if it's incriminating information?"

"Karen isn't listening to you, is she?" I immediately demand.

"No, she's flirting with the salesman. She's acting like she's actually interested in buying herself a pair of work boots."

Amusing. "When are you coming home?"

Another short pause. "It might be a while. Karen's really jerking the guy's chain and it's fun to watch."

I wish I were there to see that. I could use a laugh. "Do you want to meet me later at Burger Joint? We can go to the club from there."

"Sounds good."

"Don't invite Karen. You know this is private."

She sighs. "I'm not an idiot, Lou."

Dial tone.

I had that coming. Cindy's scatterbrained at times, but she's certainly not an idiot. Tonight I'll dress down, low-key, no attention grabbers. I decide on jeans and a T-shirt, tennis shoes and a pullover. Getting ready takes me into the evening. At seven I call down and have the night doorman order me a cab.

When I first step out on the street, I feel a moment of trepidation. I glance around me. Nothing looks out of the norm. The cab waits for me, and I find even that threatening. I get a grip and march over and open the cab door. I'm relieved when I recognize the cabby. He's picked me up several times, never sprouted fur and fangs or tried to jump me in the backseat. I climb inside and tell him where to take me.

Burger Joint is well lit and crowded. I'm relieved to see Cindy already seated. Should I tell her about the incident today? Is it even worth telling anyone about? It could have all been in my imagination. But no, my reaction to the man was not my imagination. He triggered something in me. Something bad. Maybe Cindy can help me sort through what happened today.

CONFESSION NO. 8

Rock and roll is here to stay. Or is it here to slay?

F reddie Z's is a typical smelly, sweaty rock and roll bar. The place does have a seventies feel to it, complete with wall-to-wall posters and black lights. A third-rate band is playing tonight. I hope Kane's band is better than this one.

"The only thing worse than a meat market is a less than prime meat market," Cindy says, curling her lip.

I raise my drink in salute. "Got that right. We must have come on loser night." There was a time when Cindy and I were both less than prime cut. Braces and contacts fixed Cindy. Becoming a were-wolf fixed me. Neither of us are girls a man would take home to meet Mom, however, so I guess we don't have room to talk.

"So where is this guy?" Cindy shouts over the noise. "I'm tired and want to go home. Besides, you had two outbreaks today. We probably shouldn't be out in public."

Cindy's right, and who knows where Kane is among a sea of sweaty bodies. I'm not in the mood to hunt for him, but I do want the information. "I haven't seen him yet," I answer Cindy. "I'm sure he'll shimmy out from under a rock at some point."

"Talkin' about me, cupcake?"

My head snaps up. Kane stands behind Cindy. The strobe lights in the bar remind me of the blink-blink-blink of a neon sign. They catch the blond streaks in his hair. Has he highlighted it? He wears a mesh T-shirt and black skintight pants. I'm sure he has the cowboy boots on his feet. Introductions are in order.

"Morgan Kane, this is my friend Cindy. Cindy, Morgan Kane."

Kane nods toward Cindy, then asks, "You sure you want witnesses, cupcake? I thought you wanted to keep our business private."

Cindy blinks at me and mouths, "Cupcake?"

I shrug. "She's okay. I don't keep secrets from her."

He glances between the two of us. Cindy doesn't hide the fact she's gay. She's wearing a man's sweater right now, no makeup, her brows need to be plucked, and the dial is lit up on her big ol' sports watch. Kane flashes the dimples at me.

"I see. You ladies into threesomes?"

Stefan thinking I'm gay annoyed me. Terry thinking I'm gay devastated me. I realize I could care less if Morgan thinks I'm gay.

"Cut the crap, Kane," I say. "Let's just get down to business so we can go home."

He pouts for a minute, then makes a jerking motion with his head. "Follow me. There's an office upstairs where we can talk without having to shout."

Cindy and I leave our drinks and follow him. By the time we reach a rail staircase toward the back of the bar, I wear the sweat of too many people I've had to brush up against. Heightened senses may sound like a turn-on, but in some cases they are not. This is one of them.

My ears ring and, yes, I do have the urge to howl in pain. I climb the stairs. When I reach the top landing and walk into a small room, Cindy has already seated herself on a black leather couch. The room doesn't resemble an office. There's a wet bar and lots of red velvet.

Against my better judgment, I step inside and pull the door closed. Considering what probably takes place on the black leather couch, I choose to stand. Kane is behind the bar, fixing himself a shot of Wild Turkey.

"What's the information?" I get right to the point.

Sipping his whiskey, Kane walks from behind the bar. He joins Cindy on the couch. "I was hacking around on my computer today, did a search on you, and something interesting came up."

I'm not impressed. "I've done a vanity search before. I'm a top fashion model. There are pages and pages on me."

"Yeah, on Lou Kinipski," he agrees. "No surprises there. But I'm not talking about Lou Kinipski; I'm talking about Sherry Billington."

Hearing my real name always makes me flinch. I pull myself together. "You don't think I've looked? I didn't find anything."

He takes another sip of his whiskey, and I think it's rude that he didn't offer me a shot. I could use one after the day I've had.

"That's because the average person doesn't know how to dig," he informs me. "It takes a certain skill."

Like playing air guitar? I want to ask, but refrain. I'm in the mood to humor Kane if it will get the ball rolling. "Okay, so what did you find?"

Patting the seat next to him, Kane says, "Join us and I'll tell you."

If I sit on the couch next to Kane and Cindy, in his demented mind, he's going to somehow connect that to a threesome. Humoring him is getting more difficult, but I suck it up and go sit next to him.

"Isn't this cozy?" He glances between Cindy and me.

"I think you got some scales on me," Cindy mutters, staring down at Kane's snakeskin boots. "You do know that a nice pair of leather work boots would be more practical?"

Gah! Cindy should just go to work for Red Wing.

"I'm not a work boots kind of guy, babe," Kane responds. He turns to me. "Didn't figure you for a work boots kind of girl, either, cupcake. But I like a woman who keeps me guessing."

I can't do it. I just can't keep sucking up to him. "If you call me 'cupcake' one more time you're going to find out exactly what kind of girl I am. Let's just get this over with before you make me mad enough to pull out your nipple ring."

Now Kane's the one who flinches. "Fine. While I was doing the search on Sherry Billington, I found out someone else was doing a search on her, too."

This is something new. My immediate response is to freak out. When one is a murderer, never mind being a werewolf, one doesn't like surprises, or private searches for oneself.

Rising, Kane heads back to the bar and sets his glass down. I expect him to pour himself another but he doesn't. Instead he leans against the bar facing me. "Any idea why a lab out of Nevada would be looking for you?"

A lab? I feel certain someone would like to get me and my screwed-up DNA under a microscope, but maybe I'm being paranoid. "Could one or both of my biological parents work for this lab?"

"Possible," Kane answers. "The thing is, if I contact them about you, they're going to know you've hired me to do some digging around. Sometimes people find out more than they really want to know about themselves while searching for answers about their parentage. Sometimes people only think they want to know, and once they do, they wish they had left things alone. I just want a go-ahead from you."

My first gut reaction, like Kane, is to jump at the chance. I would if I were normal. Maybe the lab doesn't have anything to do with my biological parents wanting to find the child they gave up for adoption. Maybe the lab is responsible for what I am. Maybe my parents don't work for the lab. Maybe they are in cages at the lab. Although Kane asking for my permission is the first semblance of professionalism I've seen from him, I'm torn about asking him to proceed. And he's going to find that odd.

"Maybe you should think about this for a couple of days, Lou," Cindy says. "Maybe Mr. Kane is right and you don't really want to know about your biological parents."

I glance at Cindy. I could kiss her. By expressing her opinion, she'll make my response seem more believable. "Maybe." I glance back at Kane. "Could you just concentrate on getting the records unsealed for now and let me think about this development with the lab for a while?"

He straightens from his leaning position against the bar. "You're kidding, right? This is a good, solid lead. You want me to back off before we even get started?"

So much for thinking he wouldn't find my response odd. "I want to go slow, is what I'm saying. I'm still not sure I've made the right decision in hiring you in the first place. Thinking about doing something and doing it are two different things. Like you said, sometimes it's best to let sleeping dogs lie."

Kane shakes his head. He does have highlights. A little amusing that he took my advice about that. Nothing else about the meeting is amusing, or about my day. I keep thinking about the hooded figure on the street corner. Cindy, not in jeopardy of turning into a werewolf or being involved in murders, and therefore more rational, said she thought Shay has made me paranoid. I hope she's right. I'll take being paranoid over being stalked any day of the week.

"The lab might have nothing to do with your biological parents," Kane says. "It's not unusual for people who adopt a child to have tests run on the baby before agreeing to the adoption. You know, looking for possible defects or medical conditions that might end up costing them a lot of money? I know it sounds cruel, but it is done. It could be something like that, although I don't know why they would be looking for you now."

Maybe to tell me I have a little medical condition they overlooked. Could the lab have answers for me? "What's the name of the lab?" I ask Kane. I'm thinking I can do a little research on my own without getting him involved.

He frowns at me. "When someone hires me for a job, they usually let me do my job and stay out of it."

I'm about to argue that I think my money entitles me to any information I ask for when someone knocks on the door.

"Morgan, you in there?" some guy shouts from the other side.

Kane walks to the door. "Yeah!" he shouts back. "I'm in a meeting!"

"Well, put your pants on. The cops are here asking about you. Those two ladies I saw following you up here are both over eighteen, aren't they?"

Cindy and I glance at one another. I curl my lip to let her know I'm disgusted by Kane, and disgusted that anyone would believe she and I are in here engaging in sexual activity with him. Kane swears and my attention swings back toward him.

"One of my band members got busted for coke last week. The fucking cops have been riding my ass about him. Trying to figure out if he was dealing. Like I know what all the guys do in their spare time." He takes a calming breath. "You want to wait around, ladies?"

I'm off the couch in a split second. I want no part of Kane's seedy world of rock and roll. "No, we don't. Since I'm the one forking out the cash, just do what I say. Forget the lab for now and concentrate on getting the adoption file unsealed."

Running a hand through his long hair, he says, "It's your money. I guess you make enough to throw it around. I'm not used to my clients telling me how to do my job."

In my case, he'd better get used to it. Cindy and I walk to the door. "Call me when you have more information."

Kane opens the door and Cindy and I walk out. I don't see whoever was shouting for Kane on the other side. At the end of the railing, I do catch the silhouettes of three men.

As I get closer to the men, one of them looks hauntingly familiar. The strobe hits his face and I freeze. It's Terry. What's he doing here? Following me? I'd believe that if his expression weren't every bit as surprised at seeing me as I am at seeing him. He moves toward me.

"Lou? What the hell are you doing here?"

"What are you doing here?" I shout back.

He glances past me. "You weren't just with Morgan Kane, were you?"

Not that it's really any of his business, but I say, "Yes. Do you have a problem with that?"

"You know him?"

"Yes," I answer impatiently. "Did you follow me here?"

Instead of answering, he shakes his head. "I don't like this, Lou."

Should I be flattered by his remark? Isn't it a little early in our nonrelationship for him to be jealous? Terry pulls a gun from his shoulder holster. Now I do freak out. Is he crazy?

"What are you doing?"

"You'll have to come down to the precinct, Lou.

Don't go anywhere." He starts past me and I grab his arm.

"What are you doing?" I repeat frantically.

His buddies come up behind him, guns drawn. "We're arresting Morgan Kane for the murders of Sally Preston and Lisa Keller," he answers.

CONFESSION NO. 9

Most women find a man in uniform irresistible. They do something for me, too. Like make me nauseous.

hen I was a kid, I wanted to ride in a cop car. Funny, you never hear adults say they want to ride in one. Cindy has been hauled in along with Kane and me. Morgan rode in a different car. He had two cops with him. Cindy and I only rated the one superfine, even though he has basically arrested me.

"I need to pee."

Cindy and I now sit in a little room where we've been told to stay. We've checked it out and don't see any two-way mirrors, so I'm not sweating bullets . . . yet.

"Did you see what we walked past coming in?" I ask her. "I'm sure they have public restrooms they make people use here. And I mean all people."

Crossing her legs, Cindy indicates she can wait. "You're the reason we're here, Lou. You and your murdering private investigator."

Whatever bad opinions I hold of Morgan Kane, I can't see him in the role of lady killer. He likes women too much. Whoever chewed up Sally Preston and Lisa Keller hates women. Besides, I would sense if Morgan was a killer, or a werewolf. Wouldn't I?

"Morgan Kane isn't the man in my nightmares," I tell Cindy, keeping my voice to a whisper in case the room is bugged.

"He's not exactly the man of your dreams, either," Cindy whispers back. "But he is sexy."

My head swings toward her. "Did you just say you find a man sexy?"

She rolls her eyes. "I don't mean that I find him sexy. I just mean I can see where the normal straight woman would be attracted to him."

Have I missed something? "Sexy? He's rude and conceited. He's too old to wear his pants that tight or his hair that long. He has a pierced nipple." I shudder to think how much that had to hurt.

Cindy shrugs. "He plays in a band. That voids out all the other stuff. Look at Mick Jagger. He still has women chasing him at his age."

Enough about Kane's appeal to women, or in my case, the lack thereof. What led the cops to believe he's a killer and that I am guilty by association?

"I know what they're doing," Cindy says. "They're wearing us down. Waiting until we're so tired and need to pee so bad we'll confess to anything to get out of this room."

"You watch too many cop shows. What should I tell Shay about my association with Morgan Kane?"

Obviously tired of squirming, Cindy rises and begins to pace. "Tell him the truth. There's nothing wrong with hiring a private investigator to find your birth parents. Normal people do it every day."

I'm so busy trying to cover up things lately I forget some things are normal and don't have to be lied about. The door opens and Shay steps into the room. He's wearing a five o'clock shadow that's sexy as hell. I rub my chin to make sure I'm not wearing one, too.

"Lou, Ms. Emerson, you're both free to go now."

I was geared up for serious questioning. I blink at him. "What about Morgan? Is he free to go, too?"

Shay strolls over and takes Cindy's empty seat. "We just released him," he answers.

"Why did you arrest him in the first place?" I ask.

Terry rubs his eyes. Poor baby is tired. He needs a woman at home waiting for him. I try to picture myself as that woman, but under the circumstances, I fail miserably.

"He has a connection to the case. A little too much of a coincidence."

"What kind of connection?" Cindy asks.

Terry glances at her and frowns. "This is information I'm not at liberty to share."

I feel differently. "Don't you think you owe us an explanation for hauling us down here in the middle of the night simply because we were speaking to Morgan Kane?"

"I'm sorry about that," Terry admits. "But Lou, you have all this information about the case, and then I catch you with a suspect. It didn't look good."

"What is the connection?" I repeat.

"Erotica," he answers.

"What does that mean?" Cindy asks.

"It was the name on the front of Lisa Keller's shirt the night she was murdered," I answer.

"It's also the name of Morgan Kane's band," Terry supplies.

I hadn't cared enough about Kane's musical career to ask him the name of his band. "I take it she was a fan?"

"More like a groupie from what we've heard," Shay answers. "Turns out she's slept with everyone in the band except Kane. He says he doesn't know her, might have seen her in the crowd, but wasn't aware that she's dead. I guess he doesn't have time to read the papers."

Although I see why Kane would be a suspect, I can't figure out why Shay would storm the beaches like he did unless there was more than an association between the PI and Lisa Keller. Not unless . . .

"He knew Sally Preston, too, didn't he?"

Shay glances toward Cindy. I know he doesn't feel as if she should be included, but he answers,

"She was a client of his a few years back. Wanted him to finger her ex-husband for cheating on her so she could take him to the bank during the divorce proceedings. Kane got the information she wanted. During our interview with the ex, Kane's name came up. We figured there was bad blood between the guy and Kane and didn't find any reason to be suspicious of Kane at the time, at least not until we had another connection between him and both cases."

"What about the ex?" Cindy now sits on the edge of a table corner. She looks at home in her surroundings. "Statistics prove that in most murders, the victim knew the murderer. It's usually an ex something."

Terry gives Cindy an "it's not your business" glance and turns to me. "Kane said you're a client of his. He said you hired him to find your birth parents. Is that right? And you approached him, he didn't approach you?"

Watching too much *Court TV* with Cindy pays off. I see where Terry's going with his line of questioning. He wants to make certain Morgan didn't contact me as part of his killer sex games. "I contacted him," I assure him. "A friend of mine recommended him."

Wrinkling his forehead, he asks, "Can't you find them on your own? I mean, you're psychic, right?"

Cindy comes to my rescue on this one. "Most psychics don't seem to have an ability where their own lives are concerned, just others'. Lou's tried to get a fix on her birth parents. Nothing. She draws a blank."

I'm not sure what Cindy said is true, but I know for a fact that Terry Shay wouldn't know if it is or isn't. I doubt he's done much research on the subject.

He rises without commenting. "Morgan Kane had alibis for both nights the murders took place. We checked them out before we let him go. Can I give you ladies a ride to your car?"

No wonder we've been sitting here so long. Damn Kane. I'll have bags under my eyes for tomorrow's shoot. I've had enough of the boys in blue for one night. I start to tell Shay we'll call a cab but Cindy pipes up.

"We don't have a car. You can drive us home, though."

"Sure," Terry says and walks toward the door. "Let's go."

A few minutes later I climb into Terry's restored El Camino. I've never been able to figure the love connection between men and El Caminos. They're ugly. Not really a car, not really a truck. The car is black with dark-tinted windows. It also only has one bench seat so I'm squeezed between Cindy and Terry.

At three in the morning, traffic is fairly light. Conversation is nil. Cindy's nodded off, her head resting against the window.

"So, you're adopted."

I immediately start to panic over the question but remember there is no crime in being adopted. "Yes."

"I've always been curious why people who are adopted feel compelled to find their birth parents. Most of them have been raised in a good home with loving adoptive parents. It seems sort of disrespectful of the people who raised them."

The Billingtons weren't exactly loving. They were more indifferent, which was worse than if they'd flat-out disliked me. I'm not sure if under different circumstances, I would feel so moved to find my biological parents . . . but then again, I probably would still be looking for them. I need a deeper connection with "family."

"Most people who aren't adopted wouldn't understand the need to connect," I comment. "And I'm sure there are many adopted people who aren't compelled to find their actual birth parents. People who, like you said, feel it would be disrespectful to their loving adoptive parents."

"Your parents must have been lookers," he says, and in the flimsy glow from a traffic light, I scc him smile.

I've never really thought about what my biological parents might have looked like. I've been too focused on their DNA. His folks must be lookers, too. But sometimes that is not the case. I've seen two relatively plain people produce a beautiful child.

"Do you resemble your father?"

He laughs. "No, thank God. I look more like my uncle Ned. Dad teases Mom about it all the time.

Says she got a little too friendly with the family while he was working the night beat."

I love these personal glimpses into Shay's life. A life so different from the one I had, or have. I'd love to be normal like he is. But I'm not, so I jab Cindy a little to wake her up.

"Are we home?" she mumbles.

"Almost," Shay answers. "You seem to know a lot about police procedure, Ms. Emerson."

"She watches too many police shows," I inform him.

"I've thought about joining the force," Cindy admits, stifling a yawn.

This is news to me. I thought Cindy had her heart set on construction. I turn to her. "You have?"

"Yeah. Backup plan if I never get hired on for construction work. I've tried, you know, three times and everyone just looks at my scrawny body and laughs me out of the place. Maybe you don't have to be as strong to be a cop."

"The job does require physical qualifications," Terry tells her. "Rookie training is grueling. You'd have to work out to get through the academy."

I offer what I know about the subject. "You'd have to build up your arm muscles so you can lift doughnuts all day."

Shay turns his head toward me. "Do I look like I eat doughnuts all day?"

I'm tempted to ask if I can feel his abs before I answer. He has a point. I'm sure I have just as many preconceived notions about policemen as he does about models.

"Lou could probably be a cop," Cindy grumbles. "She likes doughnuts and she's freakishly strong."

Terry laughs. "Lou doesn't look like she eats many doughnuts, and what are you?" He glances at me again. "A hundred pounds soaking wet?"

This is where I'm supposed to put on the meek act and pretend I'm a helpless, brainless female for his benefit. I'm not in the mood. "Looks can be deceiving," I quote Morgan Kane and a zillion other people who've said that. "I can probably take you down."

At least he doesn't laugh. He turns to me and says, "Tough girl, huh? Maybe you want to arm wrestle sometime?"

He's teasing. I'm tempted to say we should tongue wrestle instead. I say nothing. Terry pulls up in front of our building a few minutes later.

"Lou, before we go, you should tell Terry about what happened today. About you thinking that man was following you."

I could kill Cindy and her big mouth. Since I can't do that, I elbow her in the ribs. She makes an "oof" sound.

"What man?"

Fun and games are over. Shay snaps back into cop mode so fast it makes my head spin. I've nearly convinced myself what happened today wasn't real. Neither the perceived threat nor my reaction to it. I'm more concerned about the reaction. I can't just go turning wolfy any time my body decides that's what it should do. The possibility scares me to death. Much more than the thought of being stalked.

"It was nothing," I say.

"You thought it was something earlier," Cindy reminds me. "You were scared, Lou." She leans across me to look at Shay. "Lou was scared, and she's not usually afraid of anything."

"Let's just go in," I grind through my teeth. "I'm sure Terry is tired and would like to go home."

"I'm not that tired," he assures me. "Cindy, could I speak to Lou alone?"

Oh, great. Me and hunkalicious alone in an El Camino. Bring on the cheap booze and some country music. Maybe we can just make out instead of talking. I don't see that happening. I give Cindy a dirty look. She just smiles.

"See you upstairs, Lou." She opens the door and climbs out. Terry doesn't say anything until she's safely inside the building, then he turns to me.

"A man was following you today? When?"

I pull my hair over my shoulder and twist my ponytail, a nervous habit I've had for as long as I remember. "It was after you left me. I thought you were watching me, but when I turned to look, there was a man standing on the corner staring at me."

"What'd he look like?"

This is where I sound stupid. "I don't know. He wore a hooded sweatshirt and I couldn't see his face."

Pause. I know the question before Terry asks it.

"So, if you couldn't see his face, how do you know he was watching you?"

Since I can't tell him my werewolf radar went off, I answer, "I sensed danger from the man. It's something we psychics do."

Terry leans back against the seat and sighs. "Oh," is his only response.

His reaction should please me. It wasn't something I wanted to discuss with him anyway. Regardless of the information Terry shared with me earlier today, he's basically still a nonbeliever in psychics or things that go bump in the night unless they have a logical explanation. If I really am somehow connected to the crimes, and I must be or I wouldn't dream about them, he needs to trust me.

"You have trust issues," I say.

"I have a job where I get shot at sometimes. I have a job where people lie to me daily. It's hard to trust people."

"Well, it's also hard to get chummy with a man who arrested me earlier."

His head swings toward me. "You feel like getting chummy, Lou?"

Ironically, I do. Is it the nature of the beast in all women to be automatically attracted to men we know can protect us? I heard that on a talk show one time. Inborn instinct. "I'd think you wouldn't be interested in getting chummy with a girl you suspect is connected to murders and is crazy on top of that."

"You forgot to mention gay," he says sarcastically. "You are a puzzle, Kinipski."

I guess we're back to last names. I also think it's time to convince Shay I'm not interested in sexual relations with women. That's basically the only confusing issue for him I can clear up without digging myself into a deeper mess. I could go into a long spiel about this, but Shay's face is close to mine.

We're alone in a car at a time of night when nobody's brain cells are in full throttle. I'm still a little stung by the thought that he might not want to kiss me. I may be turning into a werewolf again, but I am still one hundred percent kissable.

I lean over and lay one on Detective Terry Shay, NYPD.

CONFESSION NO. 10

I haven't been to church since I was a kid.
Cindy and I used to pass notes to one another
during her father's fire and brimstone sermons.
I never questioned my right to be under
God's roof back then. I question it now.

The church Stefan has chosen for the shoot looks like something out of an old gothic romance novel. Crumbling stone walls, lots of arches. The only things missing when we drove up were the gargoyles and the half-naked man and woman clutching each other. The dressing room doesn't have a roof. There are about a hundred pigeons overhead just waiting to poop on my Henry Roth bridal gown. Worse than the dark circles under my eyes is the corset-style waistline on the dress that has me cinched down to about eighteen inches. If I had enough air in my lungs, I'd complain.

"One round of concealer under those eyes is not going to cut it," Cindy says, makeup kit in hand. Cindy has no room to talk. She looks as bad as I do. But Cindy isn't posing for the cover of *Bride* magazine today. I lean forward for Cindy, trying to keep my white gown pristine in a place that is dusty and moldy and just plain creepy.

"No," Stefan calls from an arched doorway. "Leave her eyes alone. She looks very Goth with those dark circles. The ringlets look great, too."

It took the hairdresser over an hour to give me all these ringlets. Scarlett O'Hara has nothing on me. "You do know I can't breathe in this thing?" I ask him, indicating my freakishly small waist.

Stefan lifts his camera and takes a couple of shots. "You don't have to breathe; you just have to look beautiful for the camera. Bridesmaids, lift Lou's dress so it doesn't get dirty."

My bridesmaids are Karen and a model named Rachel. Both are dressed in red gowns that look more like hooker wear than bridesmaid dresses. Karen kneels before me, grabbing one end of the hem. Rachel moves behind me and grabs the short train.

"This way to the altar, ladies," Stefan calls, turning to lead us into further decay and danger from a collapsing building.

Stefan and I lack our usual chemistry today. Is he sulking because I wouldn't let him take me home from the café? Or has one hot kiss in Terry's El

Camino turned my head? That kiss was a surprise for both of us. Him because he wasn't expecting it, me because I wasn't expecting it to be that good. There was a lot of tongue action, but not the "stick it down your throat, gag you" kind of action. There was also a little groping. Terry's six-pack is as hard as steel. Despite my inability to breathe, I manage a sigh.

"Why do you have that sappy look on your face today?"

I glance down at Karen. She's in a half-crouch position, holding the front of my dress while we follow Stefan. I realize the corners of my lips are turned up as if I might smile. It dawns on me that I consider smiling working and therefore hardly do it unless I'm getting paid. How sad is that?

"No reason," I answer. "I'm just in a good mood."

"Wish I could be in a good mood after only three hours of sleep," Cindy grumbles. "'Course I wasn't sitting in front of our building making out with Officer Good Body."

Karen nearly trips over the hem of her own gown. "What? You and Shay? Spill it, girl. Every dirty detail."

"Spill it on someone else's time," Stefan says, looming up before us like a prison guard. He takes my arm and steers me toward a makeshift altar. I'm sure *Bride* magazine will appreciate the dead flowers he has strewn everywhere. This setup looks more like a funeral than a wedding. But Stefan doesn't like to have his artistic eye questioned.

"Did you really go out with that caveman?"

Stefan leans close, adjusting the veil on my head. Unlike Terry with his Brut aftershave mixed with axle-grease scent, Stefan wears the three-hundred-dollar-an-ounce stuff. And it's worth every penny. He smells better than most women.

"He's not a caveman, and no, I didn't really go out with him. He gave me a ride home from somewhere. Not that it's any of your business," I add.

Fussing with the netting of my gown, he says, "I don't see him as your type. I thought you'd go for someone more sophisticated."

I can't get the kiss out of my head. The kiss alone was close to orgasmic and I have to wonder now what the sex would be like. In fact, instead of sleeping when I got home, I thought about that kiss and sex for the rest of the night. I suppose it's wrong to consider banging a man who doesn't trust me.

Recalling that Stefan is spoiling for a fight, I say, "I thought you liked Terry."

He makes a snorting noise. "Why would you think that?"

I shrug and my boobs nearly pop out of the top of the gown. "Athletic build. Broad shoulders. He sounds more like your type than mine."

Karen burst into laughter. "Good one, Lou."

Stefan is clearly not amused. He frowns at me. "Let's get to work, ladies."

We use natural light today which means we don't have a crew. Above me, half the roof is missing and sunlight streams down like an eerie mist. Despite the weak light filtering in, it's damn cold. Stefan set several portable heaters around the shoot area, but they only generate enough heat to keep our breaths from fogging the air.

He stands back and studies us through his camera lens. "Karen, take one step closer to Lou. Rachel, your position is fine, but you need to turn more toward Lou. She is the bride and the focal point of the picture."

"What's new," Rachel complains, but turns toward me.

A girl who could once easily blend in with the wall doesn't mind being the center of attention. I also don't mind the petty jealousies that arise from me having that position.

"Today, ladies, we're going for innocence," Stefan announces. "I know it's a stretch for all of you, but give it a shot."

I glance down at my sluttish gown. "You've got to be kidding. Rip the skirt off this dress and I'd be standing here in a corset and garters. From the altar to the bedroom in one easy tug."

"I know," Stefan agrees, "but I want these shots to be about contrasts. Shadow and light. Innocence and debauchery. Give me your angel look, Lou."

Debauchery? Does anyone in the twenty-first century really use that word? Angel look? To my knowledge, I don't have one. Sex sells everything and Stefan is usually egging me on with the dirty talk to get "sultry" from me. I have to dig deep to find innocence.

Oddly enough, I find it in church. Not this one. Haven Baptist Church, sitting next to my best friend, Cindy, anticipating the fried chicken her mother will serve for Sunday dinner. The Billingtons didn't do church, but they never minded if I wanted to tag along with Cindy.

In those days, I didn't yet know that I was a geek and soon would be labeled one from the sixth grade on. I didn't know I would someday become a supermodel, or a werewolf, or a murderer. In those days, my only worry was how Cindy and I would pass a lazy Sunday afternoon.

The cold rays pouring in from the missing ceiling warm me; either that, or the memory of innocence. Of blessed ignorance. I lift my gaze heavenward and wonder if God even recognizes me now. The shutter speed of Stefan's camera tries to penetrate my consciousness, but I'm not ready to come back from that time long ago, from being a normal little girl with normal hopes and normal dreams. But I do come back. Abruptly.

Peace fades and the smell of dust and mildew is replaced with the scent of . . . him. My gaze scans the crumbling balcony overhead. Beneath the Scarlett O'Hara ringlets, the fine hairs at the back of my neck bristle. My gums ache. My fingertips sting. Like the time I sensed him watching me from the corner, my body prepares to fight. I have no control, and I realize that at any moment, my friends will see that I am a freak of nature.

My body I cannot control, but my standing among my friends, I can. I have no choice but to run. Bolting from my position at the altar, I make it down two steps before Stefan asks, "Lou, where the hell are you going?"

My fingertips sting so badly I glance down and expect to see claws. Instead I see the bouquet of dead flowers in my hands. I toss it over my shoulder and rush ahead.

"I need to go to the bathroom!" I yell behind me.

Only slightly better than Stefan finding out I'm becoming a werewolf is Stefan believing I have irritable bowel syndrome. It can't be helped. I race ahead until I realize I'm not headed for the exit of the church, but deeper into its crumbling confines.

Panicked, I stop to get my bearings. To my right, more arches, darker because the roof is still intact. To the left, same scenario. Straight ahead, dead end. Behind me . . . him. I know he's there.

Veering to the left, I race down a dark hallway. I may be running to escape him, my natural instincts kicking in, but I'm also running to lead him away from Stefan, Karen, Cindy, and Rachel. I've seen what this creep can do in my dreams.

I pause to catch my breath in a dress that isn't made for breathing. The door I lean against creaks open with my weight. A musty basement smell wafts upward to me. This is the part in the scary movie where everyone boos the big-boobed blonde for going down into a dark basement alone. My boobs aren't that big and I'm a brunette.

My shoes slip on the damp stones of the stairs. I kick them off. I get about halfway down when the door above creaks. Stumbling down the rest of the stairs, I press my body up against a wall. The basement is full of boxes and junk. It's pitch-black but I have unusually good eyesight in the dark. I can make out shapes, but not details. There's a stack of boxes in front of me and I dart away from the wall and position myself behind them.

Holding my breath is easy because the damn bridal gown is cinched up so tight. I do hear breathing—loud and erratic. My fangs cut into the bottom corners of my mouth. The claws jutting from my fingertips shred the net skirting of my gown.

"Lou?"

The air in my lungs explodes out of my mouth. "Cindy, what the hell are you doing down here?"

"Where are you? I can't see a thing."

My heart hammers inside of my chest. I take as many calming breaths as the dress will allow. "I'm over here, behind some boxes."

"Why? And why did you run away like that? Stefan sent me after you."

"It's happening again," I say breathlessly. "He's here, Cindy. I sense him. He's the one who sets me off. He's the trigger."

"Huh?" she responds. "Who?"

I don't have time to explain. I'd shake Cindy if I weren't afraid my claws would cut her. "Everyone is in serious danger! Find the others, say I'm sick and they need to pack up in a hurry. Tell them I'll meet them at the cars."

"Huh?" Cindy echoes again. "I have trouble understanding you. You're lisping."

I'm lisping because of the fangs. "Just get everyone out! Hurry!"

The panic in my voice obviously spurs Cindy into action. She knows this is an "act now ask questions later" situation. "I'll get them out, but Stefan isn't going to like having his shoot interrupted."

"I think he'd like being dead less!"

"Crapola," Cindy whispers. A second later she darts toward the stairs. She's halfway up when she turns and asks, "What about you, Lou? Are you going to be all right?"

"I just need a moment to get myself back under control, then we're getting the hell out of here. Don't worry about me. I stand a better chance against this thing than anyone else."

I'm not one hundred percent sure what I've just claimed is true. I have to assume it is since I wouldn't be wearing the fangs and claws otherwise.

"Be careful!"

"Go!" I urge. Thankfully, she does. I stand still, trying to bring my fear and panic under control. That's when it dawns on me that I just sent my best friend off alone while a killer werewolf is roaming the premises. I bolt for the stairs. Fangs and claws or not, I have to make certain everyone else is safe. I'm nearly there when a noise stops me. It's a slight shuffling sound. Like a rat. Only a very big rat.

"Who's there?" I whisper. I know it was a dumb question. Like a rat, or the thing stalking me is going to answer. I decide if I'm going to be stupid I might as well be brave. "Come out," I demand. "Show yourself."

Silence.

I'm being paranoid. The murderer couldn't be down here with me . . . unless there's another entrance to the basement. I've about convinced myself I imagined the shuffling noise when very low, very soft, a laugh floats to me from the darkness. The sound is distorted, like the sound a monster would make if it were trying to be human. It raises the hair at the back of my neck again. I break out in a cold sweat.

I could stay and confront him, but besides the fact I am scared shitless at the moment, if this creep kills me, Cindy and the others will come looking for me . . . and he's going to kill them, too. I've got to make a run for it. I make a dash toward the steps. Something lashes out in the darkness. There's a sharp sting in my arm but I twist away and keep running. I bound up the stairs with superhuman speed and head out the door, running down the corridor a moment later.

If only I could have run this fast as a kid. I'd have been a track star. Instead, I could barely walk and chew gum at the same time. Is running with fangs as dangerous as running with scissors?

No time to worry over that. I move so fast I'll reach Stefan and the others at any moment. What am I going to do about the fangs? Suddenly, I remember my veil. The combs have dug into my scalp since Karen helped me put it on, so I don't know how I forgot about it. I reach behind me and flip the first layer over my face.

I skid to a halt in the chapel. It's deserted. There are no dead bodies or blood. Good. This time I know the direction to go to get out. The lingering scent of Stefan's expensive cologne guides me. When I stumble outside and down the crumbling steps of the church, I spot Karen, Rachel, and Cindy loaded up in Karen's car. Stefan stands beside his Porsche.

"Lou!" he shouts. "What's going on?"

"We've got to get out of here!" When I head toward Karen's car, Stefan intercepts me.

"Your arm is bleeding, Lou. What the hell happened in there?"

Fear dulls pain. I'd almost forgotten about the scratch I received in the basement. I glance down. Blood drips from ugly scratches on my arm.

"It's nothing," I tell him. "Let's go."

Only after I have spoken do I realize that Cindy is right. I have a lisp when I have fangs. Stefan's too distracted by the blood and the scratches to notice.

"You need emergency care, Lou. Get in my car."

He doesn't allow me a choice. Stefan opens the

passenger side door and shoves me and my ruined designer wedding gown into his car. He climbs in the other side, looks at my bleeding arm again, reaches down, and tears a strip of netting off my gown. "Wrap this around your arm," he instructs.

I wonder if he's worried about my arm or worried about his car. Now is not a good time to ask. "Punch it, will you? Let's get out of here." Just in case he is more worried about his car than about me, I add, "I feel like I'm going to puke again."

That gets him moving. Stefan pops the clutch and peels out. He does a doughnut and we're on Karen's tail in a split second. He honks and she speeds up. In the side mirror, through a filmy haze and dust, I watch the church become smaller. I expect some hideous half-man/half-wolf creature to come out of the church, bound down the steps, and chase after us.

"Where's the nearest hospital?" Stefan asks.

I'm not about to go to a hospital. "The scratches aren't that deep," I say. "I'd rather go home so I can puke in privacy."

"You aren't going to puke now, are you?"

Stefan's as white as my wedding gown once was. "I might," I say, just to be cruel. "My apartment is closer than any hospital; I suggest you get me there, quickly."

After only a moment of deliberation, Stefan shifts into third and hits it hard.

CONFESSION NO. 11

Some days start out shitty
and get progressively worse.

I sit on the toilet and stare at my dirty feet. I'm supposed to be in my bathroom puking. Stefan sits on the bed in my room. Should I make puking noises? As many models as he's worked around, Stefan should be used to that sound. I don't feel like pretend-puking, so I rise and walk to the mirror.

My fangs have now retracted. The claws are gone, as well. I'd say I look normal, but that's not the case. I still look a little like Scarlett O'Hara . . . after the fire destroyed Tara.

"I'm taking a shower!" I shout through the door. "Why don't you go home? I'm feeling better now."

"Not until I get a look at that arm!" Stefan shouts back. "I want to make sure you don't need stitches."

With my super healing powers, the arm already looks better. But Stefan isn't going to take my word for it. I turn on the shower and literally rip the ruined wedding dress off. I leave the gown in a dirty heap on the bathroom floor, slide out of my panties, and step into the shower.

The warm spray feels wonderful and I soap myself with shower gel. I use an expensive shampoo that has a wonderful fruity fragrance. Even so, it won't cover the wet-dog smell until my hair dries. Once I step out, I wrap my dripping hair in a thick towel, dry off, and grab my terry-cloth robe from a peg on the back of the bathroom door. I take a deep breath and open the door.

Through a steamy haze I see Stefan sitting on my bed. For a moment, I allow myself to imagine he's waiting for me. Okay, he is waiting for me, but I imagine he's waiting for me to come to bed. I join him.

"See, I'm fine now. You can go."

Stefan scrutinizes me. He lifts a hand and feels my forehead. "No fever. Are you going to explain what happened at the church?"

Not in a million years. "I must have eaten something last night that didn't agree with me. Suddenly, I had to puke. I ran off in search of a bathroom, a hole in the ground, anything. Then I got lost and it was dark deeper inside the church. I scratched my arm on something while trying to feel my way around."

Boy, talk about killing a man's sexual interest in me. I'd already explained in the car that the reason for the veil was to hide the vomit on my face. The sacrifices I make to save my friends.

"Let's take a look at that arm," Stefan reminds me.

I try to push the sleeve of my robe up, but the scratches are at the top of my arm. "Turn your head," I say.

Stefan smiles. "Do you really think you have anything I haven't seen before? In fact, I've seen most all of you."

"We're not at work," I insist. "When we're at work, you're supposed to be like a doctor. You're not supposed to notice things like boobs that fall out of outfits or things you can see through."

His smile stretches. "I'll try to remember that." Stefan sighs and turns so he's facing the opposite direction on the bed. I scramble out of the top of my robe, exposing only one shoulder and the arm in question. The scratch marks have faded.

"See, all better."

He turns and looks at my arm. "That was a lot of blood for those shallow scratches."

"I'm a bleeder," I explain. Ugh, is there no end to the icky stuff I must admit to in order to fool this man? "I told you it wasn't serious."

Stefan glances past me into the bathroom, frowning at the wadded, dirty gown on the floor.

"Oh, it's serious," he assures me. "Do you have any idea how much that dress costs? Not to mention the shoes you seem to have misplaced somewhere in the church."

I am now soon to own a ruined sluttish bridal gown and a pair of nonexistent shoes. I'll put them in the closet alongside my red sex shoes with the gum on the bottom. "I'll have my agency handle it."

Reaching out, Stefan runs a finger over the scratches. "I never meant for you to get hurt. Sometimes my artistic eye outweighs my common sense. Truth is, none of us should have been in that church today. The place has been condemned."

It occurs to me to wonder how the killer knew I'd be in the church. He must be watching me. Following me. It suddenly dawns on me that he's probably been watching me for six months. He's the reason for the outbreaks. I respond to some stimuli when he's around. And I realize he could have easily been around me for six months without me knowing. He can look human, just like I can, right?

"Hey, cover up, beautiful. I don't want you catching a cold on top of everything else."

Stefan interrupts my thoughts. I very much need to hear I'm beautiful at the moment. Considering the fangs and claws, I also need to feel human. Maybe I should kiss Stefan to feel human. I've wanted to kiss him for six years. Hell, I hardly know Terry Shay and I kissed him. But I don't have to work with Terry. How would Stefan's kiss compare?

"Lou? Are you here?"

Cindy. Thank God she has horrible timing.

"In here," I call.

Even though Cindy is short and skinny, she sounds like an elephant tromping through my apartment. She appears at my bedroom door a moment later. Her eyes widen upon seeing Stefan perched beside me on the bed.

"I thought you were taking Lou to the emergency room, and instead I come home to find you making a move on her."

"I'm not making a move," Stefan says, rising from the bed. He winks at me. "At least not now."

Cindy clonks past him and sits beside me. "Are you okay, Lou?"

"I'm fine," I assure her. "It was just a few scratches."

She's dying to ask me everything that happened in the church. Of course she can't while Stefan is still in the room. "You can go now, Stefan," she says. "I'll take it from here."

Not used to following orders from a lackey, Stefan lifts a brow. "Maybe Lou would prefer me to take care of her. I can fix soup."

Very clever. Pitting me against my best friend. Not clever enough. "But will you hold my hair back for me if I need to puke again?"

He flinches, then tries to act like he didn't by flexing his shoulders and rubbing the back of his neck. "Maybe you'd be more comfortable with Cindy taking care of you."

"I thought so," Cindy mutters. "Come on, lover boy. I'll show you out."

Cindy rises and moves toward the door. "Get better," Stefan mouths to me before allowing her to show him out. I close my eyes and allow myself the peace of being alone with the lingering scent of Stefan's expensive cologne. I'll have to tell Cindy what happened, what I think has been happening for the past six months. I hope Stefan's cologne is strong enough to hang around until bedtime. Maybe I'll have good dreams.

*H*e wears a mask. His eyes glow red from two dark holes. A snout protrudes from his face. His mouth is open, white pointed teeth gleaming in the night.

Above me, the moonlight casts his hairy silhouette in silver light. I want to scream but my voice is trapped inside of my throat. This cannot be real. It must be a dream. Yes, a dream. And I am once again an unwilling witness to his killing.

On the ground, huddled and shaking, lies his victim. Her fear is thick in the air, a fog that clouds her mind and robs her of the ability to run, to fight, to do anything but wait for his attack. She is a gazelle pitted against a lion. Her body has already surrendered to death.

Fight, I want to shout. Scream. Do something! I am helpless to protect her. The realization knots my stomach and forces hot bile up in my throat. I am in hell. A silent witness to a crime. There's nothing I can do but watch. Or is there?

I glance around. Leafless trees. Dead grass. In the distance, a short, long shape. I squint toward the object. It's a bench. A park? To the right, the shape of a castle. Belvedere Castle. I'm in Central Park!

Wake up! I shout inside my brain. Wake up!

With a start, I sit up, climbing my way out of one world and back into another. My alarm clock glares the numbers 2:00 A.M. in bright red. A dream. Then I remember what I must do. I scramble across the tousled covers and reach for a card. My hands shake as I dial a number my mind has unconsciously committed to memory.

The phone rings four times before he answers. "Yeah," is his response.

"He's in Central Park," I rasp. "Get someone there. Now!"

"Lou?"

"Hurry, Terry!"

I hang up. Heart pounding, covered in sweat, I escape the sheets twisted around my legs. I suddenly feel helpless again. What if Terry goes back to sleep? What if he doesn't do anything? Central Park is five blocks from my apartment. Five long blocks. I'll need running shoes.

All the sportswear ads I've done in the past have paid off. I slip into lime-green jogging suit, complete with matching jacket, throw my hair into a ponytail, slip into Nikes, and follow their slogan, "Just Do It." I don't allow myself time to think. I'm out the door, down the elevator, and running past Ralph, the night doorman, before he can rouse himself to ask what I'm doing or grab the door for me.

No holding back. Anyone on the streets this time of night is either high or drunk, and I kick it into superspeed mode as I run. I've gone two blocks before I realize I'm carrying my heavy beauty bag. Some habits die hard. No time to chastise myself for doing something that slows me down. But even slowed down, I'm damn fast.

I hear the sirens about block four. Sirens go off all over the city at all hours of the day and night so I don't panic, at least not until I hit the outer edge of the park and see cop cars and an ambulance. The action is about a quarter of a mile off.

My animal instincts tell me I'm too late, but my human spirit clings to hope. A small crowd has gathered. The junkies and partygoers out this late are being kept back from the scene by yellow crime tape and a couple of hard-faced police officers. I nudge my way through the small group. Ahead, a woman sits next to the ambulance, wrapped in a wool blanket. Shay is with her. My sense of relief is so strong my knees nearly buckle. Tears sting my eyes. She's alive. Terry believed me.

If I close my eyes, if I listen, I can hear what Terry says to the woman. "And you didn't see his face?"

The woman's trembling voice answers, "No, he was wearing a mask."

"A wolf mask, right?"

I see that mask clearly in my mind. Hideous. Like something out of a nightmare. The only thing more frightening than the mask . . . is knowing that it wasn't one.

"And he came out of nowhere? Just attacked you?"

Sobbing, the woman answers, "My boyfriend was flirting with another girl at the party. I got mad and left, decided to walk home. I cut through the park because it was shorter. He was . . . just there."

More sobbing. I open my eyes and see Terry with his arm around the woman. He motions to a paramedic and she joins them. After speaking briefly to the paramedic, Shay rises from his bent position. He glances around the area. That's when he spots me. He immediately heads in my direction. When he reaches the yellow tape, he lifts it.

"Come with me," he says.

Bending, I duck under the tape. I now see the woman being helped into the ambulance. "Is she hurt?"

Terry shakes his head. "Not physically. But she's pretty shook up. The paramedics thought it best that she spend the night in the hospital under observation."

I'm glad the woman will be somewhere safe. Her hair had been covering her face most of the time she talked to Shay. "Does she resemble me?"

"No," he answers. "He broke pattern tonight. He chose a victim randomly. Why?"

I don't know why he broke pattern, but I imagine he was simply in the mood to kill and didn't want to bother with luring a victim away from a club. I sense the beast in him is becoming harder to control.

"How did you know he was here, Lou?"

We stand in front of Terry's El Camino. I'm not sure a vision is so different from a dream. A vision just sounds more credible. "I had another vision. I saw him here."

"You saved that woman's life, Lou." Terry takes my shoulders between his hands. "I don't know what you have, but whatever it is, it's a gift."

This is where the soft music should start and Terry should apologize for mistrusting me in the first place, maybe even kiss me, but none of that happens. Instead of warm fuzzies, I'm as cold as ice. I know it's January in New York and I should be freezing, but this coldness goes deeper. It's him. He's still here. Watching . . . waiting.

Shay reaches for the handle of his door. "I'll take you home."

"He's still here."

Poised with one hand on the small of my back and the other on the door handle, Terry glances around. "We searched the park earlier, Lou. No sign of anyone suspicious."

"He's here," I insist. "I sense him."

I expect Terry to question my "gift." He is the big

bad cop and probably thinks he knows more than I do about these matters. Instead he calls to the two officers who were keeping the crowd back earlier. Both are just about to get into a cruiser a few feet away.

"Mitch, Frank, give me a hand!"

Both men change direction and amble toward us. Once they reach Terry's El Camino, one asks, "What's up, Shay?"

"I'd like to take another turn around the area. If we split up, it won't take long."

One man groans, but neither argues.

"Guns off safety," Shay instructs. "I'll meet you by that park bench and we'll split up from there."

I like a man in control.

"Wait in the El Camino, Lou."

Correction, I like a man in control as long as he doesn't think he's in control of me. I want to go with Terry, but of course that will look suspicious. A model, in his mind, would rather stay somewhere safe and out of the way.

Shay opens the door and waits until I climb into the El Camino. "Just keep the doors locked and the windows rolled up. You'll be okay."

He hits the door locks and slams the door before I can say anything. Then he walks away. I'd dig in my beauty bag for a piece of chocolate but my stomach is churning so bad it would be a waste of calories. I worry about Terry. He might be a tough guy, but he has no idea what he's really dealing with.

Another chill races up my spine and I wish Shay had at least left me the keys. I could turn on the heater. My breath steams up the windows. I rub the dew off and squint into the park. Even with my superior night vision, it's hard to see anything but shapes of trees and bushes. Someone knocks on the passenger side window. I slide across the seat thinking it's Shay and wipe the window off.

It's not Shay. It's HIM. His eyes glow red. His face is not a face at all, but a misshapen mess, half human, half wolf. His mouth is open, fangs gleaming in the moonlight. He's hideous. A scream claws its way up my throat.

He bangs on the window again and I jump. He nearly smiles, which pulls his face sideways and makes him more grotesque than he already is. His lips twist back and, through the glass, I hear him growl. I want to growl in response, but nothing comes out of my clogged throat. None of the previous responses I've had toward him occur. Why?

Maybe because I can see and hear him, but I can't smell him. He corrects that problem by banging so hard a third time that glass flies. His clawlike hand comes through the window. Glass cuts my face. The sting hurts, but not as bad as my scalp when his hand grabs a fistful of my hair. Frantically, I reach for something to anchor myself, hoping I can clutch the steering wheel and blare the horn. I come up short and only manage to clutch my beauty bag.

Another hard tug and my head is nearly out the window. I fumble in my beauty bag, grab the first thing my hand closes around, then he pulls me outside. I land hard on the pavement, knocking the breath from my lungs. He stands over me.

His scent is strong now. A smell of decay, as if his soul is rotten. He leans down beside me. I come nose to snout with him. "I wanted more time with you," he says in a garbled voice. "Time for you to see what it's like when it all slips away."

His breath is fetid. It nearly makes me gag. I lift the bottle clutched in my hand and give him a good dose of hairspray, right in the eyes. I've been spritzed before accidentally. I know it stings like hell. He rears back with a howl. I bring my knee up between his hairy thighs. He's a man in that department, anyway. Another howl and he doubles up and rolls to the side.

I wish I were wearing my red sex shoes. I'd give him a kick to the side, maybe puncture his lung with a stiletto heel. Since I'm not wearing the right shoes, I lift the hairspray to give him another spritz. That's when I notice the claws jutting from my fingertips.

I'd welcome their return, but Shay could come upon the scene at any moment. He wouldn't know which monster to shoot first.

"Lou?"

There goes that psychic thing again. I glance to my left. Terry stands in the street a few feet away. At that distance, he can't make out more than my shape.

Distracted, I'm taken off guard when Dog Breath rolls away, jumps to his feet, and takes off. Terry breaks into a run, headed toward me, gun drawn. I have no idea if I have fangs and thick body hair in places I shouldn't. Terry can't see me like this. I turn away and take off after Dog Breath.

Ahead, the monster ducks into an alley. My sane side says not to follow him. It could be a trap. My insane side says I have to follow. This creep is not only a woman killer, he's messing with my life. Do I have the ability to deal with the werewolf? Glancing at my claws, I realize I might be the only person who *can* deal with him. I suppress my fear and follow him in. Sane side warns that I could be his next victim.

CONFESSION NO. 12

*One thing you never hear about cops is that
they have a good sense of humor. Come to think of it,
you never hear that about werewolves, either.*

I t's your typical scary alley. Dark, wet, and there's lots of garbage sacks stacked next to the Dumpsters. Lots of places for a werewolf murderer to hide and jump out at me. Although the place looks deserted, I don't follow my first instinct to race down the alley, panicked that I've lost sight of a killer. Instead, I move slowly, the hairspray still clutched in my hairy hand. My tongue seeks and finds the fangs that have extended in my mouth. I itch everywhere and can only assume I might be wearing a fur coat under my stylish jogging suit.

A noise to my left makes me wheel in that direction. A rat scurries from beneath a sack of garbage. I have no inclination to chase the rat down and have him for a protein snack. I am as repulsed by the rodent as any normal red-blooded woman would be. That's comforting to me. At least I know even when I have fur, fangs, and claws, on the inside, I'm still me.

A figure lunges from the shadows on my left. I wheel toward it, thinking it's Dog Breath. It only takes a good whiff to figure out the man isn't Dog Breath. He's Alcohol Breath. The drunk stumbles up to me, a half-smoked cigarette butt hanging from his lips.

"Watcha doing out here all alone, pretty lady?" he slurs, then fumbles with a matchbook, tears out a match, strikes it, and brings the flame to the tip of the stogie. His bloodshot eyes lift to me in the flimsy light of the match. They widen. His mouth drops open and the stogie falls to the ground. The matches follow. "Hey, how come you have a beard?"

Oh, great. Facial hair. I didn't expect to be dealing with this issue until menopause. "Did you see a strange-looking man go down the alley in front of us?"

The lisp is so bad I hardly understand myself. I'm sure a man drunk on his ass has even more trouble. Instead of answering or asking me to repeat the question, the drunk's face screws up and he lets out a bloodcurdling scream. He evidently sobers up quickly because he makes a mad dash for the alley entrance and disappears.

Surely I don't look *that* bad. No time to worry about it; from somewhere down the alley that creepy laugh floats to me. He materializes a couple of yards away. His eyes glow red in the darkness. His shadow looks bigger and hairier. He starts toward me on two legs, then crouches down and continues on four. This totally freaks me out. I'm too scared to run and realize, even if I did, he'd easily catch me. I have no weapon except the hairspray.

Wait, all those *MacGyver* reruns are not just a waste of time. I bend and frantically search for the book of matches the drunk dropped. I find the book, but peeling it open with claws slows me down. A glance up and those red eyes are only a couple of feet away. Hands trembling, claws hampering me, I pull the only remaining match free, strike it, hold the hairspray up and place the flame in front of it before pressing the spray button.

I expect a blowtorch. I get an explosion. A fireball that hits Dog Breath directly in the face. He yelps and rolls backward. The smell of singed hair fills the alley. He's still on fire. With an eerie howl, he jumps to his feet and runs in the opposite direction, looking like a human torch. He disappears around a corner. Did I wound him enough to kill him? I'm out of hairspray, out of matches, and my saner half says this is not a good time to follow him and find out.

If I killed him, the nightmares should stop. If I didn't . . . he's going to be one pissed-off werewolf. I back out of the alley and take to the streets. It's around four in the morning now and there are still cars on the street, though very few. People, too.

That's one thing I love about New York. It never completely shuts down. I head for home.

I keep hearing Dog Breath's distorted voice in my head. What did he mean when he said he wanted more time, time for me to see what it's like when it all slips away? My career? If he's the trigger for me, and he knows it, I can see where he could easily ruin my modeling career ... my whole life. I hope I killed him.

A couple approaching from ahead brings me from my thoughts. They're arm in arm, cuddled together, laughing. I figure they've had a late night of partying somewhere. He kisses her and they both laugh again. It's very sweet and I experience a pang of envy. I wish I were simply out walking with my boyfriend. I wish I even had a boyfriend.

The guy glances up, spots me a few feet ahead, and skids to a halt. The girl stumbles but he quickly pulls her behind him. I stop. His bravery lasts only a second before he takes the girl's hand and they run for the other side of the street.

"Oh, my God, what is that?" I hear the girl say frantically as they race away.

For a moment, I am transported back to Haven High School. I am a dorky sophomore. Sometimes the more popular girls press themselves against the lockers when I pass like I have something catching. They laugh and everyone laughs with them. On days like that, I would walk home from school crying. Even Cindy couldn't cheer me up.

My eyes sting now. I blink back tears. Dog Breath has managed to transport me back to a time when I felt like more of a monster than I do at this moment. It's not even a nice place to visit and I damn sure don't want to live there again. I try to take comfort in the thought that I may have killed Dog Breath and now all this werewolf business with me is going to stop. I try, I don't say I succeed.

Once I reach my apartment building, I have a new problem. How am I going to get past the night doorman without sending him running for his life? I look at my hands. The claws have retracted. I run my tongue over my teeth. The fangs are gone. I touch my face. Uh-oh. I still have a beard. I rub the fur and, surprisingly, it comes off in my hands. What the hell is this? I keep rubbing and it keeps falling off.

I rub until my face feels smooth again. The fur might still be on my body, but having it off my face will at least allow me inside and up to my apartment. Luckily my jogging suit has a hood and I pull it up, walk to the door, and go inside. The night doorman stands with Terry Shay. Both glance up. Terry has a phone stuck in his ear. His face drains of color when he sees me.

"Lou," he breathes. "Thank God you're okay." He says into the phone, "I've got her. You can stop looking."

He hangs up and walks toward me. Now his face flushes with color. I swear I see steam coming out of his ears. "Where have you been? I was going crazy trying to find you. I've got guys out trolling the streets. Searching the park, the surrounding area. Why the hell did you take off after him?"

"I'm okay," I say.

His face darkens a shade and he sticks a long finger in my face. "What were you thinking, Lou? Chasing him? If you hadn't been in the way I could have dropped him! You're lucky to be alive!"

Behind us, the night doorman's eyes are wide. He hangs on our every word. "Let's go upstairs, Terry," I suggest. "My feet hurt and I need a shower."

I walk to the elevator, push the button, and assume Shay is coming along for the ride. The doors open, I step inside, and Terry slides in beside me.

"I'm very pissed at you right now," he informs me. "I was beginning to think you not only had beauty, you had brains to go along with it, but now I have to reconsider."

I'm too exhausted at the moment to let his temper spark my own. "I had hairspray. I thought I could take him." Which reminds me. "Hey, did you find my beauty bag?"

When I look at him, Terry's eyes are as cold as my ass was the day I met him on the roof. "Yes, I found the damn thing. I put it my car. It weighs more than you do."

"I want it back," I assure him. "Don't want you borrowing my beauty products."

This fails to get even a hint of a smile from him. He has no sense of humor. Mine's a little on the weak side tonight, as well. The elevator opens and we step into the hallway leading to my apartment. That's when I remember that my keys are in my beauty bag. I can't recall if in my haste to leave, I even locked my door. I try the knob when we reach my apartment and the door swings open. Cindy's asleep on my couch, the television blaring. *Court TV.* I should have known.

"Don't wake her," I whisper to Terry. I'll deal with Cindy after I deal with Terry. I motion for him to follow me into the kitchen. He's in my face in a heartbeat, although he keeps his voice low. "This creep who broke out my car window and you chased after with hairspray, did you get a good look at him?"

Should I tell him the truth? Jack Nicholson's voice screams in my head, "You want the truth? You can't handle the truth!" I figure I should listen to Jack. "No, he was wearing the mask. I did manage to set him on fire, though." I drop that little bomb while fixing us both herbal tea.

"You did what?"

"Shsss," I warn him, nodding toward the living room where I'd like Sleeping Beauty to remain in a coma. "He came at me in an alley. I had the hairspray and a match and I set his face on fire, or rather, his mask. He ran away."

Terry's mouth drops open. "You actually confronted this guy? A killer? One I suspect is really after you?"

Popping a mug into the microwave, I shrug. "I think I was in some kind of shock. Normally, I'd have been too scared to do anything like that. Maybe you should have the hospitals checked for anyone coming in with burns to the face or head for the next couple of days."

Shay is right behind me when I turn around. "Chasing bad guys is my job. I've been trained to take care of myself. You had no business doing what you did tonight. Swear to me you're never going to do anything that stupid again."

That's a tall order. Instead of swearing anything I take the cup out of the microwave, dunk a teabag in the water, and shove it in Terry's hands. "I need a shower. Enjoy your tea."

After undressing to find my clothes fur lined, I take a hot shower, hide the hairy clothes in a hamper, brush my teeth, and put on my old terry-cloth robe. I have nicer robes, but this is my comfort wear. I'm surprised to find Terry sitting on my bed, my phone in his ear.

"Yeah, I want all reports from the local hospitals of any men coming in with head or facial burns. That's from tonight for the next month."

While showering, I thought about Dog Breath and those burns. If I didn't kill him, and if he's like me, he'll heal at a fast rate. He won't need a doctor. Dammit.

"Sorry, your friend woke and I asked if I could borrow a phone. My cell is dead. She told me to use the one in here."

Cindy sending Shay to my bedroom is probably another unconscious effort on her part to hook me up with some good sex. Terry looks like the kind of guy who can deliver. He's also pissed at me so I'm thinking he might not be in a delivering mood. "Speaking of Cindy, I'd better check on her."

"She left," Shay says. "Said three's a crowd and she'd talk to you later. I wanted to make sure you're all right before I go. And to rake you over the coals a little more about putting yourself in danger."

Surprisingly, I'm not nearly as upset about being pulled from a broken window by a murdering werewolf as I am about the couples' reaction to me on the street. It brought back all my old insecurities about myself. I need to feel pretty.

"What I did tonight was stupid," I admit.

"You got that right," he assures me. "You took ten years off my life, Kinipski." Terry rubs the back of his neck and sighs. "It's not supposed to be personal for me. I don't think straight when it gets too personal."

I move forward and allow myself the indulgence of running my hands through his hair. It's soft and thick. "You like me," I tease him.

"I don't like you at the moment," he says, but his big blues soften on me and I know his anger has cooled. "But okay, yeah, I like you a little. You're different than I thought you'd be when I first saw you. You're a bit of a geek, Kinipski. For some reason, that appeals to me."

"So my looks don't matter?" I want confirmation of this. If they don't, one way or the other, he's the first man I've ever met who had that opinion.

Terry shrugs. "I'm not saying the package isn't nice. I'm just saying there's more to the package than most people probably realize."

He's spot-on about that. He's also about to get his bones jumped. I need to feel like a woman tonight. Desirable in every way. I'm glad I didn't promise him earlier that I'd never do anything stupid again, because I'm getting ready to. I untie my robe and let it fall open.

"You wanted to make sure I'm okay before you leave. Do I look okay?"

Terry is probably a hard person to shock. He's a New York detective and I imagine he's seen more in his thirty or so years of living than most people see in a lifetime. His gaze widens, but only slightly. He takes a good long look before his eyes lift to meet mine.

"You look fine, Lou. More than fine."

This is the validation I need. Terry knows I'm not perfect. He knows I have faults. And he wants me anyway. I see that he does by the way he looks at me. He stands, steps forward, and pulls me into his arms. When he kisses me, I taste the peppermint tea I fixed him earlier.

He slides his hands inside my robe and splays them across my back to pull me closer. Then he groans and steps away. "I don't have anything with me," he says.

I lift a brow. "What? Terry Shay unprepared for any emergency?" Tsking as I walk past him, I move to my nightstand, switch off the baby monitor, open a drawer, and remove a couple of condom packages. I'm obsessive about birth control. I won't take any chances when it comes to passing my screwed-up DNA along to some poor kid. "Lucky for you, Shay, I'm prepared."

He gives me that lopsided half-smile that gets my juices flowing. "No. Lucky for you, Kinipski."

Once the armor has been supplied, the troops get moving. Terry grabs me and pulls me down upon the bed with him. He rolls on top of me, staring down. Then slowly, he bends to kiss me. The kiss starts out soft and heats up in a hurry. I tug at Terry's shirt. I hear it rip. He laughs and pulls the shirt off over his head, tossing it across the bed. I'm afraid to go for his pants. He rolls away, stands up and unbuttons his jeans, slips off his shoes and socks, unzips and shimmies out of his pants. He has a nice package, too. Really nice.

I shrug out of my robe and he's next to me on the bed. He touches me, I touch him. His abs are as hard as I remember. He's hard everywhere. Like I said, very impressive. Together, we get the armor on. I don't know if the werewolf factor plays into my responses, but Terry's touch, his kiss, drive me wild.

He eases me down to the mattress. When he slides on top of me sparks fly from the contact of skin against skin. Something beastly takes over and I switch our positions. He looks surprised I got the drop on him. Sliding down his body, I bend and nip at his nipples. He has very little hair on his chest. Earlier, I had a lot more, but I'm not going to brag.

Terry pushes me up. His hands close over my breasts, kneading gently. That starts a fire deep inside of me. He leans up and teases my nipples with his tongue. My female part presses against his male part and he groans softly. I'm wet and ready. Angling my hips, I bring him inside of me. We both gasp, then I bend and kiss him.

His hips arch upward, deep. I move against him, our kisses shorter, wetter, more breathless as we move with the rhythm of sex. Terry takes my hips between his hands and tries to slow me. I'm not in the mood to be suppressed. I grab his hands and lift them over his head, pinning them there against the pillows. Then I have my way with him. This way, that way, every way.

I'm sweating when the first tremors of climax take me. This is my first one with an actual man. Bob, the battery-operated boyfriend in my panty drawer, knows how to please me in bed, but mortal men have always fallen short. I'm completely blown away. Terry picks up the pace as I spasm around him, driving deeper until I feel him shudder. That shudder pushes me over the edge. I'm not sure, but I might have howled before I collapse on top of him. He grunts, like I've knocked the breath from him.

I lie there like a rag doll, listening to the wild hammering of Terry's heart. Finally, a man who knows his way around the bedroom. But then I realize I have never been so uninhibited with a man before. I guess Cindy is right. It's different with someone I actually have a relationship with . . . not that I'm sure what exactly my relationship is with Shay.

"That was something," he says.

"Hmm," I respond, nestling closer to him. My elbow pokes him in the ribs and he grunts again. He'd better toughen up. We only have about two hours until morning . . . and I'm going to take advantage of every minute of it.

CONFESSION NO. 13

There's one way that I realize I am
perfectly normal. Even beautiful girls sometimes
wake up to a note on their pillow.

Somewhere in the far recesses of my exhausted mind I hear the phone ring. I think it has rung more than once. I'm too tired to answer it. Maybe it's because I ran five blocks last night in superspeed mode. Maybe because I was dragged through a broken window, then I chased down a murderer and set him on fire. Maybe it's because then I had to walk my hairy self home afterward. But more probably, it's because of the mind-blowing sex I had with Terry Shay. Three times!

I smile and turn to the other side of the bed, hoping he's awake and ready to go again. He's neither of those things. He's gone. I sit up and listen to see if he's still in the apartment, maybe in the bathroom or in the kitchen making me breakfast. The place is as quiet as a cemetery. My beauty bag sits on the bottom of the bed. There's a note attached. I crawl forward and snatch the note.

"Didn't want to wake you. Had to go to work. I'll call you later. Terry."

Was the signature really necessary? And couldn't he have added some flowery romantic crap to make me feel as if last night weren't just a one-night stand? Considering the man in question, the answer is no. No-nonsense Terry is also no-nonsense in the sack. He gets right down to business, and he's good at it.

I grin again. I can't help myself.

"Lou, are you alone in there?"

I scramble out of bed, grab my ratty robe, and slip into it. "Yeah, I'm alone!"

"Then I guess my plan didn't work," Cindy grumbles upon entering my bedroom. She stops short and sniffs. "I think it smells like sex in here."

A comment from me is not immediately forthcoming.

"Please tell me that's sex I smell," Cindy persists.

The grin breaks out on my face again. "That's not just sex, my friend. That's mind-blowing sex you smell."

Cindy glances around the bedroom. "He is still alive, right?"

My grin stretches. "Yes, he left me a note." I raise my hand to high-five her. She leaves me hanging.

"He left you a friggin' note? That's never a good sign."

I finally lower my palm. "No, you don't understand," I stress. "It was good. I finally got mine, you know?"

Cindy's brow lifts. "So Bob gets to retire?"

Glancing at the top left drawer of my dresser, I say, "Well, not just yet. It's not like Shay even asked me out."

Shaking her head, Cindy says, "And at least Bob has never left you a note."

Okay, so the afterglow of great sex has worn off and I'm staring at a note. I'm sure Terry will call me later, just like the note says. He's a cop. He's not supposed to lie.

"By the way, what happened last night that you even ended up with Terry over here?" Cindy asks. "And where did you go? I woke up and didn't hear anything on the monitor. No breathing, no tossing and turning like I usually hear. I thought I'd better come over and check on you, and you're gone."

My euphoria continues to fade. Now I have to think about the bad part of last night. "I had a nightmare," I answer, moving out of the bedroom toward the kitchen to fix coffee. "This time, I looked around to see where the victim was." I fiddle with the coffeepot as Cindy slides onto what I now think of as Terry's stool.

"And you could figure it out?" Cindy asks.

I nod. "He was in Central Park. He was going to kill a woman. I woke myself up, called Terry, then raced to Central Park hoping to get there in time to stop him."

"Lou, are you crazy?"

After dumping the last scoop in the filter and turning on the pot, I face Cindy. "What did you expect me to do?"

Her face is pale. "Let the cops handle it. Lou, you know this creep is after you. I can't believe you went to a location where you knew he'd be. You could have been killed!"

Now I realize I can't tell Cindy what happened after I reached the park. I also understand that the one person I thought I could tell all my secrets to has basically turned into my mother. Like all good daughters, I have to start lying to Cindy. The less she knows, the less she has to worry about.

"As you can see by the fact I'm standing in my kitchen making us coffee, I didn't get myself killed. The police arrived in time to save the woman, the bad guy of course got away, and Terry finally believes all this psychic crap I've been dishing him."

She chews on her lip before saying, "It's not good to lie to your lover, Lou."

I don't think a few hours of mind-blowing sex and a note puts Terry in "my lover" category. But yes, I am lying to him. Now I'm lying to Cindy. It's the fact I've gotten so good at it that bothers me.

"Coffee?"

"You're changing the subject," Cindy grumbles. "But yeah, coffee sounds good."

After pouring her a cup, I go off to the bedroom to check my messages. And yes, I'm hoping there's at least one from Terry telling me that he's never had sex as good as it was last night and he is now my love slave for life. A girl can hope, at least on her way to find out. There is a message. It's from Morgan Kane.

"Hey, cupcake, a man nearly gets arrested and you don't call him anymore? I found out your mother's name. Meet me at the office today if you want the information."

My heart lurches. I wish I'd answered the phone when Morgan called. I could already know my mother's name, something I have wondered for years. I pick up the phone and dial Morgan's number. I get his answering machine. Why does he always insist on seeing me? Because he's a perve, I'm thinking, and he wants to annoy me with his perviness. My mother's name is worth a meeting with Kane. I head for the shower.

Ironically, Kane is on the phone when I walk into his office. I have a feeling he ignored my call earlier after the caller ID showed my number. He wanted me to have to come all the way downtown to his dirty office. He holds up a finger to indicate one minute. I walk over and sit across from him. The highlights really are nice. He looks . . . somehow sexier.

While he talks, I watch his lips move. I'm not really paying attention to what he's saying, just noticing that his mouth is shaped nicely. What's wrong with me? Has one night of wild uninhibited sex turned me into a nympho? Kane hangs up and nods toward me.

"Good to see you, cupcake."

I must wipe away all thoughts that Kane is in any way attractive to me. "Wish I could say the same. Was it really necessary for me to come down here?"

"Most people don't like personal information left on their answering machines," he answers. "I thought you wanted to keep this private."

He has a point. Not that I usually have anyone around listening to my messages, but I might start having someone around. Like a certain hot detective who doesn't need to know my private business. "Okay," I agree. "What's her name?"

Morgan opens his desk drawer and takes out his Wild Turkey and two glasses. He pours each glass half full and shoves mine toward me. Normally, I would refuse, but what he's about to tell me requires a shot of something strong. I snatch up the glass and take a sip. It's horrible. I wish he'd drink something else.

"I got a copy of your birth certificate. Her name is Wendy Underwood."

Wendy? It's funny how when you're a kid, you dream that your parents have some exotic name, maybe foreign, mysterious. "What about my father's name?" Surely he has a more mysterious name.

Kane throws back his drink in one gulp. "Unknown."

Well, that's certainly mysterious. "She didn't know who got her pregnant?"

In a surprise move, Kane reaches across the desk and pats my hand. I snatch it away and he smiles. Then he gets back to business. "I'm sure she knew. A lot of unwed mothers put 'unknown' on the father's identity. Makes the adoption process easier, or maybe their lives, depending on the relationship and the circumstances."

I take another drink of Wild Turkey and find myself thinking it's not so bad after all. "Do you know where she is?"

"I'm working on it, cupcake. She was once employed by that lab I told you about. She's probably the one who did a search on you."

My stomach feels warm, either from the liquor or the knowledge that at least my mother is curious about me. She wants to know where I am. "She doesn't work there now?"

He shakes his recently highlighted head. "No. I called and asked for her. She's been gone for about two years."

"What about the Billingtons? Have you contacted them for information?"

Sitting back in his chair, he sighs. "I thought you didn't want me messing with them," he reminds me. "Has that changed?"

I don't want Kane messing with anything that has to do with Haven, but I can't help but wonder if my birth mother might have contacted them in the time I've been gone. That would be logical since she had to have known my adopted name to do the search for me.

"I didn't and I don't," I admit. "But I also told you not to contact the lab, and you did anyway."

Morgan holds up his hands in surrender. "Hey, if I hadn't lifted your mother's name from the birth certificate and traced her to the lab, I wouldn't have contacted them. All I did was ask for her by name. Talk to someone in personnel to see if they knew where she'd gone. Sounds like she didn't give notice. Just disappeared."

Kane's eyes are really sexy when they're not bloodshot. Why am I noticing that? I shake my head in an effort to clear it. "She might have left to look for me. I'll call the Billingtons and ask if my birth mother has contacted them. I just didn't want to talk to them again. We didn't part on good terms."

Kane reaches for his glass again. "Pass whatever information you get along to me. I need the money, cupcake."

"So, what happens next?"

After pouring another shot, Morgan answers, "I stay on the trail of your mother. Do you want me to go to Nevada, snoop around down there?"

It seems to me that people would be more forth-coming with information to a daughter looking for her mother than to a rock star asking questions. I can't go myself, not now, but I like the thought of seeing where my mother lived and worked. "No, I'd rather you not go there. At least not without me. I'll let you know when my schedule is clear."

He stares at me from over the top of his shot glass. "Or whenever whoever it was that kept you up all night and put the glow in your cheeks says you can go?"

My supposedly glowing cheeks start to sting. I can't remember the last time I blushed. "I'm talking about my work schedule. And just for the record, I don't answer to anyone. And if my cheeks or any-thing else is glowing it's none of your business."

Kane leans back in his chair. He puts his hands behind his head and smiles at me. "I see getting some hasn't improved your mood. He must not be doing something right."

As far as I'm concerned, Terry did everything right. It's Kane who sours my mood. "Been arrested lately?" I ask sweetly.

His shit-eating grin fades. "I can't help it if I just happened to have a connection to those two poor women. That was a low blow."

He's right, but he's also annoying. "I never said I play nice." Rising, I gather my beauty bag and slide it over one shoulder. "You do owe me one for helping to convince Terry you're not the murdering kind."

Morgan raises his brows. "Terry? Terry Shay? Don't tell me that cop who hauled your sweet ass to jail is the same one who got a piece of it?"

When he puts it that way, I no longer feel warm and fuzzy over our night together, but more embarrassed than anything. Would another woman go to bed with a man who had just a few nights ago suspected her of having something to do with a murder? If he looks like Shay, I decide, yes, she would.

"I told you it's none of your business," I remind him, hoping I'm not blushing again.

His chair makes a loud scraping noise when Kane gets to his feet. "At least now I know you're not all that picky. Gives me hope."

A growl escapes me before I can control it. Morgan throws back his head and laughs. "You are one of a kind, cupcake."

Yeah, one of a kind all right. And the only person who can tell me why is a woman by the name of Wendy Underwood. "Keep searching online to see what you can dig up on Wendy Underwood's trail after she left the lab. I'll contact the Billingtons and let you know if they have any new information."

I turn and walk toward the door.

"You know where to find me if you can't reach me by phone."

Without commenting, I walk out and close the door. The thought of calling the Billingtons churns bile in my stomach. I can't imagine what they thought when I didn't come home on prom night, or the night after or the one after that. Just because they weren't capable of openly expressing love toward me didn't mean they didn't care. Where was the bond that should have driven me home to throw myself in their arms and sob out everything that happened? Maybe neither the Billingtons nor I allowed ourselves to care too deeply. Maybe on some level we all knew there was something unnatural about me.

I brood over it all the way home. Once I'm in the apartment, I brood over the unblinking light on my answering machine. Why hasn't Terry called like he said he would? I catch myself before I become too pathetic. I have enough to worry about at the moment.

Like calling the Billingtons after seven years without a word from me. I pick up the phone and stare at it. The number is still etched into my brain. Then I realize I can't do it. At least not without moral support. Instead of dialing my old phone number, I dial Cindy's cell.

CONFESSION NO. 14

They say you don't miss something until you've lost it. What they don't say is that even though you lose, sometimes someone you care about ends up winning, which makes it almost all right.

While I wait for Cindy to arrive from an outing with a new friend, I'm forced to chow down on stale cereal. I wish I hadn't finished off the pretzels and yogurt. I'm in serious need of food around here. Half a box and one episode of *Psychic Detectives* later, Cindy uses her key to enter my apartment. I don't get up; I'm embarrassed to say that my knees are shaky.

"What's up, Lou?" Cindy flounces over and plops down beside me. Before I can answer, she notices what I'm watching. "Oooh, is this the one where the psychic actually gets arrested because they think she must have been involved in the murder to know so many details about it?"

It is the episode, and I see a strange parallel to the psychic's circumstances and my own. "Yeah, it is that one," I answer. I'm about to launch into my dramatic tale about having to contact the Billingtons when I notice a heavenly smell. Cindy has a McDonald's sack in her hand. "Please tell me that's for me. I'm starving."

She smiles and hands over the bag. "I know you don't have any food around here. Figured you could use some greasy meat."

I'd hug Cindy if I weren't busy tearing into the sack. "I adore you," I say before taking a big greasy bite.

"So, you never said why you need me here. What's going on?"

"I have to call the Billingtons," I answer, without bothering to chew and swallow first.

Cindy actually turns away from the television to stare at me. "Why in the hell would you do a crazy thing like that?"

It is crazy. But some small part of me wants to talk to them. Okay, a big part of me wants to talk to them. I'd like a few tears exchanged between us. I'd like for them to tell me they love me. "Wendy Underwood is why the hell I'm doing a crazy thing like calling them."

Cindy frowns. "Who is Wendy Underwood?"

Now to drop the bomb. "My mother."

Either the news or a fry Cindy snatched makes her choke. I thump her on the back. "I think she's looking for me," I explain. "She might have contacted the Billingtons after I ran away. She might have left contact information for them in case I come back or call."

"When did you find this out?"

"Morgan told me this afternoon. He got hold of a copy of my birth certificate and that was the name listed under 'mother.'"

Earth-shattering news obviously doesn't affect Cindy's appetite. She digs in my bag and takes another fry. "What's your father's name?"

"The certificate says 'unknown.'"

"Bummer," Cindy responds. "What makes you think your biological mother might be looking for you, Lou? I mean I know you hope she—"

"She worked for that lab in Nevada that was doing a search online for me," I interrupt. "The one you heard Morgan tell me about at the club. It had to be her trying to find me."

Cindy sits back against the couch cushions and sighs. "So, what are you going to say to them?"

As good as grease tastes to me, I put the half-eaten burger aside. "I don't know. But I do know I need you here with me when I make the call."

She reaches forward and pats my hand. "I'm here. Just don't mention me when you talk to the Billingtons. I'm sure my folks don't care where I am or if I live and breathe."

The pain in Cindy's voice breaks my heart. She tries to act tough, like me, but deep down, we're both still little girls who grew up in a little town in Texas. It hurt her deeply, tragically, when her father kicked her out. I thought he was all about compassion and forgiveness. Guess I was wrong.

My hand trembles when I reach for the phone resting on the sofa table. It takes almost more courage than I have to dial a number I have not dialed in years. When the phone starts to ring, my heart hammers hard against my chest. I realize how badly I want to hear Norma's voice, or even Clive's. I realize that I love them. I miss them. The phone picks up and an automated voice informs me that the number I have dialed is no longer in service. I hang up.

"What's wrong?" Cindy leans forward to look at me. "No answer?"

"Disconnected."

Her brows shoot up. Damn, I'd like to get a hold of those brows. "That's kind of weird."

"Kind of weird" pretty much describes everything about my life these days. Cindy snatches the phone from me and punches in a number. A moment later I realize she's called information. She gives them the Billingtons' name and the town and state. I dig in my beauty bag for a pen and notepad but she hangs up.

"No listing."

Have they moved? Gotten an unlisted number? A horrible thought occurs. Has something happened to them? I've spent seven years worrying that they might worry what had happened to me, if I was alive or dead, and it never occurred to me to worry that something might happen to them. I have to know, and not just because I need information from them about my birth mother. I care. There is an easy way to find out.

As if sensing my thoughts, Cindy glances away from me. "I can't call them, Lou. Don't ask me to. I am dead to them."

We sit in silence for a moment. "You could say you are the ghost of their former daughter."

My comment fails to get a smile from Cindy. "I'm not kidding, Lou. I can't call them. I won't."

More silence.

"I guess you can call them and ask," she finally says. "It makes more sense than me calling."

I knew that before silence break number two, but I needed Cindy's permission to call her parents. It's a given. No matter how selfish I want to be, I can't unless Cindy gives me permission to dig up her past hurt.

"You're sure?" I ask.

Instead of answering, Cindy punches numbers into the phone and hands it to me. Then she promptly leaves the room and heads into my kitchen, which she knows has nothing good in it.

Mrs. Emerson answers on the second ring. Her voice brings back memories, the good kind, and I feel a catch in my throat. "Hello?" she repeats.

"Ah, hello. Mrs. Emerson, this is L—Sherry Billington."

Silence. The shocked kind, I imagine. I forge ahead.

"I tried to get in touch with my folks earlier and their number has been disconnected. I called information but they didn't have a listing for them in Haven anymore. Can you tell me where they are?" More silence. I wonder if Mrs. Emerson hung up on me. "Mrs. Emerson?"

"Are you all right, Sherry?" her small voice finally asks. "No one has heard from you since you disappeared on prom night."

Guilt. It rushes up and takes my breath away. What happened to me was not the Billingtons' fault. I should have called them. I should have at least mailed them a note saying I was all right . . . but I foolishly believed I could leave my past behind and start over. Now my past is catching up with me. Fast.

"I know," I whisper. "I'm sorry."

I hear movement, like Mrs. Emerson had to sit down. "I have some bad news about your parents, Sherry."

Now I need to sit down, but I already am so instead I stand up. My heart hammers again. "Has something happened to them?" I force myself to ask.

A pause, then a sigh. "I don't know, Sherry. No one knows. They just up and disappeared one night two years ago. Took everything and were just gone. The house is standing empty. They owned it and there haven't been any For Sale signs posted, so we all assume they might come back."

Clive and Norma were predictable people. They were not spontaneous. Not impulsive. I can't imagine them packing up and moving in the night and telling no one what they were doing, or why. Something niggles at me. Something Kane said. My birth mother disappeared from the lab in Nevada two years ago. She just up and left without telling anyone where she was going. At least no one she worked with. Coincidence? I don't think so.

"Would you give the Billingtons my number if they do contact anyone in Haven, or if they come back?"

"Of course, honey," Mrs. Emerson says. She always called me "honey" and I feel a catch in my throat again. I give her my cell number, the one that should say "blocked call" if they've moved into the twentieth-first century and have caller ID. "Thank you, Mrs. Emerson." I almost hang up when she says, "Do you know where Cindy is?"

I'm silent, which is not a good thing. A definite indication that I do but am not saying anything.

"Please," Mrs. Emerson whispers. "Is she all right? It's eating me up inside. Please just tell me that she's all right."

Am I betraying Cindy's trust if I say anything? Agony. I hear agony in Mrs. Emerson's voice. It is not the voice of someone who has turned her back on her only child. It's the voice of a desperate mother.

"I should have told her father that he couldn't stop loving someone just because they did not turn out to be who he wanted them to be. I shouldn't have let her go."

I hear Cindy banging around in the kitchen. I think she's trying hard not to listen to me. To distract herself so she won't be tempted to try to hear her mother's voice.

"She's all right," I say. "She's here, with me."

"Thank God." Mrs. Emerson's voice catches on a sob. "I've been so worried about her."

What else can I say? Nothing. The ball is in Mrs. Emerson's court.

"Can I talk to her?"

I hesitate.

"Please," she begs.

I walk into the kitchen, go over to Cindy, who is staring into an empty pantry, and slap the phone in her hand. "She wants to talk to you." Then I leave and go back into the living room. I turn up the TV because this is not my business. An hour later I'm glad that I make a lot of money because Cindy is eating all my minutes. When she comes back in and sits beside me, laying the phone on the sofa table, her eyes are red and her nose runs.

"Am I in deep shit with you?" I ask.

Cindy draws a sleeve across her nose and shakes her head. "No. You know I wanted to talk to her. I just didn't know if she would want to talk to me, and finding out she didn't would have killed me all over again."

I put an arm around Cindy and pull her close. She gasps and pushes me away. "You're cracking my ribs. You don't know your own strength sometimes."

A vision of me holding Terry down and climbing on top of him last night flashes through my head. Was that a groan of pleasure or a grimace of pain? Oh, yeah, Cindy. Back to the matter at hand. I turn to her.

"Sorry, I just want to give you comfort."

The sleeve goes across her nose again. There's a damn box of tissues right there on the end table, but I won't split hairs over it.

"I'm okay. Mom and I are at least speaking. She has my number. She says she'll call."

I don't want to ask, but it will seem odd if I don't. "What about your dad? Did you talk to him?"

The waterworks come on. I should have just stuck with being odd. However, now it's perfectly acceptable to reach across Cindy and snag the tissues. I hand her the box.

"No," she answers. "He's still pretending I don't exist." Cindy removes a tissue and blows her nose. She wads it up and tosses it on my sofa table. Again, I must contain myself and pay attention to the important issues.

"The sad thing is, I really want to talk to him. I want to forgive him for what he said, what he did. And I want to forgive my mother for letting him. Does that make me pathetic?"

More gently, I put my arm around Cindy and pull her close. "No, dear friend, it makes you a better man than your father, and stronger woman than your mother. They could both learn a thing or two from you."

"Damn straight they could." Cindy hiccups. She rises and stomps toward the kitchen again.

"Amen!" I say for good measure, following behind her.

Cindy has her head in my empty fridge when I catch up to her. "Watch what you say," she warns. "I'm the only one allowed to talk trash about my folks. And why in the hell don't you ever have any food in this place! I'm starving."

When she's upset, Cindy's blood sugar gets low and if she doesn't get something to eat quickly, she's liable to kill someone. I'm the someone at the moment.

"Why don't we go out? Have some booze and red meat."

Slamming the fridge door, Cindy smiles for the first time in an hour. "Now you're talking."

CONFESSION NO. 15

*Due to circumstances beyond my control,
I have learned a lie is more often kinder than
the truth. Now if everyone else could just learn
the same thing, we could all be happy.*

Two apple martinis later, two steaks, one rare, and a decadent chocolate creation that Cindy and I felt we should share, we sit in sated satisfaction in the greatest steak house in Brooklyn. We're both too stuffed to talk. I imagine Cindy is thinking of her mother and their conversation earlier. I have so many thoughts rolling around in my head it's hard to focus on just one.

What happened to Dog Breath? Did I kill him? Or will I dream again tonight? I glance out the windows to the streets beyond. He could be out there right now. Watching me. I don't want to think about that.

Or the fact that my cell hasn't rung all day. I try to ward off the insecurity seeping in—feelings that were so much a part of my life when I was Sherry Billington. Just where are the Billingtons? Where is Wendy Underwood? Why the hell hasn't Terry called me?

"Haven't heard from him, have you?"

Glancing back at Cindy, I say, "That obvious, huh?"

She gives me her sad smile. The one that's supposed to make me feel better for reasons I can't fathom. "You're wearing the same look you did the day you lugged that stray cat home. Clive and Norma said you could keep it and it ran off the next day."

"Damn cat slept with me the night before he ran off, too," I grumble.

My cell rings. My heart skips a beat. It's been an emotional twenty-four hours. I let it ring three times before I answer. I sound calm and collected.

"Hi, Lou. Terry."

When I spend the wee hours having sex with a man who signs his notes and identifies himself when he calls, it's not a good sign. "Terry who?"

He laughs. "Busy day. Just now got a chance to call. What are you doing?"

"Cindy and I are at Pete's in Brooklyn, wondering if we can undo our pants and pick our teeth."

I get another laugh. "Can I come by and give you a ride home? Cindy, too, of course."

It's weird to be a supermodel, lusted over by millions of men, the object of most fourteen-year-old boys' wet dreams, and suddenly feel like I've never had a relationship with a man before. I guess I haven't, not really. "We're finished eating. Cindy might be anxious to leave."

A pause. He wasn't expecting me to decline the offer.

"I can put on the siren on top of the El Camino and be there in ten minutes. I was over at my folks' for dinner."

Good enough for sex. Not good enough to meet the parents. I know I'm being a total geek about this and decide to chill. "Ten minutes," I say and hang up.

Cindy nods approvingly. "I do believe you've finally become cool, Lou. Way to put him in his place."

"Thanks for the reminder that I'm still a geek at heart," I mutter. "Terry will be giving us a lift home. He's even putting on the siren for us."

She fake-claps her hands. "Oh, goody, but sorry, I have to go. You two should be alone." She gathers her coat.

"Wait," I insist. "You don't have to leave. We're both going to the same place. Don't be silly."

Her eyes are still puffy and I'm not sure Cindy doesn't have snot in her eyebrows. "We're not both going to the same place. I'm supposed to meet someone and I'm already late."

Cindy's love life is starting to sound more interesting than mine. Well, who am I kidding? It's always been more interesting. "Same chick you were with earlier?"

She frowns at me. "Lesbians do not refer to themselves as 'chicks'. We are women . . . and, well, sometimes we're men."

"She's the dyke, right?"

I get another dirty look. "She's actually quite beautiful if you must know. She puts me to shame."

Now is a perfect opportunity to make Cindy more aware of her own looks. "You have great bone structure, Cindy. Nice features. With a little effort, you could be gorgeous, too. If you let me work on you a little, I can help you get any woman you want."

Her face turns splotchy red. Cindy rises from her chair. "Is that supposed to be some kind of compliment, Lou? A girl who has to wax her facial hair, and whose hot new lover left her a note this morning, shouldn't be telling anyone how to get whoever they want."

Cindy stomps off and I'm not only stuck with the check, I'm stuck sitting alone. I had that coming. Cindy has never been insecure about her looks. She doesn't care about being attractive. She's more interested in a person's insides than their outsides. That's why she was always my best friend. Even during my Sherry years. I could learn a thing or two from her.

Another drink sounds good and I glance up to hail a waiter. I am confronted by a tall drink of water in a leather jacket who makes me realize I'll always be into a person's looks. I have become shallow. That's the sad truth.

Terry slides into a chair across from me. He glances around. "Where's Cindy? I thought she would be here."

For a second, I get a vibe. It's almost as if Terry is nervous to be alone with me. After what we did together last night, I realize I'm being silly. Self-doubt can still do a number with my head. It usually only takes a long look in the mirror to straighten me out.

"She had a date. You just missed her."

He tilts his head to one side and rubs his shoulder. A grimace crosses his face. "I needed to talk to you about business, so I guess it's better that she's not here."

Business? Do we really have to get right to that? How about a kiss, a smile, something that lets me know I didn't imagine we had great sex last night, or rather, early this morning. Since I'm new at the actual relationship game, I play the "last night never happened" one that he's playing. "Have any hospital reports come in on the creep I burned last night?"

Terry shakes his head. "Nothing. No one who matched the kind of guy we're looking for."

I'm disappointed by the news. "Maybe he crawled off somewhere and died. I torched him pretty good."

He stares across the table at me, his deep-set, long-lashed blue eyes absent the proper amount of lust I wish were there. "He's not dead, Lou. When I left your building this morning, Gus the doorman was outside sweeping the sidewalk. He commented to me that someone must have gotten a haircut in front of the building. There was hair all over the sidewalk. I bagged it and took it in for analysis."

The nearly raw meat I ate for dinner rolls around in my stomach. It wasn't Dog Breath's hair all over the sidewalk. What if the analysis ties the hair to me? How the hell do I explain that? I paused while running for my life to give my hair a trim?

"So, that's why you wanted to see me?"

I hope my question will get us on another subject, a more personal one. No such luck.

"I didn't talk to the lab until tonight. I was at the hospital all afternoon. Lou, it was fucking weird. The analysis reports that the hair was actually wolf fur."

At least he didn't say wolf hair combined with *my* hair. Instead of sighing with relief, I lean forward and put my elbows on the table. "I told you he thinks he's a werewolf. The mask he wore could have very well been made of real wolf fur. I read somewhere that practicing lycanthropes often use actual wolf fur to summon a transformation."

Terry reaches forward and grabs my half-empty water glass, takes a drink, and sets it back down. "That's what the profiler said. It gives me the creeps."

So would finding out that he slept with a werewolf last night. I feel guilty that I must deceive him. But lovers lie to each other about a lot of things, right? For example, being faithful, being married . . . being human.

"I hope I at least slowed him down if I didn't kill him. He might still need medical care for his injuries at some point. We can hope anyway. That's why you were at the hospital all afternoon, right? Checking things out?"

Terry's gaze slides away. He studies my water glass again as if it holds all the secrets of the world. "Actually, I had a couple of broken ribs I had to have taken care of."

I gasp. "What happened? Did you get hurt at work?"

His face flushes. "No, not at work."

I know he has brothers. He'd said he'd been at his parents' house when he called. "Let me guess," I tease him. "A friendly game of football with your brothers turned deadly."

He smiles and rubs his shoulder. "I got the cracked ribs last night, Lou, or I guess it was early this morning."

I'm trying to process what he's telling me. He was with me early this morning. Another vision of me elbowing him in the ribs flashes through my head. Oh, my God.

"I hurt you."

He laughs as if it's nothing, but it's something to me. "Cindy was right. You are freakishly strong."

My face is on fire. I had hoped he'd be reliving our hot sex all day in his mind, and instead he was at the hospital having his ribs taped. To my knowledge,

I have never sent one of my former lovers to the hospital the next day . . . but then, I had never stuck around long enough to find out.

Now I stare at the half-empty water glass as if I find it as fascinating as Terry did a minute ago. "I guess that's a real turn-on," I say.

He laughs again. "Let's go. I'll take you home."

I have to give him points for bravery. Uninhibited sex with me is obviously dangerous. Terry is willing to be alone with me again . . . but is he willing to have sex with me again?

Terry stands. I grab my beauty bag and my coat. We walk from the steak house. Terry's El Camino is still warm, which is good since I'm sure he's not brave enough to cuddle with me. Clear plastic and duct tape replace the glass on the passenger side. I thought last night had one bright spot. That spot is getting darker by the moment.

We don't speak. I can't think of anything to say in my defense. Terry pulls up along the curb in front of my building a while later. Was I the only one having a good time in bed? I had an orgasm with a man, which is a first for me. Should I invite him up, or would that just be setting myself up for rejection?

"I suppose a repeat of last night is out of the question?" There, I go ahead and set myself up.

His hand is warm against the back of my neck. I turn to look at him, expecting him to pull me close and kiss me. Instead, he says, "Maybe after the bruises heal."

I'm bad in bed. No one would guess that to look at me. Not even me. "I didn't realize you weren't having a good time."

Terry gives my neck a squeeze. It doesn't make me flinch. He can be strong and be gentle. Why can't I? "I wouldn't say that, Kinipski. Despite the cracked ribs and a few bruises, I've been thinking about you all day."

A warm feeling settles in my stomach then moves lower. "So I wasn't that bad?"

He laughs. "You were incredible. I'm just not in good enough shape to go another round with you. I'll have to buff up first."

Terry is buff. Who do I have to sleep with? Superman? Does Superman exist? I didn't think that werewolves existed at one time in my life. I've learned a lot since then.

"There's another reason we should cool things down, Lou," Terry says, his tone serious.

It had better be a good one or I might be traumatized for life. "I'm listening."

His thumb brushes the side of my neck, sending a little shiver through me. "What I said about it getting personal, I meant that. It's harder to do my job when my emotions are involved. Until we catch this weirdo, I don't think it's a good idea to be having sex."

"You mean with anyone, or just each other?" This is something I did even as Sherry Billington. Joke when someone hurts my feelings.

He frowns. "Just each other."

"Oh, that's good to know." About now is when I need to vacate the El Camino. My cool only lasts so long and then Sherry breaks through with all her insecurities and geekiness. I should be thankful Terry has given me an out. It isn't smart for a werewolf to date a cop. Not if she has any self-preservation instincts. I reach for the door.

"Lou." Again, Terry's touch is gentle as he grips my arm. He pulls me back and kisses me. If it's a goodbye kiss, it's a damn good one. "Now you're just rubbing it in," I say against his lips.

He laughs and pulls away. "Resisting you is going to be a challenge, Kinipski."

"You got that right." And I intend to make certain Terry regrets choosing job over sex. I open the door and climb out. Terry will watch me until I get inside. The building has good security. Cameras alert both the day and night shift doormen about whoever is coming and going, and they never open the door to someone they don't know lives in the building. Since I feel secure, I put a little extra swing in my walk.

Cindy is still on her hot date, so I can't unload on her, or apologize for wanting to make her more attractive to the same sex. I take a shower and go to bed. When a girl has nightmares, going to sleep isn't a high priority. After an hour of tossing and turning, I manage to fall asleep, and stay asleep. I wake to the sound of my alarm. I reach to turn it off but someone beats me to it. I sit up, a scream in my throat.

Cindy perches on the edge of my bed. "I need your help."

Once I swallow down the scream, I shove the hair out of my eyes and throw the twisted covers back. "Cindy, you have a key in case I need you and the humane society to intervene on my behalf, not so you can just come and go as you please. Did it occur to you that I might not be alone?"

She smiles. "I listened in on the monitor. I didn't hear extra snoring or anything."

I turned on the monitor before I went to bed in case I had the nightmare again. All I have to do is remember to turn it off when I have company . . . and I plan to have company again. "So what do you need?"

"I've been thinking about what you said last night."

It doesn't surprise me that Cindy won't let that go. One of the things I admire about her is that she stands up for her beliefs. "I shouldn't have said that. I planned to apologize to you today. You look great just the way you are."

"I know," Cindy says. "But last night I noticed how my date kept getting hit on and stared at, and I thought, what the hell, it wouldn't kill me to pluck my eyebrows."

"Damn. Who is this woman you will pluck your eyebrows for? I've got to meet her."

Cindy shakes her head. "Not yet. I want to see if it's going to work out first. My batting average hasn't been too good lately."

At least she has an average. One up, one down; not a good season for me, either. "Okay, we'll get started right away. I'll get the tweezers and the Vaseline."

"Sounds kinky." Cindy wiggles her unibrow. "Why are you alone this morning, by the way? Terry did pick you up, right?"

It's too early to talk about beating Terry up in bed. "Put coffee on while I get everything together," I say, rising to search for the needed beauty tools. "I do have some, don't I?"

"I brought some over with me," Cindy calls, headed toward my kitchen. "It should be ready. I'll get us a cup."

While I have Cindy at the mercy of her well-hidden vanity, I decide a facial is in order, maybe even a manicure and a pedicure. Depends on how long she can take the girlie stuff.

"Here we go, nice and hot," Cindy says upon reentering the bedroom. She holds two steaming mugs. "I'm assuming we'll do the torture in your bathroom under the bright lights."

"You assume right, come in and sit on the toilet, we'll get started."

"You do understand that I could do this myself?" Cindy joins me under the bright lights.

"I know, but the problem is that you won't." I take my mug and have a sip. "You feel better when forced into good hygiene. I remember your mother had to yell at you several times to get you to even brush your teeth when I spent the night."

Plopping down on my toilet seat, Cindy says, "You were all about looks even when you didn't have any. You've always wanted to be Barbie."

Placing my cup on the bathroom counter, I grab the tweezers and the Vaseline and approach Cindy. "At least I didn't want to do Barbie. Your folks should have seen the foreshadowing when I had Barbie and Ken and you had Barbie and Midge, who now that I think about it was obviously gay."

Cindy tilts her face up and I smear Vaseline on her eyebrows. "Midge was a tomboy, not a lesbian."

"Yeah, right."

"A few freckles and pigtails does not a lesbian make," Cindy insists. "Although my Midge was definitely hot for Barbie."

"I know, she hit on my Barbie when your Barbie wasn't looking."

Cindy laughs, and I figure that's the last one I'll get from her for the rest of the morning.

CONFESSION NO. 16

A little truth women hate to admit. A man can make
you feel good, then make you feel bad, but it only
takes another one to make you feel good again.

Cindy only allowed me a couple of hours of torture before she talked me into taking off for soup and salad at our favorite café. We're nearly finished when I notice Cindy's gaze move across the room and dart back. This happens several times before I rouse myself from a food-induced stupor and take a look for myself. Stefan and Natasha Somethingorother sit across the room having coffee.

Great. Kick me while I'm down. I realize this is why Cindy hasn't pointed out their presence. "You can stop doing that," I say. "I see them. And the only way to cheer me up now is if we can make fun of them."

"Lou," Cindy warns. "That's about as mature as fifth grade. I'm sure they're just discussing business, so don't get your panties in a wad."

"Business." I snort. "Probably more like a reconciliation. Why does he always wear that orange stocking cap? He knows I don't like it."

Cindy shrugs. "Maybe his head is just cold. It is winter and he is bald."

"He shaves his head. He is not bald," I snap.

"So he says." Cindy snorts. "I thought you wanted to make fun of him."

She should know me better. "I really wanted to just make fun of her."

Leaning back, Cindy sighs. "Give it a rest, Lou. She's really nice if you'd take the time to get to know her."

That statement immediately pricks my curiosity. "When did you take the time to get to know her?"

Fumbling with a napkin, Cindy wipes her mouth. I was going to tell her she had salad dressing on her chin but figured a girl who had snot in her eyebrows last night would consider it a minor offense. "I've worked with her, remember? She doesn't like you because you're snotty to her."

"I'm not snotty," I argue. "And it's hard to be nice to a girl who rubs it in that she's sleeping with your man."

Cindy's brows shoot up. I did a nice job on them. Her skin glows. She's fixed her hair and she really is a knockout. "Your man? I believe it's because he's been everyone's man except yours that you won't take the relationship to the next level. Stefan and Natasha only slept together once. She's a one-night stand. Show a little compassion."

Kick number two, and from my best friend. Cindy really knows how to preach. Maybe it comes natural to her, like it does to her dad. I am currently on the one-night-stand list even if Terry says he doesn't want it to be that way. How do I know that's not what he says to every girl he sleeps with? Maybe it's an excuse to keep from alienating me since we're basically involved in a case together. Okay, a little compassion won't kill me. I glance toward Natasha and find her looking at me.

My first instinct is to arch my back and hiss. I smile instead and give her a wave. "See, I'm making nice," I say through my teeth.

Stefan stares at me, too. He says something to Natasha, grabs his cup, and rises from the table. The next thing I know, both are heading in our direction.

"Shit," I mutter.

"Remember, you said you'd be nice," Cindy says.

I said that when we were talking about some point in the future. Twenty years from now or something. I owe Cindy one for letting me torture her all morning. Truth is, some of the things I did to her didn't have to hurt as much as they did. I took out my frustration about Terry on her.

"Hi," I nearly shout when Stefan and Natasha reach the table.

Both draw back as if startled. I decide this could be amusing, if only for myself. "Sit down," I urge them. "Wow, imagine running into you two here. Have you eaten?"

"No, well, yes, I ate earlier," Stefan says, taking a seat across from me. "Natasha and I just met for coffee. I asked her to be part of an upcoming ski shoot in Vermont."

Stefan knows I hate to be cold, and I don't really like snow. I'm from Texas and we didn't get much of it in Haven. So why does it bother me that he hasn't asked me? Under normal circumstances it wouldn't. I'm feeling insecure.

"Sounds like fun," I say, unable to keep up my earlier level of enthusiasm.

"It does?" Stefan laughs. "You hate cold weather and snow, Lou."

"Yes," I admit. "But I bet it's beautiful in Vermont."

"It is." Natasha speaks up. "I love to ski. I know the perfect little inn where we can stay during the shoot. I am friends with the owners. They have family still in Russia, like me."

"Sounds like fun," Cindy says. "Any chance I can come along to do makeup for the models?"

Stefan doesn't answer for a moment. I glance at him and find him staring at Cindy. "You look different," he finally comments. "I never noticed what delicate bone structure you have, Cindy. Or how big and beautiful your eyes are."

Cindy bats her lashes. "Thank you, Stefan. So, do I get to come?"

My mouth may be hanging open in unattractive fashion. I've never seen Cindy do flirty. Especially with a man.

"Sure, I'll count you in," Stefan answers. "What about you, Lou? You want in? I'm sure the advertisers would be thrilled to have you in the ad."

Now is when I have to decide if I really want in, or if I just want to be asked so I don't feel left out. I haven't dreamed about Dog Breath. Could he really be dead?

"When?" I ask.

"A couple of weeks."

That gives me time to see if the nightmares have ended for good, and if Kane finds out anything else about Wendy Underwood.

"I'd like you to come," Stefan says.

Those eyes. So dark and deep, like my favorite chocolate. How can I say no to Stefan? My savior. My friend. The man I haven't beat up in bed yet. At least in Stefan's eyes, I'm still the most perfect woman on the planet. "Okay, I'll go."

If I'm not mistaken, I hear both Cindy and Natasha groan their disappointment.

After two more nights without nightmares, I allow myself to believe I killed the monster. It was self-defense and he was killing women, so no guilt to follow me around on this one. It's strange to think I will never suffer another nightmare with the killer's passing. Then it occurs to me that I've been dreaming about him for seven years.

Does that mean he's been killing women for that long? I also realize my dream settings have been different places. Different cities. Different states. I grab a notepad and sit, trying to remember those early dreams. After an hour of working, I call Terry and tell him I need to talk to him.

He arrives thirty minutes later. I alerted Gus that Terry would be coming and to let him in. When I open the door to his knock and see Terry standing there, my heart does a lurch and my knees go weak. He wears baggy jeans and a form-fitting T-shirt. His form looks damn good. Business, I remind myself. This meeting is about business.

"So, what have you got for me?" he asks.

There's another loaded question. "Come in, I'll show you."

I turn and walk to the sofa where my notepad rests. I hear the door close and Terry joins me on the couch. "I've been thinking about the killer. About visions that I've had during the past seven years. He's killed other women. Women in other states. Not all of the victims have been found. I thought that together, we might give the victims' families closure about their loved ones and what happened to them."

Terry glances up from my notes. "I don't know, Lou. What you have here is pretty vague. I need specifics before I can dig around in someone else's jurisdiction."

It's not like I see signs in my head. I couldn't even read the tattoo on Dog Breath's back shoulder. "I remember that one place where I saw him murder a woman had pictures of Elvis everywhere. It was like a shrine and it was too cheesy to be anything but a cheap hotel."

"Memphis?" Terry suggests.

"Can you check if a murder happened in a hotel there that resembles the murders that have happened here? She would have been a brunette. All the women he's killed in my visions have been brunettes."

Terry flexes his shoulder beneath his jacket. "I'll dig around a little. See if I can come up with a match."

Now that the reason I asked Terry to drop by has been set into motion, the moment grows awkward. "Would you like coffee? Herbal tea?"

"No, thanks," Terry answers, which is good since I have neither. "I should get going. Can I take your notes with me?"

I nod. "You'll let me know if you find anything?"

He rises, so I do the same. "I'll be in touch." Terry walks toward the door. Once he reaches it he turns back toward me. "Lou, you know you're not out of danger, right? Just because this creep hasn't murdered a woman for a couple of days doesn't mean he's no longer a problem. You understand that, right?"

Deep inside, I do know that. I figure real life is

just like the movies, and about the time you think the bad guy is dead, he jumps out at you. "I understand," I say. "Guess I'll see you around."

"I'll be around," he assures me. "Stay alert to your surroundings. Until I have a body, I still consider the man you blowtorched alive and dangerous. You had better do the same. In fact, I'd like you to check in with me daily."

Interesting. "Do you always go above and beyond the call of duty like this with everyone?"

He glances at the carpet and runs a hand through his hair before glancing back up. "You're not just the job, Lou. You know that."

I do know that. I also know that Terry's right and we have more important issues to deal with besides sex. He's someone I would like to get closer to, but until I'm sure that Dog Breath is dead, and until I know more about where I came from, and where I'm going, I have to keep some distance between us. He turns and walks down the hall. I close the door and lean with my back against it.

The door suddenly bursts open and knocks me forward. Cindy stands on the other side, her eyes wide. "Hey, what were you doing blocking the door like that?"

Rubbing the sore spot where the door banged my head, I say, "Hey, what are you doing just barging in here? Ever heard of knocking?"

"Sorry, too excited," she says, rushing into the

living room. "My mom called today. She actually called like she said she would, and guess what? She wants to see me. She wants me to come home."

I'm stunned, and not just by the door hitting me in the back of the head. "You're going home?"

Cindy plops down on my sofa. "I'm considering it. There's a problem. She hasn't told my dad she's been in contact with me. She says I can't stay at the house."

There are no hotels in Haven. There is one grocery store and a gas station. And there used to be a barber shop. I can't imagine Clive walking away from his business. From everything.

Moving to the couch, I sit beside Cindy. "She let your dad throw you out, Cindy. I'm not sure running home the minute she suggests it is a good idea. Shouldn't she suffer a little, like you've suffered?"

The happy look on Cindy's face fades. "She has suffered, Lou. We've both suffered because of my dad's decision. Why can't you be happy that she wants to see me?"

Why, indeed. Could it be the sudden paralyzing fear I have that Cindy will leave me? "You won't stay, will you?"

I see the lightbulb pop on in Cindy's head. "Lou," she says softly. "I could never live in Haven again. I've made my home here, with you. We're a team. I'm only talking about a short visit. I'll be coming back."

Relieved, I lean my aching head against the couch

cushions. "Then you should go. I know you'd love to see her."

Cindy leans back with me. "Yeah, but where will I stay? I haven't kept in touch with anyone, and the fewer people who know I'm in Haven, the less likelihood that my dad will find out about my visit."

Now I get an idea. "You can stay at the Billingtons' house. They're not there and I still have a key."

Chewing her bottom lip, Cindy considers my suggestion. "I don't know. That would be weird."

It would also give Cindy time to snoop around the house and possibly learn more about the Billingtons' disappearance. "You have to go," I decide. "And you have to see if Clive and Norma left any clues about where they went, or why."

"I can do some detective work for you?"

This is right up her alley. "Yeah," I answer. "Now, when do you leave?"

She grins. "I booked a flight for day after tomorrow. I'll stay in Texas until the Vermont shoot and fly in and meet everyone there."

Two weeks without my sidekick will be tough. "I'll help you pack."

CONFESSION NO. 17

*I tell myself I'm popular now. Most of the
time I even believe it. If that's true, why do all the
people in my life keep running away?*

The nightmare is different this time. There's no
woman involved, no murder. No sex or blood.
Just him and his distorted, burned face staring
at me, laughing at me, taunting me. I wake in the
usual cold sweat, the covers twisted around my legs.
It's four in the morning, Cindy has gone to see her
mother, and there's no one to comfort me. I climb
out of bed and head for the kitchen.

Food will calm me. Cindy made sure we went to
the grocery store before she left. She had arrived in
Dallas earlier and had called to say her mother had
driven to the airport to pick her up, telling the good
reverend she had a doctor's appointment. I thought

Cindy might call me from Clive and Norma's later this evening, but no such luck. Opening the fridge, I decide on a ham sandwich.

I pour a big glass of milk with shaking hands. Just because I saw Dog Breath in my dreams doesn't mean he's still alive. The fact it was different from the usual nightmares allows me to believe this one was simply a dream. I keep telling myself that while I scarf down a sandwich and drink my milk. An hour later, I fall asleep on the couch watching *Court TV*. The phone wakes me. I fumble for the phone I left lying on the sofa table.

"Hello."

"Lou, do you have any idea where Cindy is?"

Stefan sounds like he hasn't had his Starbucks yet. I glance at my watch. It's seven in the morning. "Do you know how early it is?"

"Sorry, sweetheart, but I have a shoot about to get under way and my makeup artist called in sick. One of my models can't make it, either. I hoped Cindy could fill in for me."

I have serious morning brain fog. Could be because a nightmare woke me up at four, and it took me an hour or two to go back to sleep. "Sorry, Cindy's out of town. What kind of shoot?"

"Low budget. Catalogue stuff."

I gave up catalogue modeling five years ago. The pay isn't that good and supermodels have certain standards. "Anyone new coming down the line who looks promising?"

"A couple of girls. They could use some guidance."

He's tricky. "Like someone who's been in the business for a while?"

He laughs. "You interested?"

I have no desire to sit around thinking about the dream or missing Cindy today. I need to work, and I don't care if it's work beneath my usual standards. "I'll fill in. Maybe you can get Tina for makeup. She's decent."

"You're an angel. Tell you what, I can pick you up. You're on the way."

Since I told Terry I'd be cautious, I realize going to the shoot with Stefan would be safer than chancing a cab ride. "When will you be here?"

"Twenty minutes."

Ugh. I'm sure my eyes are puffy again. I'll brew myself a quick cup of tea and use the tea bags to soothe the puffiness. "See you then."

The catalogue shoot has been good for me. It's taken my mind off my problems and allowed me to be worshiped and adored like every supermodel needs. I've been helpful to the other girls, offering suggestions about makeup tips and natural poses. I've modeled everything from underwear to bathrobes today, and by the time we finish, I'm pleasantly exhausted. Stefan suggests we get a bite to eat together.

Since I have no one to go home to, I gratefully accept. We end up at a little Italian restaurant off the beaten path. Stefan is obviously a regular. The staff treats him like royalty. We're seated at a romantic table for two in the back. Stefan orders wine. I'm wondering if this is a good idea.

Candlelight, wine, a good-looking man who clearly adores me? Sounds like a recipe for trouble. I'm still exploring my feelings for Terry. Just because he confirmed we should only avoid sex with each other doesn't mean I should run out and have it with the next available guy who comes along. Recalling that Stefan's been on the waiting list for a long time is still no excuse. My reasons for resisting haven't changed.

"How are things in Stefan's world?" I ask.

He glances up from his menu. "A little lonely at the moment. Having a dry spell, I guess."

I taste the wine. It's a sweet red and warm on my tongue. "You might have to start at the bottom and work your way up again," I suggest dryly. "Or you could actually have a serious relationship with a woman. That would be something new and different."

Stefan smiles at me and sips his wine. "I'm waiting for the right girl." His smile fades. His dark eyes stare into mine. "I've been waiting for a while now."

I need another drink. Maybe something stronger. The way he's looking at me, I have no doubt that I'm the girl he's waiting for. His timing to finally take off the gloves couldn't be worse. "You've always been a sucker for a pretty face," I say quietly.

He lifts his glass and swirls his wine. "I have to do something while I'm waiting."

Glancing at him from beneath my lashes, I say, "Most guys just take up golf."

My comment makes him laugh out loud. "I love your sense of humor, Lou. Most beautiful women don't have one, you know. It's like a trade-off. Beauty for personality, but you, you've got them both."

And a mustache at times lately. I need to change the subject. I have been harboring feelings for Stefan for years, but now is not the time to finally explore them. I've always imagined when we come clean with each other, we'll come clean about everything. I can't do that. I haven't been able to do that for six and a half years. Maybe I'll never be able to. At least not without the answers I need about myself.

The waiter appears with bread sticks and Stefan and I order spaghetti and meatballs. We both reach for a bread stick. Our fingers brush and I can't ignore the surge of electricity. It's always been between us. Definitely time for a subject change. I snatch my hand back, but of course not without a bread stick clutched between my fingers.

"Catherine Shaw showed a lot of promise today. She has great skin."

He salutes me with his glass in acknowledgment of the subject change. "Great skin. Small breasts. I told her today a little cleavage would take her a long way. She said she'd contact a plastic surgeon next week."

Stefan carries a lot of weight in the industry. Too much, maybe, I'm thinking. "Do you feel right about asking women to go under the knife to further their careers? I wouldn't. So she has small breasts. Why should that really be a factor in modeling? A lot of women have small breasts. I'm sure they would appreciate seeing outfits on someone built more realistically."

His gaze moves up and down me. "You're not built like the average woman, Lou. Women would kill to look like you. Going under the knife is a small price to pay for perfection."

Since I wasn't always built like this, and even though the transformation was not one of my choosing, I figure I should shut up about this particular issue. Remembering what it was like to be Sherry Billington reminds me that it's hard to measure up to the women featured in magazines and movies. It's unfair really for young women to think they have to look like those women to get what they want in life, or be worthy of getting it. I need more wine.

"This is good," I say, raising my glass for another sip . . . or two . . . or three.

Stefan smiles indulgently at me. I'm sure he doesn't mind if I get plastered. The better to take advantage of me. Stefan has a nice build, but he's not buff like Terry. I would squish him like a bug. But what about a kiss? Would one kiss hurt anything? Would a kiss re-

veal my true feelings for Stefan? Are they real, or have
I made them more than what they are?

B y the time Stefan drops me off at my building,
walks me in and rides the elevator to floor ten
with me, I've sobered up enough to reconsider a
kiss. Our evening together was fun, playful, and just
what I needed. A kiss might ruin the whole night.
What if Stefan isn't a good kisser? Sometimes it's
better to wonder than to know for a fact. Not that he
doesn't have references, and plenty of them. Okay,
for sure I shouldn't kiss him.

I turn to him at the door. "It's been fun. Thank you
for taking me to dinner and for involving me in the
catalogue shoot. I'm exhausted. I should be able to
sleep tonight."

He leans toward me, resting his arm on the doorframe. "I've got something to help you sleep. Don't
you think it's time, Lou?"

His scent invades my nostrils and clogs rational
thinking. I shake my head to regain my senses.
"Time for what?"

He runs a finger down my nose. "You know what.
We've been having foreplay for six and a half years.
Aren't you ready to get down to business?"

Stefan pressed against me, staring down with those
dark, hypnotic eyes, is hard to resist. But can I really
sleep with one guy, then turn around two nights later
and sleep with another? Wouldn't that make me too

much like a man? I don't want to be just another of Stefan's conquests. I don't want him to be one of mine.

What we have is special. Or that's what I've been telling myself all these years anyway. Every girl dreams of a knight in shining armor. Stefan has been mine, but deep down, I'm afraid he will let me down. I'm afraid he'll prove that he's just another man.

"No," I say softly. "I'm not ready. Our friendship and our working relationship mean too much to me to mess it up with a quick roll in the hay."

The sensuous smile on Stefan's mouth fades. Very seriously, he asks, "Who said it would be quick?"

I laugh, thankful for a break in the tension between us. "Okay, 'quick' wasn't the right word. I've heard about your sexual prowess in bed. One girl or another is always talking about it."

He flinches. "Ouch. You know, it will only take the right woman to make me give up all my bad habits."

I'm not falling for his lines. I hear he's good at those, too. "Happy hunting."

Against my better judgment, I lean forward and kiss him on the cheek. He turns his head and our lips touch. We stay that way for a moment, neither pulling away. We stare at each other until his lashes lower, his mouth moves against mine, and the cell in my beauty bag rings.

I jump and step away. Divine intervention? I dig in my bag, pull out my cell, and see by the caller ID that it's Cindy. "I have to take this," I say. "Ah, thanks for a wonderful evening."

He sighs. "One of these days we're going to have to talk about us, Lou." He turns and walks away. I watch him, my cell ringing over and over. He reaches the elevator and pushes the button. It opens and he steps inside. He's gone. The moment is gone. I unlock the door while answering the phone.

"Hi, Cindy."

"Hey, what took you so long to answer?"

"What took you so long to call me?" I ask in turn.

"I spent the day with my mom. I just now had a chance."

I immediately feel guilty that I think I am the center of Cindy's universe when she's dealing with a reunion with her mother after a three-year separation. "Sorry, Cindy. How'd it go?"

She sighs. "A little forced at first, but by the end of the day we were laughing and talking about old times. It was great, Lou. Of course she had to go home to Dad and I'll have to wait to see her again until she makes up an excuse to get out the house."

Cindy's mom should stand up to her dad, but I guess one step at a time. "That's wonderful, Cindy. I'm so happy for you."

Silence for a moment. "Lou, it's weird being here."

Cradling the phone between my ear and neck, I lock up and move to the couch. "Haven is nothing like New York. I figured it would seem even smaller to you, now that you've lived in the city."

"Not Haven, Lou, your old house. They didn't take anything. There's still food in the pantry. Milk that's two years old in the refrigerator. Their clothes are still in the closet."

The hair on the back of my neck prickles. "Their car isn't in the garage, is it?"

"No, it's gone. I checked after I saw all the stuff still in the house."

This news greatly disturbs me. Again, this is out of character for Clive and Norma. I hope they're not in the house . . . dead. "You've checked everything out, right?"

"Yeah, Lou, no dead bodies if that's what you mean. I did find something in your old room."

I'm on the edge of my seat. Literally. "What?"

"An envelope with your name on it."

My heart misses a beat. "Did you open it?"

"Of course not," Cindy says with an indignant snort. "I'll bring it when I meet you in Vermont."

Vermont isn't for two more weeks. I can't wait that long. Cindy is the one person I've never kept secrets from. "Open it, Cindy," I instruct. "Read it to me."

"You're sure?"

"I'm sure." I take a calming breath while listening to Cindy fumble with the envelope. A moment later, she clears her throat.

"'Dear Sherry. If you're reading this, you've come home. Leave immediately. You're in danger. They're looking for you. We accepted the money they offered to adopt you, to take care of you, always understanding that someday they would come for you. They said you are special. They said not to get too close to you. We tried, but over the years, we came to care for you, Sherry. We came to love you. You're not like the others. We know you have a good heart. You're not a monster. Change your name if you haven't. Stay away from Haven. Stay safe. We must go. We fear for our lives. We know too much. Follow the signs we left you."

Silence. I'm in shock. Tears stream down my cheeks, the words "we love you" echoing in my head. A declaration of love is late in coming, but even so, for one brief moment, I feel a moment of pure joy. Then I focus on the rest of the note.

"Lou, are you okay?" Cindy's voice echoes. She sounds like she's in a tunnel.

"A bit much to take in," I respond. And it is. I wish I had the note in front of me to read again. "It doesn't make a lot of sense," I say.

"No, it doesn't," Cindy agrees. "But they made one thing clear, Lou. You're in some type of danger."

That's nothing new. Not lately. Who am I in danger from? Who are the Billingtons afraid of? What freakin' signs?

"There's more."

I snap out of my shock. "More in the note?"

"No, someone has come in here and rifled through things, Lou. Mostly in Clive and Norma's room. Papers and stuff."

A chill races through me. "You need to get out of there," I realize. "Now."

"We're going," Cindy assures me. "I'll grab a few of your things, and we're gone."

It dawns on me that Cindy said "we." "Who's with you?"

Silence.

"Oh, my gosh," I say. "You took your girlfriend with you."

"She's here in the house wanting to leave. I'm in the bathroom so I could talk to you in private."

I can't deal with the note right now, or with the fact someone has been in the house looking around for information. I can deal with Cindy's personal life. "What'd your mom think of that?"

"She likes her," Cindy says in a quiet voice. "I needed moral support to make this trip. And I made this trip for you just as much as me, remember?"

I'm not going to argue with Cindy about the issue at the moment, and really, is it any of my business that she took her girlfriend home to meet her mother? It does sting a little. Cindy and I have always been each other's moral support.

"Look, I have to go, Lou. I'll get some of your stuff and have it for you when we meet in Vermont. We'll go back to Dallas tonight and get a hotel, and tomorrow, I'll ask Mom if we can stay with them. She has to tell Dad I'm here at some point."

Despite being a little freaked out, I say, "I hope it works out for you, Cindy. When are you going to tell me your friend's name?"

"Vermont, maybe," Cindy answers. "We'll see how things go while we're here."

"Check back in as soon as you can," I say. "And good luck with your folks."

"Cindy out."

Even though I'm in shock, her coplike goodbye makes me smile for a minute. I sit and think about the note for a while. Who are the "they" I might be in danger from? How much do the Billingtons know? Where are they? Where is Wendy Underwood? I'll have to put Morgan on the Billingtons' trail, even if I don't want to. I rack my brain trying to figure out what signs the Billingtons spoke of in the note. Nothing. I get nothing. About now I wish I really was psychic.

Moving into the bedroom, I go to the bathroom and turn on the shower. I'm now thinking about Dog Breath. If he's like me, he might heal quickly, but bad burns to the face would put him out of commission for a while. Maybe he isn't dead. Maybe he's just lying low until he looks human again and can attract women. If he's alive, he'll start killing again. And I'm probably the first woman he's coming after. I'm in danger from an unknown source, and I'm in danger from a killer. That should help me sleep.

CONFESSION NO. 18

Girls just want to have fun . . .
and live to tell about it the next day.

Terry calls the next morning. He needs to talk to me about some files he's been looking through and picks me up in front of my building an hour later. The window is fixed in the El Camino. I'm getting a little attached to the car. And the driver. Today I wear Gap jeans and a Lucky T-shirt. I tried to dress down since Terry's not really into fashion. And this is business. What I'm wondering is why he didn't just bring the files with him. Is he considering going back on his word?

"I appreciate this," he says while he drives. "I would have just gathered it up and brought it with me, but if the files stay in one place, there's less likelihood of losing the information inside of them."

Is he a mind reader? I flip my hair and smile. "Of course," I say, like I knew that. "Listen, I hope this won't take long. I promised Karen we'd shop today."

"Shouldn't take too long," he responds. "When we're finished, I'll give you a lift to wherever you need to go."

Besides shopping, Karen has also agreed to go to Freddie Z's with me tonight. I need to put Morgan on the trail of the Billingtons and don't want to wait until Monday to speak with him.

"That will be great. Thanks," I say. Turning toward him, I stare at his profile. He has a great jawline. Square and masculine. He looks a little nervous under my scrutiny. "What type of files do you want me to look at?" I ask.

"Missing women," he answers. "That tip you gave me, about the sleazy hotel with all the Elvis pictures, it paid off. It's a dump called Heartbreak Hotel in Memphis. A woman was killed there in the same style. Something came up in the Washington area, too. And there's a hell of a lot of missing women all the way from Dallas to New Jersey who resemble you, Lou. Brunettes. Young. Some pretty and some not so pretty."

This is one instance when I wish I had been wrong, but I knew I wouldn't be since I've been having the nightmares for seven years. Too bad this wasn't just a ploy to get me into bed again. I'm still a little shook up from my phone conversation with Cindy last night. I'll have to suck it up and look at the files. I feel somehow responsible for the killer's victims.

The ride to Terry's place isn't far. He lives in an apartment building on Fifty-seventh. The building isn't nearly as nice as mine and I have to climb three flights of stairs. Once we reach his apartment, he unlocks the door and escorts me inside.

The first thing I notice is that the place is clean. I figured a bachelor cop who is at work more than he's home wouldn't care too much about being tidy, but I'm pleased to find Terry proves me wrong. His living room furniture is black leather, tasteful and yet masculine. The entire apartment has polished hardwood floors and bright area rugs. I glance in the kitchen. No dirty dishes in the sink.

"Want a beer or something?"

"A soda would be great."

"Make yourself comfortable on the couch. The files are there on the table next to it. I'll grab our drinks."

I sit and take the first of several files stacked on an end table next to me. The file contains the photo of a woman missing in the Oklahoma City area. I don't recognize her from my dreams. That doesn't mean she isn't a victim. I realize sometimes the women in my dreams aren't at their best. Hair tousled, naked in bed with a man who intends to rip their throats out during orgasm. That is a very different image from a photo probably supplied by a concerned family member.

"Recognize her?" Terry sets our drinks on coasters and settles beside me.

"No."

I put the folder aside, reach for my soda, take a sip, and replace the glass on the coaster. "I like your place," I say, glancing around.

Terry laughs. "It's nothing like yours, but thanks. My mom decorated for me. She says I have no taste."

Not sure that's a compliment to me, but I don't say anything. "I think it's great that you're so close to your family."

"Sometimes it's great," he agrees. "Sometimes it's a pain in the ass."

I laugh, even though I'm thinking being part of a loving family, a normal family, could never be anything but wonderful. I pick up another file and get a jolt.

"She's one of the victims," I say. The reason I recall this particular dream and this particular girl so vividly was because of the location. I wasn't in a hotel room. I was in a car. The backseat. "This woman was murdered in the backseat of her car. She's still in the car wherever it may be."

Terry grabs a pen and notepad and writes down the information. I go through six more folders before I see another victim I recognize. This one is from Virginia. The reason she's still missing is because she was murdered in a wooded area. Again, in the backseat of her car. I'm sick to my stomach.

It was one thing when I thought the dreams were about me, because I would wake up and know it was just a nightmare. Now I know differently and looking at the photos only brings back the brutality of the crimes committed against the victims.

"I can't look at any more," I tell Terry, placing the folder aside. "This victim was murdered in a wooded area, I remember there being a dam and a reservoir in the vision. Remembering makes me sick."

"That's enough for today," he says, staring at me with concern etched across his handsome face. "I appreciate you taking a look, Lou. You were right. These women's families need closure. You're doing a good thing."

I'm not sure he's right. I mean, he is right about the victims' families needing closure, but I'm wondering if their loved ones would still be alive if they didn't in some way resemble me. But maybe it has to do with the fact that I resemble them. Maybe this creep came after me because I fit his criteria. It's confusing. Thinking about the connection gives me a headache.

"Where do you need me to take you?" he asks.

"Let me call Karen and see where she wants to start. I imagine Jimmy Choo since she bought out Manolo Blahnik last time we were out."

Terry gives me a blank look. "You do know you're speaking another language."

I laugh, which feels good after all the sobering things going on in my life at the moment. "Maybe

I'll buy you something today," I decide. "Maybe a Prada dress shirt."

Terry indicates his T-shirt and jeans. "Do I look like the kind of guy who'd wear a designer dress shirt?"

"You'd look hot in Prada," I insist. "Maybe an Italian silk in cherry red."

He flinches like I socked him. Which isn't funny. Then he leans closer and asks, "Know what you look best in, Kinipski?"

I figure this is another loaded question, but I bite. Then I have to wonder if I really do bite. I look at his neck for teeth marks and thankfully don't see any. "What?"

"Nothing."

His mouth is within kissing distance. Maybe the files weren't the only reason Terry invited me over. "You look good in that, too," I say. "Maybe we should change."

His mouth comes a little closer. He suddenly groans and pulls back. "I knew this wouldn't be a good idea. You and me alone in a place that has a bed. We might have to stick to coffee shops to discuss business."

Part of me might be ready to jump Terry again, but part of me is gun-shy. Not shy of his gun, but shy of sending him to the hospital again. He removes the option by removing himself. He grabs our empty glasses and heads for the kitchen.

"Need to use the little girl's room before we go?"

"Do you have one?" I ask. "I figured you just had a little boy's room."

I hear him laugh from the kitchen. "The *big* boy's room is first door to the left in the hallway."

I'm shallow enough to want to see the bathroom. If there are any fungi, my infatuation with Terry is over. I'm just weird about those things. I find the bathroom and call Karen from inside. Just as I suspected, she wants to meet at Jimmy Choo on Fifth Avenue. I hang up and scout out the bathroom in search of fungi. Lucky for Terry, there isn't any. Once I leave the bathroom, I snoop in his bedroom.

A picture of a beautiful sunset hangs above his king-sized bed. The room is painted steely gray with a black bedspread and curtains. His dresser is scattered with an assortment of pictures. One is of him and a couple of guys who resemble him enough that they must be his brothers. I pick up a picture of an older couple I assume are his parents. They look nice. I rejoin Terry in the living area.

"Ready?"

I grab my beauty bag, glancing at the files still resting on his end table. I need some fun.

Karen is a marathon shopper and my dogs are yelping by the time we finish shopping, have dinner, and head to Freddie Z's. The place is packed but we have no trouble getting past the lines. I might play my looks down when I'm out and about, but not Karen. She's always on the runway. We walk past men who whistle and women who wish they could kill us with a single dirty look. Once inside we're greeted by the loudest rock and roll music I have ever heard.

I shuffle toward a spot where I can see the band. Morgan sings, he's playing a real guitar, and he's pretty damn good. He wears the cowboy boots as usual, and tonight he's shirtless, although I see what might be a T-shirt hanging from one of his back pockets. His tight pants are slung down low on his hips. The nipple ring flashes with the strobe lights.

"You say you know that guy?" Karen stands next to me, staring at Kane, who is doing a fine rendition of "Hotel California."

"Yeah, he's, well, kind of a friend of mine," I shout over the noise.

A waitress appears and hands us two drinks. I can't believe Karen had time to get to the bar and order. The line at the bar is as long as the line outside to get in. "Did you order?" I ask her.

"Of course not," she says. "I never buy my own drinks."

We take the drinks and the waitress nods toward a couple of losers who grin like a five-dollar drink is going to get them in our panties.

"Come on," Karen says, moving toward the losers.

"Huh? Please tell me we are not going to join them."

"They have a table. I'm not standing around all night. My feet hurt."

She has a point. My feet hurt, too. I follow. The two men who sent us drinks nearly upset the table in their excitement to seat us. Introductions are made. Karen gives fake names. I'm Sunny and she's Velma Sue. The men are Bill and George. Bill has a receding hairline and George has an overbite. Neither have a personality. I let Karen make small talk and turn my attention to Morgan.

The way he pumps his guitar while plucking out the tune to "Hotel California" is . . . well, it's damn sexy. There's a group of women standing below the stage screaming. Cindy was right. This is a guy who doesn't have a problem getting girls. That makes me wonder if I'll have trouble getting a chance to speak to him.

The waitress who brought our drinks pauses before the table and asks if everyone is set. Another round is ordered even though I've only had one sip of my drink. I excuse myself and follow the waitress, catching up to her when she pauses because the area around the bar is packed.

Tapping her on the shoulder, I ask, "Does the band take a break and could I get a message to Morgan?"

She laughs. "Yeah, they break in about fifteen minutes, but honey, you'll have to take a number to see him."

I open my beauty bag and pull out a fifty. "Will this get him a message?"

She blinks. "Sure, honey. Here's a pad and pen."

I scribble off a note and hand it to her along with the fifty. I'm not that excited to go back to Bill and George, so I walk around. Like the last time I visited the club, the sounds, sights, and scents get to me, but as I watch couples move on the dance floor, I realize they don't care about the sweat, or the noise, or anything else. They're lost either in each other or in the music.

For the first time, I understand what Morgan does when he's on stage. He provides release from everything else going on in these people's lives. He gives them an escape from the day-to-day. I long to find that escape, if only for a little while.

I'm drawn to the dance floor and find myself among the dancers, moving to the music. It doesn't matter that I'm dancing alone, the floor is so crowded no one will know, or care.

Swaying to the music, eyes closed, I forget my troubles. I heard Kane sing that first day I visited his office, but I was so freaked out by the sight of him playing air guitar and dancing around, I didn't pay much attention to the voice. I pay attention now.

Kane's voice is a cross between Rob Thomas and Bryan Adams. There's just enough grittiness in it to be sexy. I move deeper into the crowd, closer to the stage. Before I know it, I'm standing with the groupies, staring up at Kane like he's some kind of god.

He walks to the edge of the stage and sings down

to his adoring fans, spots me, and nearly forgets the words. I smile over that. He bends and extends his hand to me. I stare blankly at it for a moment.

A girl nudges me. "Take it!" she shouts.

I do. The next thing I know, I'm hefted up on stage. Kane sings to me, but I have no idea what I'm supposed to do except stand there like an idiot. A moment later the modeling training kicks in and I strut my stuff. The crowd goes wild.

Kane rubs against me a time or two and gets in my face to blast out his song. I realize the song has changed and he now sings Billy Joel's "Uptown Girl." That makes me laugh. It's not very rock and roll, but the crowd is in the moment and so am I. This is what I do. And although Kane investigates besides singing with a band, I realize this is what he does, too. We entertain.

The song ends and Kane shouts to the crowd that the band is taking a break. He grabs my arm on the way past and, laughing, we walk offstage.

"I thought this wasn't your kind of place, cupcake," he says. "What are you doing here?"

Still high from actually having fun, I answer, "I need to talk to you. It can't wait until Monday."

Morgan hands his guitar to another band member and leads me down a dark hallway, past a set of doors, and we're suddenly outside in a back alley. It's cold and he's not wearing a shirt.

"You're going to freeze to death out here," I tell him.

He shrugs, reaches into his back pocket and pulls the T-shirt out, slipping it over his head. It has the band name scrawled across the front and I have a flash of Lisa Keller. Kane then reaches down and retrieves a pack of cigarettes and a lighter from his boot. He lights up. "I always come out here during break to cool down and have a smoke. What's going on that you have to come slumming, cupcake?"

"My friend Cindy went home this weekend and she was going to check on the Billingtons for me. They've disappeared. Up and left everything behind. I want you to expand your search to include finding them."

Kane stares at me through a haze of cigarette smoke. His eyes narrow. "Why would they cut out like that and leave everything behind?"

Good question. I can't tell Kane the truth. I can only tell him a portion of the note's contents. "Cindy said they'd left me a note. The impression I get is that the adoption might not have been entirely legal. Something they could have gotten in trouble for."

"Baby black market?"

I shrug. "Could be. Something wasn't on the up-and-up. They may have information on Wendy Underwood, unless you've already found something on her."

He shakes his head. "That woman doesn't want to be found. It's like she dropped off the face of the earth after she left the lab."

Everyone in my life seems to be dropping off the

face of the earth. "Maybe the Billingtons won't be as careful about covering their tracks."

He throws his cigarette on the ground and snuffs it out with a cowboy boot. "It's why these people in your life feel like they have to cover their tracks that has me curious. You're sure you're telling me everything?"

"I'm telling you everything I know," I lie. "If both Wendy Underwood and the Billingtons were involved in some type of baby sale, they could all get in trouble, couldn't they?"

"Yeah, they could," he agrees. "You do remember it will be another thirty grand to find your adoptive parents?"

Now I don't feel bad about lying to Morgan. I'm paying a lot for the privilege. "I remember."

"Leave me information about the Billingtons on my machine. First names, family members. Where they're originally from."

Problem is, I don't have much information on the Billingtons. I'll think about it hard and try to come up with something.

"Got to get back to work," he says. "Want to stick around? I'll buy you a drink when we finish for the night."

Funny, I want Terry to forget we're all business, and I want Kane to remember it. "No, thanks. As soon as I find the girl I came with, I'm heading out."

He flashes the dimples. "Your loss, cupcake. I personally think you need to have more fun."

He's right. I do need to have more fun, but with werewolf outbreaks, murderers on the loose, and unanswered questions, it's difficult. For one brief moment onstage with Kane, I had fun. I forgot everything and allowed myself to live in the moment. I guess I owe him for that. Then I remember I'm paying him sixty grand if he finds all the parties I want found.

"Let's go. It's been a long day."

Morgan opens the door and I follow him inside. He has a nice ass. I'll give him that. His band buddies are poised at the stage entrance, drinking and flirting with groupies. I'll wager most of those women are waiting to talk to Morgan. I won't cramp his style, and keep walking once we reach the stage entrance.

I'm back out on the dance floor a moment later. A disk jockey plays old rock and roll tunes. I make my way through the dancers until I leave one crowd and join another. Getting back to the table where I left Karen might take me a good thirty minutes. As I work my way through the crowd, a scent suddenly teases me, barely noticeable combined with all the other scents—body odor, perfume, men's cologne, beer. It draws me up short. It's him.

CONFESSION NO. 19

*Whoever coined the phrase "what you
don't know can't hurt you" was an idiot.*

My gaze darts frantically to the right and left—
in front and behind me. People. They're everywhere. I close my eyes and focus on the scent
and which direction it's coming from. It wafts in and
out, teasing me. About the time I decide I imagined it,
I catch another whiff. In front of me. I think that's the
direction the scent comes from. I move forward . . .
hunting.

Directly ahead, I see a man walking away, his arm
draped around a girl with long dark hair. He wears a
thin muscle shirt, the style that shows most of the
backs of both shoulders. A word is tattooed across
the left one. The shirt covers all but the letters *I N E S*.
I try to catch up, but the bottleneck of people gath-

ered around the bar hold me back. He's headed toward the front entrance, which means he's on his
way out. Since I have freakish upper body strength, I
figure now is a good time to use it. I start shoving my
way through the crowd.

Foul language explodes around me. I send one poor
guy crashing into the bar where the shatter of glass
says he's overturned several drinks. More cussing.
I keep moving. The man in the T-shirt is almost to the
door. I can't let him get away. What if it's him? What
if the dark-haired girl is his next victim? A hand grips
my arm. I try to twist free.

"Lou? Where the hell you been, girl? I've been
looking for you."

Karen's nails dig into my arm. I try to shake her
off but she holds on. "Where's the damn fire? Hold
up, Lou."

"Let go!" I growl the words. "He's getting away!"

"Huh?" Karen releases me. I shove my way
through people and finally reach the door. The dark-
haired girl stands talking to another girl. I glance
around. No sign of the guy with the tattoo. Since I
don't see him, I assume he went outside. I do the
same.

The line is shorter now to get in. I race past it,
looking at faces illuminated by the flashing sign
above the door of Freddie Z's. I reach the street and
glance in both directions. There are people walking
down the street, but I don't see a guy in a muscle
T-shirt.

"Lou, what's wrong? Who's getting away?"

Karen huffs as she speaks because she's winded from chasing after me. I don't know what to say. Then I remember the girl. I'll question her about the guy I thought she was leaving with. Without explaining to Karen, I walk back to the entrance. The big black doorman blocks my way.

"You come out, you get back in line to get in," he informs me.

This calls for quick thinking and serious flirting. I bat my lashes at him. "I left my purse in there. I just want to go back in real quick and get it."

He eyes my big beauty bag.

"It's a little purse that I keep in my big purse."

"You yanking me?"

"Lou, I thought we were going." Karen now stands beside us.

"I left something inside," I explain. "This nice gentleman was just about to let me go back to get it."

"Well, hurry up," Karen snaps. "I want to go home."

The doorman glances between the two of us and sighs. "Go on," he tells me.

"I'll get the car," Karen calls.

I scramble past him. Once inside, I expect to see the girl where she was when I left. She's gone, and so is the girl she was talking to. I move a few feet, looking around. I don't see her anywhere. Not that I would spot her easily in this packed place. Shit. It could take me all night to track her down. I might never track her down the way the crowd mills around.

Who knows if the guy with the tattoo was him? Lots of guys have tattoos. I don't know if the scent I caught was real or simply a product of my subconscious. What I don't know can't hurt me. Yeah, right.

Deflated, I go back out. Karen waits at the curb. I climb into her car and she takes me home. By the time we reach my apartment building, a hot shower sounds good. A familiar El Camino is parked in front of my building.

"Well, well," I say to Karen. "That man just can't stay away from me."

"Who is it?" Karen asks.

"Terry, you know, the cop?"

"Lucky girl," Karen mutters. "I never knew you had so much man action going on. I thought you were saving yourself for Stefan."

"I might if he was saving himself for me, but we both know that is not the case."

Karen nods. "Two can play his game," she agrees. "Is that cop as hot as he looks like he'd be in bed?"

Men kiss and tell . . . women are worse. "Yes," I say with a grin and climb out of the car. "Thanks for spending the day with me." I close the door.

Walking to the passenger side of the El Camino, I open the door. "What's going on?"

"Do you know what time it is?" he asks.

I glance at my watch. "It's one-thirty and you really should get your own watch so you don't have to

stake out apartment buildings hoping to ask someone coming home."

"Funny," he says sarcastically. "I've been trying
to call you. I wanted to check up on you and you
wouldn't answer your phone."

If my phone rang in Freddie Z's, I would have
never heard it over the noise. I climb inside the El
Camino, which is at least warm. "Karen and I were
out all day. We went to a club tonight."

Terry frowns at me. "Do you think it's smart to go
to clubs when you know the killer considers them
his hunting grounds?"

There are a zillion clubs in New York. What were
the odds that I thought I spotted Dog Breath at the
one I was at tonight? Slim to none . . . unless he had
been following me all day. "I'm not giving up my
social life over this creep," I say. "We don't even
know if he's still alive, or even still in the area."

"Exactly," Terry snaps. "We don't know, so why
are you out running around at night, putting yourself
at risk?"

Although in my opinion, it's none of his business,
I answer, "I had a meeting with someone tonight. I
had to meet him at a club because that's where he
works."

His pretty blue eyes narrow. "Who. Kane?"

I'm starting to get pissed. Just because Terry and
I are basically working together on the missing
women files doesn't mean he can stick his nose in
my personal life. "He is conducting an investigation

for me, remember? Sometimes that's the only place I can catch him."

Terry snorts. "That guy has a rap sheet a mile long. Breaking and entering. Car theft. You shouldn't be involved with him."

Okay, so I'm not surprised Kane has a rap sheet. I imagine there's not much he won't do to get the information he needs. That might be a bad thing in Terry's opinion, but since I'm a person needing information, it's not necessarily a bad thing in mine. What is a bad thing is Terry telling me who I can hire to do my personal business and who I can't. "Just because we slept together doesn't mean you now have the right to order me around. Where I go and who I see is none of your business."

I open the door to get out, but Terry grabs my arm. "It is my business, dammit!"

Glancing down at his hand wrapped around my arm, I say, "If you don't want me to beat you up again, you'd better let go."

He releases me. A second later he shoves the same hand through his hair. "Look. I was worried about you. I've been looking at those files all afternoon. Women missing. Some of them dead. I don't want you to be in a file."

No matter how hard Terry tries to keep our relationship impersonal, it's not working for him. It's not working me for me, either. I was mad a minute ago, but I've never seen him look vulnerable. He's a control freak and he's hooked up with a freak who is out of control. Two freaks, actually. Me and Dog Breath.

"You want to come up for coffee?" I ask.

He shakes his head. "I'll take you to have coffee. I'm not coming up."

I'm tired, but Terry looks like he could use some company. "I get the impression you don't trust me, Shay."

He finally smiles. His teeth flash in the darkness. "I don't trust myself, Kinipski. My ribs are healing up pretty good. Getting beat up by a girl isn't always a bad thing."

I laugh and close the door. "Let's go have coffee."

An hour and three cups of coffee later, I'm so wired I won't be sleeping anytime soon. Terry and I keep the conversation light. I don't tell him about my earlier suspicions that I smelled Dog Breath in Freddie Z's. I'm not sure I did smell him. I know for sure I don't want to explain my abnormal sense of smell.

Terry's curious about my background so I do some more lying to him. I tell him I grew up in a small town in Texas close to Dallas. There are a hundred small towns in Texas close to Dallas. I tell him a couple of funny stories about me and Cindy growing up. Mostly, I let him do the talking. Despite the caffeine pumping through his veins, Terry yawns.

"Guess we'd better get going. I have to be in early tomorrow."

He pays the bill and we leave, climbing into the El Camino parked in front of an all-night diner. No one seemed to recognize him at the diner. He didn't take me to a cop hangout and I know they have them. If he's ashamed of me he has standards so high he's never going to find a woman. I think more probably, he just doesn't want to be razzed for spending time with a supermodel. Or maybe a professed psychic. Neither are probably people he had a high opinion of in the past. I think I'm changing his mind.

As soon as Terry fires up the engine, his police radio goes off. The dispatcher reports a 242 in progress in the vicinity of Canal Street in SoHo. A caller reports screams coming from the vicinity.

"What's a 242?" I ask him.

"Assault." He picks up the receiver. "This is Detective Terry Shay, I'm in the vicinity and will proceed to the location."

"Use caution, Detective. Backup is on the way."

He glances at me. "Get out and go wait for me in the diner. Stay inside."

I don't want to sit in the diner and wait for no telling how long for him to come back. "Just take me with you. I'll stay in the car."

He gives me a look. We both know what happened last time I stayed in his car alone. "No civilians are allowed with me on a code call. Go, Lou, it's just a couple of streets over and I'm wasting time."

Being stubborn may cost someone their life. "I'll call a cab," I tell him. "Go do your cop thing."

I climb out. Terry peels away from the curb. I stand outside watching his taillights. He turns on the next corner. I'm about to go back inside and call a cab when I hear it. A woman's scream.

My hearing is so much more acute than the average person's; I imagine the scream could have come from as far as two streets over. I also imagine I can follow the screams and locate the victim before Terry can. A few minutes might mean the difference between life and death for the woman.

I'm not wearing my running shoes, but I take off. As usual, the ten-pound beauty bag is slung over one shoulder. It must be the reason I have such freakish upper-body strength . . . that and the fact I'm a werewolf.

The neighborhood is deserted. I'm not scared. Dog Breath scares me because he's a freak like me. A normal man assaulting a woman I'm not afraid of. I think I can take him. I round one corner and charge down the street to the next. Ahead, I see Terry's taillights, moving slowly. He shines a spotlight out his window down the alleyways. I close my eyes and listen.

I hear a muffled scream. Terry has passed them. I lunge across the street into an alleyway. Nothing is noticeable except the usual Dumpsters and trash bags stacked everywhere. I know how Terry missed the attack. Heavy breathing sounds from behind the third Dumpster on the right. I move toward the Dumpster. The strange sound of a sucking noise reaches me. What the hell is this guy doing to the woman?

I'd call out, but that would give him the advantage of knowing I'm here. He might be armed. Instead I creep up on him. Attacker and victim are huddled on the ground next to the Dumpster. I reach out, grab the back of the guy's coat, and haul him off her. He turns to face me and I nearly pee my pants. Blood runs in two streaks down the sides of his mouth. His face is deathly pale in the darkness.

"Oh, shit," I say.

His smile reveals long white fangs. The man whips a knife from his coat pocket. I take a step back. He quickly bends beside the woman and slashes her neck. Instincts take over and I lunge at him. He's strong, but I'm stronger. This surprises him. His dark eyes widen when I shove him against the brick wall of a building. He bares the fangs at me again. I growl in response. The knife in his hand slices past my face, barely missing me. When he lifts it again, I grab his hand and pin it against the building. I notice that I now have claws. He notices the same thing.

"Who are you?" he hisses at me.

"I'm your worst nightmare," I answer, and I feel the change coming over me. It's a survival instinct, I realize. Anytime I'm in danger, this is what will happen. Just like it happened on prom night. I had never been attacked or felt as if I were in danger before that night. Maybe the werewolf side of me had been dormant all my life, and it only took one traumatic event to release it.

The woman moans, distracting me. At least I know she's alive. The fanged creep uses the distraction to shove me away. He runs. I'm torn between helping the woman and going after him. Then I hear Terry's truck lumbering toward the alleyway. He's going to shine that big spotlight on me in a minute. I bend and pull the woman from behind the Dumpster where he'll be able to spot her, then I run like hell.

Punching it into superspeed, I'm at the end of the alley in about ten seconds flat. I'm not sure which way to go. Do I just run, or do I go after Fangman? I catch the scent of blood to the left. Fangman. Is he really a vampire or a pervert who likes to wear fake fangs and bite women? What the hell. I might as well find out. I go left.

I question my decision two blocks later when I catch up with Fangman. He isn't alone. There are now two other fangmen with him.

"That's her," he says to the others. "She's a synthetic. I can tell by the smell of her."

Synthetic? Is that another word for "werewolf"? "What do you mean by that?" I demand.

One of the fangmen laughs. "She doesn't know what she is."

I lift my hand, claws extended. "I know what I am," I correct him. "I just don't know why."

"Because you were made that way, baby," the fangman I chased says. "You're an unnatural."

I take offense. "More unnatural than you?"

All three move closer to me. "We're natural monsters. Made by another of our kind. You were created by science."

Is this a bunch of shit? Are they trying to distract me with conversation so they can bite me? Is this even happening? Am I at home dreaming?

"Weres, synthetic or natural, are not welcome on our turf. Understand?" the fangman says.

Is he insinuating there are others besides me and Dog Breath? If I'm not dreaming, this is too bizarre for even a werewolf supermodel to handle.

"Cops are scouting the area," one of the fangmen warns. "We'd better find cover."

I'm thankful for the tip. It wouldn't do for one cop in particular to come across me. Especially not in the condition I'm in. But I have more questions, and some strong advice.

"You shouldn't kill women," I inform the group. "I don't like that. I might come back and bite your balls off if you do that. You do have balls, don't you?"

One of the palefaces grabs his crotch. "Yeah, we got balls. We got big balls. And for the record, we don't kill our victims if we can help it. We give them a little throat slash to hide the bite marks and they go on their merry way. Now, you end up in Queens and it's a different story."

There are vampires in Queens? There are vampires period? My cell rings. The sound startles me. I glance at my beauty bag, and when I glance back up, the fangmen are gone. I stare into the shadows, wondering if I'm delusional and if I ever saw them to begin with. The phone keeps ringing. I fumble in my bag, having trouble grasping the phone while wearing claws.

"Hello," I say.

"Lou, you made it home okay, right?"

"I'm home," I lie to Terry. I'm a couple of streets over and in shock from having just conversed with three vampires. "Did you find the woman?"

"Yeah, she's okay. A superficial knife wound to the throat. My spotlight must have chased the attacker away. The woman says she doesn't remember a thing after the guy grabbed her. Shock. We get that a lot with victims."

"I'm glad she's all right."

"Why are you talking funny?"

Damn fangs. I hope they retract soon. "I'm doing a whitening treatment. I have something in my mouth."

"Oh. Guess I'll go so I can wrap up here and catch a couple of hours' sleep before I go in. Night, Lou."

"Night, Terry."

But I hope I'm already asleep.

CONFESSION NO. 20

*I figure about ninety percent of the
people in America don't live in the
"real world." I wish I were one of them.*

The phone wakes me. I turn over in bed to reach
for it, glance up, and see Dog Breath standing
over me. I scream. Then I wake up. The phone
really is ringing. I grab it and answer.

"Lou, are you all right? Why didn't you return any
of my calls last night?"

It's good to hear Cindy's voice. I was so wiped
out and freaked out when I got home last night, I
went straight to the shower and then to bed. "Long
night," I answer. "Weird night," I clarify. "I didn't
get in until late. Real late."

"Well, I was worried about you," Cindy grouses.
"You never stay out late, at least not unless I'm with
you. Where were you?"

Is Cindy ready to learn the city is overrun with bloodsucking fiends? I think she has enough on her plate at the moment. "I went out with Karen. We went to Freddie Z's so I could tell Morgan he needs to look for the Billingtons as well as my birth parents. We stayed out late."

"How is Karen?"

I know Cindy is having a jealous moment. Friends do, there's nothing weird about it. "She's fine. Not nearly as fun to hang out with as you. What happened with your folks? Did your mom tell your dad, and where are you staying?"

"Mom didn't get up the nerve. We're staying at a hotel in Grapevine. Mom's coming in to have lunch and do some shopping with us. I guess it's okay. Not sure I'm really ready to introduce Dad to my girlfriend."

My nose itches and I scratch, hoping I don't find a mustache under my lip. I don't. "So are you still staying until we're supposed to meet up in Vermont?"

"Yeah, Mom wants me to stay as long as I can. She says we have a lot of catching up to do. My friend can't stay that long, so I figure when she goes home Mom and I can work on a meeting with Dad. I got some stuff for you, by the way. Not much, but some photos and stuff from school I thought you'd want."

"Thanks. I appreciate what you've done for me, Cindy."

For the first time in our lives, Cindy and I seem at a loss for words. I want to tell her about the fangmen just to turn her back into the motormouth I know and love.

"Guess I'd better go, Lou," Cindy finally says. "Mom will be here shortly to pick us up. I'll call you in a couple of days."

"Okay. Talk to you later."

She hangs up.

I'm glad Cindy has something to do. I have nothing to do but think about my weird night. I remember I'm supposed to leave information about the Billingtons on Morgan's machine. Bad thing is, I don't have much information about them. Neither talked about their lives before Haven and me. I do remember Norma saying she grew up in California. I saw something one time in the papers they kept in a metal box with the name Norma Ford on it.

I'll start there. My understanding was that neither Clive nor Norma had any family left. Either that or they were estranged from their family members; they never bothered to explain which it was.

I call Morgan and leave him what little information I have. He's got to earn his money. No matter how hard I try, I can't get the vampires out of my head. I'd like to pretend last night was just a dream, but I know it wasn't. So what do I do with this strange knowledge that I acquired last night? I can't very well share it with Terry. He'll think I'm crazy. Then I wonder which he would find more repulsive. A werewolf or a vampire?

Taking my thoughts a step further, I wonder whether Terry would be more open to the possibility of werewolves if he were forced to accept the existence of vampires? Real werewolves, of which I am supposedly not one. Synthetic? What the hell did they mean? I have to set Terry on the path of enlightenment, even if my motives are purely selfish. If he discovered for himself that, like in all cultures, there are good and bad, maybe he can learn to accept me for who I really am.

Maybe the fangmen were putting me on. Should I venture onto their turf and find out? Maybe they'd be willing to give me more information. If not, and things get ugly, I will turn wolfy again. I still haven't managed a complete transformation since prom night. If I'm going to do it again, I'd like to be prepared. Before I do anything, I need to call Terry. He has trouble accepting psychics? I'll see how he does with vampires. I pick up the phone and dial his number.

"Yeah." His standard answer.

"Terry, it's Lou. I need to tell you about a vision I had concerning the woman who was attacked in the alley last night."

Silence. He's still creeped out by the psychic stuff.

"Okay," he finally says.

"Have the wound to her neck rechecked. I think they'll find bite marks."

Another pause. "Are you saying this case is related to the other cases? The serial killer who thinks he's a werewolf?"

"No," I answer matter-of-factly. "This guy's a vampire."

Silence again.

"Terry?"

"You know, I'd think you were full of crap but the tip you gave me about the woman in her car, the one you said was hidden in a wooded area, panned out. I gave the authorities there the information and they found her. Her family was at least glad they had a body to bury. Like you said, it gave them a certain amount of closure."

"Have the hospital recheck the woman's neck," I repeat. "And check your files for unsolved murders in Queens where the victims had their throats slit. Those murders are being done by vampires, too."

"Lou." Terry groans. "If you're psychic, why do you only see weird shit like this? For your information, I don't have to check my files. I'm aware of several murders in Queens where the victims had their throats slit. We suspect the killings are gang-related executions."

"Think again," I say and hang up.

I spend the rest of the afternoon giving myself a facial, a manicure, and a waxing even though I don't need to wax. My agent calls and we go over job offers and details of the Vermont shoot. After I jot down my schedule, I prepare for the evening. I've decided to have a date with vampires.

In case I need to make a transformation, I try to prepare. I remove most of my makeup from my beauty bag, making room for extra clothing. I include a trash bag, as well. My closet is packed full of clothes. A lot of times I get to keep the outfits I model. I sort through them, deciding what I wouldn't mind losing. One outfit I can part with is a black leather jacket and pants that I've always considered a little too catwomanish to actually wear in public.

It's perfect for a late-night meeting with vampires. Now all I have to do is wait for nightfall.

The neighborhood in SoHo is mostly warehouses, but a few run-down apartment buildings are scattered along the streets. The lighting is poor. It's late and most of the apartment windows are dark. A car lumbers my way, the rap music so loud it vibrates the pavement. I figure vampires don't ride around in cars and step into an alley so I won't be seen.

Footsteps click against the pavement at the end of the alley. I can't be lucky enough for whoever's coming to be the three amigos. I'm surprised by who it is. If I'm not mistaken, it's the same woman who was attacked last night. I know it's her, she has a big white bandage on her neck. She spots me and draws up short.

"Don't worry. I won't hurt you," I call to her.

She stomps toward me. "Get lost, sister. This is my alley."

What does that mean? She lives in the alley? I

know people live on the streets. I glance around looking for a cardboard box or sacks full of belongings. "You live here?"

The woman rolls her eyes. I'm sure she thinks I can't see her reaction in the darkness. "Hell, no, I don't live here. I live down the street. But this is where I meet someone."

I'm confused. "You got attacked here last night. Why are you back this time of night where it might happen again?"

"Attacked?" she echoes. "What makes you think that?"

The woman was unconscious by the time I pulled the bloodsucker off her. She told Terry she didn't remember anything after the guy grabbed her. "It's why you woke up in the hospital this morning with a bandage around your slashed throat, remember?"

"How do you know this stuff?" she demands.

I reach out and place a hand on her shoulder. "I was here. I'm the one who scared your attacker off."

She knocks my hand away. "So you're the one who interfered."

I have the feeling my mouth is opening and closing like a fish out of water. "Interfered?" I finally manage. "I saved your life!"

"Maria, I told you not to come see me for a few days."

I wheel around. Fangman stands directly behind me. He walks past me and pauses to touch the woman's cheek. "I took too much last night. You need to regain your strength."

In the moonlight, she stares up at him adoringly, then pouts. "Then you'll get what you need from someone else. You know I'm jealous."

"You're also married. Go home to your husband."

Tears sparkle in her eyes. "He can't make me feel the way you do."

Bring out the violins. I think I'm going to puke. "Excuse me," I say. "You were screaming. That's why someone called the cops."

Fangman steers the woman toward the street. "Go home, Maria. I'll explain to the gringo."

Maria looks me up and down. "Yeah, I know what you'll explain to her. She's pretty. Maybe you want to suck her neck."

"She's tainted," Fangman says, curling his lip as he looks at me like I'm liver and onions. "Her blood is no good to me. I'll wait for you, but two days. Promise you will rest for two days before you come back here."

"You'll be weak if you wait that long to feed," Maria argues. "Just take a little." She offers the side of her neck that isn't bandaged.

Fangman shakes his head. "Don't tempt me, Maria. You know your blood is the sweetest to me. Go now."

With a sigh, Maria walks past him, pausing in front of me to glare. "Leave my man alone," she mutters under her breath.

I've entered a strange world. And I thought I already lived there. I wait until Maria makes it down the alley and turns the corner before addressing fangman. "What the hell is going on with her?" I ask.

He shrugs. "She loves me. I feed on her. She likes it."

"Then why was she screaming last night?"

The vampire walks to where I stand. "They were screams of ecstasy, not of fear. I warned her to be quiet but she makes a lot of noise."

I must have a "HUH?" look on my face. Fangman smiles and says, "If it's done right, a bite from a vampire can be better than sex to a woman. Of course, not all vampires do it right. Some have no regard for human life. They look at humans as they would cattle. A meal. Nothing more."

"Like those in Queens you told me about last night?"

His lip curls again. "Barbarians," he spits. "They have lost their humanity. They are thugs, rapists, and murderers. They give the rest of us a bad name."

Which brings me to the reason I'm in a bad neighborhood dressed like catwoman. "I don't understand what you said to me last night. About being synthetic. Are you saying someone made me what I am?"

"Let's walk," the vampire suggests. "He or she who stands in one place too long in this neighborhood soon becomes a victim."

I fall into step beside him. "Why am I tainted to you?"

He laughs, and I would say he looks nice when he smiles, but he still has the fangs. "You are curious now that you understand it can bring you pleasure."

"Wrong," I assure him. "I'm not into fang hickeys."

"The blood of a werewolf, even a synthetic one, can kill a vampire. We need pure human blood."

I'm still having trouble accepting the existence of vampires, although why that should be is beyond me. "Do you know of a werewolf roaming the city killing women?"

The vampire sighs. He pauses beside a broken streetlamp. "There are many werewolves and vampires. There is an underworld, but like sticks with like. We are not part of your world. We have our own struggles. Our own ways." He eyes my outfit and adds, "You would not fit in there."

It's been a while since I felt like part of the "out" crowd. "So you don't have answers for me? You can't point me in the right direction?"

He shakes his head. "No. Synthetics are not allowed in our world. You must be a natural to gain entrance to the underworld."

Great. Denied access. Besides possibly finding answers about myself in the underworld, maybe it would be nice to be with those who share something in common with me. What am I thinking? I want to rub elbows with monsters?

"You should go," Fangman says. "I need to feed and you are cramping my style."

I'm appalled. "You told Maria you wouldn't."

He shrugs. "What Maria doesn't know won't hurt her. I get hypoglycemic if I don't feed."

He's just like Cindy. Okay. Not. "Why aren't I turning?" I wonder. "I did last night when I was around you."

"You thought you were in danger last night," Fangman says. "It is a trigger for you. For all werewolves, obviously even synthetics."

"Do you know of other synthetics?"

He frowns. I get the impression he's becoming impatient with me. "I know they exist. Like I told you, I don't mix with werewolves. They have their own place in the underworld, and it is far from ours. We don't usually get along."

To say I'm disappointed is an understatement. This is the closest I've come to finding someone who might have answers about why I am what I am.

"How do you exist in the world of normal humans?"

Adjusting the skintight catwoman jacket, I answer, "I do what I have to do. I'm not different from everyone else except for the claws and fangs and fur, and those are evidently only triggered by certain factors . . . or others like me."

"It has been a long time since I walked in the sunshine. Since I enjoyed being human."

"So, it really is like the movies? You can't go out during the day?"

He laughs. "No, we can go out during the day. We simply choose not to. Unlike you, our fangs do not retract. We cannot hide what we are the way that you can."

I guess I could have it worse than I do. "Bummer," I say.

The vampire suddenly cocks his head and places a finger against his bloodred lips. "Someone is coming. You should go so I can feed."

My stomach rolls with the thought of what he's about to do. "I'm glad you don't hurt people. But blood. Yuck."

"It's like a fine wine to me. Now go. You are not welcome in this neighborhood."

I've been thrown out of a strange world. At least a relatively safe strange world. Deflated, I walk away from the scene of a future crime. I'll head home, or at least to a section of the city where I can hail a cab.

I take a few steps and turn around. "What's your name, Fangman?"

"Rick," he answers. "What about you, werewolf?"

"Lou," I answer, then move on.

CONFESSION NO. 21

Denial is a nice place to visit,
but living there can cost you your life.

The trip home was strangely uneventful. I was prepared to transform if the need arose. I had my beauty bag packed to stash somewhere so when I turned back into myself, I'd have somewhere to get clothes. And yes, the outfit I packed was an Yves Saint Laurent wool jumpsuit that makes me look like a clown. But I didn't get rid of the outfit and I didn't transform so I might experience what actually happens to me when I go completely werewolf.

I'm aware of the fact I might kill in werewolf form; I did that the only other time I made a transformation. But it was self-defense and I recalled very little about the actual time I spent as a werewolf. I need to know if my thoughts are completely my own. If I'm dangerous to more than someone trying to harm me.

I fish for my keys as I approach my apartment door. When I get ready to stick the key in my lock, I notice the door is slightly ajar. The hair on the back of my neck stands on end. Normally finding my door ajar wouldn't bother me. Cindy's the worst about coming in and making herself at home. But Cindy is in Texas. No one else has a key.

I push the door open. The apartment is dark like I left it. A noise comes from the kitchen. My heart rises in my throat. I grip my beauty bag tighter, prepared to use it as a weapon if I need to bash someone over the head. Then I move toward the kitchen. Whoever's in there isn't quiet. I hear the fridge open and close—the rustle of a paper bag. Lifting my beauty bag higher, I enter the kitchen.

A dark shadow digs in a bag sitting on the bar. I sneak up behind them, bag held high. The shadow turns, bumps into me, and screams. I scream, too.

It quickly dawns on me that it must be a vampire come to kill me for knowing too much. Dog Breath would not scream.

"Who are you and what the hell are you doing in my apartment?"

"It's Natasha," she gasps. "Cindy gave me the key to your apartment. She said I could ask you for the spare to hers, but I couldn't get a hold of you."

Natasha? Why would Cindy give someone I don't like the key to my apartment, especially considering

I'm not always at my best and shouldn't be barged in upon? And why would Natasha need the key to Cindy's place? I walk over and switch on the light. It's Natasha Somethingorother, all right. Then I notice the suitcase sitting at her feet.

"What's going on?"

Natasha places a hand to her heart. "My apartment is being fumigated. I mentioned this to Cindy and she said I could stay at her place while she is out of town. She gave me the key to your apartment and told me to contact you and ask for the spare key to hers. I couldn't reach you and I have these groceries that would ruin."

As much as I miss Cindy, I could clobber her at the moment. Just what I need, broad shoulders living next door. "Nice of her to mention that to me," I mutter. "How'd you get past Ralph, anyway?"

"Cindy told both doormen that I would be staying at her apartment for a few days. I just had to show identification."

Sighing, I place my beauty bag on the counter. I remove Cindy's spare key from my key ring. When I hand it to Natasha, she says, "Cindy said you might want to go over and tidy up before I see her apartment. I told her it didn't matter to me, but she insisted."

The monitor. She wants me to get rid of it, which is a good idea. If Natasha switches it on, she's going to hear me in my bedroom and wonder what the deal is. "I'll be right back," I say. "You can repack your grocery bag."

Taking my beauty bag to stash the monitor, I leave the apartment and go next door. Cindy is a messy person. I grab a few clothes she's left lying around and put them in her bathroom hamper. I'm not making her bed. She should have told me about Natasha coming to stay at her place. But then I would have probably pitched a fit and told her I didn't want her here. I unplug the monitor and stick it in my beauty bag and return to my apartment.

Natasha waits by the door with her grocery bag and suitcase. I hand her the key. "Knock yourself out, but don't bother me. I don't like to be disturbed."

She frowns. "Cindy said this would be a good time for us to make amends and become friends."

I try not to roll my eyes. "Cindy is often wrong." Opening the door wider, I indicate she can go. That's when I notice the draft. I glance toward the French doors leading from the balcony and see the drapes flapping in the wind.

"Were you born in a barn? First you leave my door open and then you open my balcony doors and leave them open? It's cold outside, you know?"

Natasha glances toward the open doors. "They were like that when I came in. I thought you were airing the place out or something."

Prickly sensation at the back of the neck number two. I didn't leave my balcony doors open when I left. "Oh, I might have left them open now that I think about it. I had them open earlier when I burned something and wanted to get rid of the smell. You can go now." I shove her into the hallway. "Good night."

After I close the door, I lean against it and sniff the air. My gaze darts around the dark apartment, looking for a shadow that doesn't belong. The cold, crisp air washes away any scent from an intruder, but someone besides Natasha has been in my apartment. I'd sense that even if the doors had not been left open. It's just a feeling, a creepy one. My sanctuary is fast becoming a zoo. What kind of animal has been in my apartment sniffing around? And is it gone, or still here?

The heaviest thing in my beauty bag is the monitor I just stuffed inside. I take it out and grip it firmly, moving through the dark apartment. Sure I can switch on a light; but not only does that allow me to better see someone lurking in the shadows, it allows them to see me. Nothing looks out of place in the living area. I've already been in the kitchen. Nowhere to hide in there. My bedroom seems the most logical place that an intruder might lie in wait for me.

I creep into the hallway leading into my room. The bedroom door is open, which is the way I left it. As soon as I step into the room, I catch a scent I have tried like hell to convince myself no longer exists.

The bed is a total wreck. It wasn't made when I left, but even in the darkness, I see that the mattress has been ripped up, stuffing everywhere. Not only do I smell the foul odor that belongs to Dog Breath,

I smell urine. He's marked the mattress. I'll kill him! I see red. No, really, I see red. My eyes glow back at me from the dresser mirror. I didn't know they glowed red in the dark. Creepy, but not nearly as horrible as what has taken place in my room.

I've been defiled. Rage builds inside of me and I let it come. If he's still here, hiding, I'll need the fuel to make a transformation. My teeth don't ache. My skin doesn't itch. My fingertips do not sting. He's not here or they would. As angry as I am, I have the sense to make certain. I switch on the bedroom light.

The carnage infuriates me further. He's not under the bed, in the closet, or in the bathroom shower. But nothing takes away from the fact that he was here. He did this to taunt me. To let me know he's still alive and stalking me. It's worse than if he'd waited around and attacked me. It's worse because he knows I'll worry about when he's coming back.

While I'm full of rage, I throw down my beauty bag and the monitor and use my freakish upper body strength to grab the mattress, haul it through the apartment, take it through the open doors of the balcony and pitch it over. Gus will freak out when he sees it lying on the grounds tomorrow and have it immediately hauled away. Next I go to the kitchen, find the air freshener and use the whole can when I return to the bedroom. I retrace my steps to the kitchen, get a pair of rubber gloves, and go through the apartment picking up stuffing that fell out of the mattress; then I return to the balcony and pitch that over, as well.

Once I close the doors and lean against them, I've used all my rage and I shake uncontrollably. True, it feels about twenty degrees in here since the doors have been open, but I know that isn't why I shake. Dog Breath is alive. He's done worse than attack me, he's invaded my space. He's defiled my property. And I'm scared shitless. I hate that more than anything. I'm on the verge of tears when a soft rap sounds against my front door. I don't think Dog Breath would bother to knock after what he's done, but I'm not ruling it out. I remember the door isn't locked anyway and he'd come on in or bust it down, so I go and answer it.

Natasha stands outside. "Is everything all right in there? I keep hearing you bang around. It sounds like you're rearranging your furniture."

I never thought I'd see the day when I was glad to see Natasha Somethingorother. It has arrived. Instead of offering an explanation, I step out into the hall and pull the door closed behind me. "Hey, do you mind if I crash on Cindy's couch? I can't get that burned smell out of my apartment no matter how hard I try. It makes me sick."

She shrugs. "Okay. Don't you want to get some pajamas?"

Cindy is the only person I know who sleeps in leather. "Actually, I like to sleep in this. Let's go."

Natasha eyes me oddly but doesn't question my decision. I follow her into Cindy's apartment, glad to see the TV switched on and no signs that she's ready to go to bed despite the late hour. A bag of pretzels and a cup of yogurt sit on Cindy's sofa table. My favorite. Dog Breath might kill me, but he'll never kill my appetite.

The werewolf freak might not have killed my appetite, but he killed my ability to sleep. I don't want to examine the fact that I could hardly bring myself to return to my apartment this morning. I hate to give him credit for that. I love this apartment. At some dark point during the early hours just before dawn, I even found myself thinking I should move.

Like hell I will. I also thought that I should call Terry and tell him my apartment had been broken into, and that I know who it was, and he cannot cross the werewolf killer off his list of people to worry about. I'm reconsidering that, as well. Terry would insist I stay somewhere else. His place? I'm thinking he'd be too smart to offer me that option.

I made myself coffee earlier because it was a normal thing to do. Now I sit on my couch that thankfully has not been peed on, and sip the rich brew, wondering what my next move should be. The first thing I did when I came home was go out on the balcony and look below. Just as I predicted, no sign of the defiled mattress or any stuffing. Gus is good.

How can I move when Gus is so good? I can't. If I move, Cindy will have to move and she likes it here as much as I do.

I'm still not happy with her for letting Natasha stay in her apartment while she's gone, but I guess if she hadn't, I wouldn't have had someone to sit up and watch TV with last night. Someone I hardly said two words to. I can count being upset over having my apartment broken into, my mattress peed on, and the confirmation that denial does not make something so or not so, as consolation I wasn't being totally rude. A little voice inside my head argues that I would have been rude regardless.

So Natasha likes pretzels dipped in yogurt as much as I do? That's hardly reason enough to forget she slept with my man. And why am I dwelling on this when I have so much else to dwell upon? That's a no-brainer. I don't want to think about the other. But I have to.

Setting my cup aside, I rise and move to the balcony doors. I'm sure they weren't locked. I don't expect someone to scale the side of a building to the tenth floor and slip into my apartment to murder me or trash my stuff when I'm not home to murder. My thinking has to change. So do my doors. I get the phone book and call one of those security door places. I'll have iron barriers on the other side before nightfall.

I'm fairly certain that Dog Breath won't try getting into the building from the front entrance. He has to either have a code to punch in, or a doorman would have to let him in. Neither would. I'm also fairly confident the five locks on my door will keep Dog Breath out. The only other way I know to be safe . . . is to kill him for good. There's only one way I can kill him. I have to be one hundred percent certain I can do a complete transformation.

Ready or not, I must venture to Queens and see if my life being threatened will turn me. Of course if it doesn't, I'll be in deep shit. I need a superhero as a sidekick instead of a lesbian.

My phone rings. I answer. It's sort of a superhero. "Hi, Terry."

"Thought I'd let you know the woman you wanted me to check for bite marks was released from the hospital before I could have her neck looked at again. But we got another body last night at the morgue. Woman with her throat slit. Happened in Queens. The coroner who did the autopsy confirmed what you told me. There were bite marks."

I'm not surprised and see no reason to act like I am. "So, what are you going to do?"

"Off-duty stakeout," he answers. "Thought I might head over to Flushing, 147th Street along Northern Boulevard, where a lot of gang action has been going on. I want to check it out for myself. I'm not about to tell my captain I think vampires are murdering these people, not gang members. And really, it has to be some type of ritual thing. I mean, there aren't really vampires."

So Terry likes to visit denial as much as the next person. "When are you going?"

"Tomorrow night."

"Can I come?"

He laughs. "Absolutely not. It's dangerous over there. It wouldn't be safe for you to tag along."

"How about coffee before you go? I need to talk to you about something." There. I have to tell Terry Dog Breath is still alive, even if I might not tell him exactly how I know that. I need time to come up with a story.

"Okay, I'll pick you up and then drop you back home before I go. Around eight?"

"That will be fine."

"See you then. Stay out of trouble."

I hang up. Trouble has suddenly become my middle name. Which reminds me of Morgan. I give him a call. As usual, he doesn't pick up and I get his machine. "Morgan, this is Lou. Found anything? Feel free to leave the information on my machine."

I'm not going to the club again until I figure out if I can transform and what happens when I do. Maybe Dog Breath wasn't there when I went with Karen, but I strongly suspect that he was, and I know he has picked up at least one woman there. And killed her afterward.

In the next two days I plan to Dog Breath–proof my apartment, have the carpet in the bedroom replaced, and buy a new mattress. If I get too desperate for company, there's always my new next-door neighbor. It'll have to be a cold day in hell before I stoop to visiting Natasha. By six-thirty that evening, I declare it a cold day in hell and go next door. Natasha looks surprised to see me. She should be. Something wafting from the apartment into the hallway smells delicious.

"Are you expecting company?" I ask. "I smell cooking."

"No, I cook for myself. I get tired of takeout food." She leaves the door open and heads toward Cindy's kitchen. I'm not sure Cindy even has dishes or pots and pans. I guess she has pots and pans or Natasha wouldn't be cooking something that jumpstarts my salivary glands.

Neither Cindy nor I can cook worth a damn. That's why we eat out so much. I make sure I lock the door before following Natasha.

She lifts the lid of a big pot and stirs. "Do you want to eat? There is plenty."

I take a seat at the bar. "You sure you're not expecting someone? That's a big pot."

Looking over her rather broad shoulder, Natasha laughs. "I come from a big family. I never learned to cook for one. I usually eat a lot of leftovers."

"When did you come to America?"

"I was fifteen," she answers. "I came as an exchange student, but didn't want to go home once I graduated. I got in with an agency in Los Angeles, did some modeling for them, became an American citizen, and moved to New York."

"Do you ever miss living in Russia?"

She shakes her head. "No. But I miss my family. Someday I'll make enough to bring them all over to live. In the meantime, we write letters."

Okay, I feel a little guilty for joining in the fun when Karen gave Natasha a hard time about looking like a dyke. I know how it feels to be separated from your family. Of course, there's still the Stefan issue between us.

"He wasn't worth it."

I glance up and catch Natasha staring at me. "What?"

"He wasn't worth having all the other girls hate me."

"Who, Stefan?" During uncomfortable moments, always pretend confusion over the conversation topic.

"I thought if I slept with him, it would make me one of you. I would be allowed into your snotty club. I wanted to belong."

Damn her. I can relate to that, too. My dislike of Natasha fades. If the food is as good as it smells, it might cinch the deal. "I can see where sleeping with him would make you believe you were one of the crowd," I say dryly. "It was the gloating part that got you in trouble. It would have been better if you did what everyone else who sleeps with Stefan does, pretend you haven't."

"Ah." Natasha nods and turns back to her big pot. "No one tells me these things."

While she stirs, I reconsider hating her.

"Do you still have a thing for him?" I ask.

Natasha moves from the stove and takes two bowls from the cabinet. The bowls are plastic. "I never had a thing for him. I only wanted to be accepted. I thought that was the way."

I withhold judgment until Natasha dishes me a big bowl of what appears to be goulash. She hands me a spoon. I take a bite. After closing my eyes and savoring the combination of meat, noodles, garlic, and tomato sauce, I swallow and say, "Natasha, I think this is the beginning of a beautiful relationship."

She smiles. Her bowl brims to the top. Another girl who likes to eat is always welcome in my club. Even if there's something odd about Natasha. Any model who has never had a thing for Stefan is not a normal red-blooded straight girl.

CONFESSION NO. 22

Girls who like to eat are welcome in my club.
Vampires who try to eat me are not.

Terry and I sip coffee in a shop that's in a better location than the last one. I still don't see any cops hanging out.

"What did you want to talk to me about?"

Setting my mocha aside, I answer. "It's about the werewolf killer. I've had visions. He's not dead. He's just waiting."

Terry raises a brow. "Waiting for what?"

I can't meet his eyes. "I don't know."

Terry is quiet. I feel his steady gaze on my face. "He's waiting for you. Isn't that right, Lou?"

It is right, but if I admit that, Terry is going to be on my ass twenty-four/seven. And not in a good way. I won't be able to talk to vampires or walk around the city with a five o'clock shadow or a midnight beard. "I don't know what he's waiting for," I lie. "I just want you to be aware that he's still out there."

"Thanks for the tip." Terry finishes his coffee. "Now here's one for you. I want you to stay home until we catch this guy. No shopping. No modeling. No chance for this guy to get his hands on you, understand?"

Blinking back at him, I say, "I told you I won't rearrange my life for this creep. He'd like that—thinking he had me so scared I just stay in my apartment and tremble at the thought of going out. He feeds on fear and I'm not so much as tossing him a crumb. Got that?"

Now Terry blinks at me. "I admire your bravery, Lou, but it borders on stupidity. I've seen what this psycho does to women. There's no question now that he's marked you as a target. Do you want to end up dead?"

I can't move past the stupidity remark to consider Terry's questions. Why is it all right for a man to be brave, but if a woman is, she's labeled stupid instead? "I'm finished. I'd like to go home."

He glances at his watch. "Yeah, I've got to get to Queens and start my stakeout. At least consider what I said. I've seen your place; I think you can give up a few pairs of shoes and do without a paycheck for a while. Better yet, do you have out-of-town relatives you can stay with until we nail this guy?"

Shoes? Does he think that's all I buy with my pay-check? I'm starting to wonder if following Terry to-night in case I need to save his ass is good idea. At the moment, his ass is not worth saving. I rise from the cozy two-top table situated in the back of the coffee shop and gather my beauty bag. "I'm going to Vermont on a modeling shoot at the end of the week. I'll be gone three or four days if that makes you feel better."

"That's good," Terry decides, rising also. He puts a hand against my back and steers me to the door. "Try to lay low until then, okay?"

"Sure," I lie. "Whatever big strong policeman says."

When he issues a grunt of disapproval behind me, I figure he doesn't appreciate my sarcasm. That's okay. I don't appreciate his macho attitude at the moment, either. I suppress the urge to remind him that I beat him up in bed. The only reason I suppress it is because I might want to beat him up in bed again at some future date.

The ride to my apartment is chilly despite my lustful thoughts, the warm heat blowing from the vents, and the hot coffee sitting in our stomachs. The only comment I make is telling Terry to be careful, before I climb out of his car and go inside my build-ing. I wait until he drives off before asking Ralph to call me a cab. The cabby, unless he's crazy, will not take me all the way to the stakeout point, but as long as he gets me within walking distance that's all right.

My beauty bag is packed with the clown jumpsuit I don't mind losing.

I'm nervous. And I'm not feeling all that brave at the moment. I question the sanity of calling a beast forth that I'm unsure I can control. My near-transformation the night I confronted Dog Breath assures me I'll be able to control myself, but the recollection of what happened on prom night still haunts me. Should I experiment when a man I care about is involved? But knowing what I know, can I leave Terry to fend for himself in a neighborhood overrun with vampires?

The cab pulls up outside. I'm torn about my earlier decision. Saying I'm brave and actually being brave are two different things. Then I think of Terry alone on the dark streets, unaware of what he's really up against. I wanted tonight to be an eye-opening experience for him. I don't want it to be a neck-sucking or -slashing experience for him. That decides the matter. I go outside and get in the cab.

By the time I find Terry's El Camino parked along Northern Boulevard, my nerves have taken a beating and my feet hurt. I don't like what I see. Terry is not inside the car. I've already stashed my beauty bag behind some trash in a nearby alley and I'm ready to confront whatever vampires might consider me a late-night snack.

Is Terry out scouting the area, or has he already become a victim? When I draw closer to the El Camino, I notice that the smell of his Brut/axle grease aftershave still lingers in the air. I follow the scent. It leads me five blocks down to an alley where I see Terry lying on the ground and four figures huddled over him.

"Hey!" I shout. "Back off him, bloodsuckers!"

Four palefaces turn toward me. They rise from their bent positions. "Women stupid enough to hang out in this neighborhood after dark either have a death wish, or are looking for a meal," one of the vampires says. He eyes me up and down. "Go find your own cocktail, this one is ours."

They think I'm a vampire. By the ache of my teeth, the itch of my skin, and the sting in my fingertips, I can soon assure them that I'm not. "I'm not a bloodsucker," I say. "If you don't leave him alone, I'm going to kick your asses."

My statement gets a laugh from all of them. "You and what army, little girl?" the same one who spoke earlier taunts.

"Her and this army."

I wheel around. Rick and his two buddies stand behind me. I thought they steered clear of this turf. "What are you doing here?"

"Decided to come over and try to reason with these guys about their activities. The cops are going to catch on sooner or later, and it will make things hard for all of us," Rick answers.

The click of switchblades being opened draws my

attention back to the four thugs planning to make a meal out of Terry.

"We don't want to play nice," one of the fangmen crouching over Terry says. "You three go back to your own turf or die along with these two."

Shit. I brought everything but my switchblade. I look down at my hands and see claws jutting from my fingertips. Guess I don't need a switchblade after all. I'm not the only one to notice the claws.

"She's a werewolf!" the leader of the bad vampires shouts. "Kill her!" he orders his gang members. "Kill them all!"

I'm not up to speed on gang protocol. I expect them to count to three or something before attacking us. Wrong. I suddenly have a vampire in my face. He slashes out with his knife and barely misses gutting me. It's not that I try to hurt the guy right off, but I bring my hands up to block another knife attack and slash his face open. He must be really hungry because there's not much blood. I think what little he has drains right out. He crumples to the ground.

I glance up to see the leader pulling Terry's head up by the hair. His fangs flash white in the darkness, then he descends toward Terry's neck. In superspeed I rush him. I kick out and land a blow to his face. He stumbles back. Terry's forehead hits the pavement. Hard.

"I'll kill you, bitch," the leader growls up at me, wiping blood from the corner of his lip. He licks his fingers afterward. Ewww.

He lunges at me. He hits me so hard I fly backward

and hit the side of a building, knocking the air from my lungs. About the time I manage to gasp, his hand closes around my throat. He chokes me. My claws slash out at him. Blood spurts from an injury on his neck. It splatters my face and hair. That really pisses me off. It's yucky. The bloodsucker leans in and bites me. It hurts like hell. I'm not the least turned on by it like Rick said women were.

Then I remember something else Rick said. The vampire is about to move in for another bite but suddenly his face pales. He's pretty white anyway. I'm talking the color of milk here. He stumbles back, gagging while holding his throat. He crumples to the ground, jerking and convulsing until he finally lies still. Biting a werewolf killed him. I guess he didn't know that would happen.

Thinking of Rick, I glance toward him. His two friends lie dead on the ground. The other two bloodsuckers have him cornered. Rick's decent, for a vampire. If I don't do something, he'll die. My hands are fur covered. I have the claws and the teeth, now I need the whole package. I think about prom night. I think about Terry and what will happen to him once the vampires have killed Rick. I think about the shadows creeping into the alley. The scent of blood having drawn them.

My face hurts. My whole body hurts. I hear the awful sound of bones crunching—rearranging themselves. My clothes rip. I grow taller . . . bigger. Then I let out a roar that would scare the dead. And it does. The two vampires huddled over Rick wheel in my direction. Their eyes widen. They leave Rick, hold their switchblades in front of them, and stalk toward me. When one gets within knifing distance, my hairy arm shoots out and knocks him ten feet through the air. The other one flies at me. I swat him as easily as I did the other one.

Suddenly, I'm surrounded. Four more vampires have slunk from the shadows. I lunge forward and attack the one closest to me. This is sickening, even to me, but I tear his throat out. Another comes at me and I rake his face with my claws. Rick jumps into the fray. He handles one vampire while I pick up the other and snap him like a twig. I'm prepared for another attack, but it doesn't come. Rick stands over the body of the vampire he killed. The blood and carnage around me makes me sick.

I'm on all fours. My clothes lie in shreds around me. I'm not cold because I am covered by fur. I look down my face at a long snout. I am a wolf . . . but am I still me? I think so. I hear my thoughts inside my head. Glancing at Rick, I feel no urge to hurl myself at him and rip his throat out. I watch as he moves to where Terry lies.

"He's unconscious," he calls toward me, as if it's perfectly normal to converse with a wolf. "I guess we need to get him to a hospital." Rick scoops up Terry in his arms. "Where's his car?"

I'm afraid to speak. Afraid it will come out like a bark or a howl, or worse, all distorted and creepy sounding like Dog Breath. I have no choice but to do the Lassie thing. I take off, stop and turn to look at him, run back, turn and run a few steps, turn to look at him.

"I get it," Rick says. "Take me to his car."

Once we reach the El Camino, Rick digs through Terry's pockets and gets his keys. He unlocks the door and slides him inside the passenger side. I follow him around to the driver side.

"What, you think you're driving?" Rick asks. "Get in the back. I have allergies to animal fur."

I growl but he ignores me, climbs inside, and slams the door. He starts up the El Camino. I race to the alley where I stashed my clothes, grab the bag in my mouth, and race back and jump in the back of the car.

I've done a lot of things since I came to New York seven years ago. I've done runway, commercials, catalogues, multimillion-dollar advertisements to push every kind of product imaginable. I've never ridden in the back end of an El Camino with the wind in my fur, the moon full above, looking at the world through wolf eyes. It's cool.

I look around, mesmerized by the sights, as if I'm seeing them all for the first time. My senses are sharper than they have ever been. I see, smell, hear, and even feel more than I ever have. It's wonderful until the hair starts flying. Literally. The fur starts coming off. My bones hurt. My face hurts. It's excruciating. By the time Rick pulls into Elmhurst

Hospital, I'm naked and shivering. I fumble through my bag to remove the clown suit. Rick pulls into the back of the parking garage where no one wants to park due to the distance to the elevators.

He gets out and catches me squirming around on the freezing metal bed of the El Camino, trying to get the jumpsuit up over my hips.

Rick's eyes about pop out of his head. If they did, it wouldn't surprise me. Not on a night like tonight.

"Whoa," he says, turning away. "I'm a vampire, not a gelding. Damn, girl, you look like a supermodel."

"I-I-I a-a-a-m a s-supermodel."

He turns back around. "No shit? I thought you looked familiar. I've probably seen you on billboards, right?"

"Y-yes." A few shifts to the right and left and right again later, I pull the jumpsuit up and zip it closed. I'm glad it's wool, even if it's itchy. I pull on boots and hop over the side of the El Camino.

"You'll have to handle it from here," Rick says. "I can't go in."

"I'm sorry about your friends."

He nods. "They knew what they were up against. Those freaks in Queens are ruining things for the decent vampires."

When I told Terry to look for bite marks, I didn't realize I'd be putting Rick and those like him in danger along with the bloodsuckers killing people. Maybe it wasn't such a good idea to alert Terry to the problem. Maybe it's better if the world stays ignorant about the monsters who roam the streets at night. They have enough human monsters to deal with.

"Thanks for your help tonight. I'm not sure what would have happened if you hadn't come along."

He shrugs. "I think you could have handled it. You are one badass when someone gets your fur up."

I suppose he considers that a compliment. "See you around," I say.

Rick walks off into the shadows. I grab my beauty bag from the back and hop into the El Camino. I'll take Terry to the emergency entrance. Then I have to figure out how to explain to him how I just happened along and saved his life tonight.

CONFESSION NO. 23

*I like making new friends as much as the
next person . . . but girls with broad shoulders
and boys with fangs are not my preferred
choice for breakfast companions.*

The smell of bacon wakes me. For a moment,
I'm back in Haven, waking for school to the
smell of Norma cooking breakfast for me and
Clive. I savor that memory. Life in a simpler time. A
time of innocence. Then I realize the smell is so
strong it can only be coming from my kitchen. I
shoot out of bed and plow through the apartment,
skidding to a halt in the kitchen. Natasha stands at
the stove. Rick sits on Terry's bar stool.

"What the hell is going on?"

"Wake up, sleepyhead," Natasha croons. "I found
your friend outside loitering around on my way back
from the market. I asked if he'd like to join us for
breakfast."

My head snaps toward Rick. "I thought you weren't a morning person."

"I wanted to show you something. Ask your opinion."

Immediately I know what he wants an opinion on. He's wearing makeup to give himself color and he's done something to his teeth.

"Not bad," I say. "What'd you do?"

"Filed them," he answers.

I slide onto the stool next to him. "Won't that affect your ability to . . ." I glance toward Natasha. She has her back to us, scrambling eggs. "Feed?"

He shrugs. "I didn't care. All night, I kept thinking about you, living a normal life, and it made me hunger for more than blood. It made me think maybe I could be normal, too."

"Toast?"

We glance across the kitchen toward Natasha. She has no clue she's serving a werewolf and a vampire. "Sure," I call back. "Hey, how did you get in here?"

Natasha walks over and shoves a plate of bacon and scrambled eggs in front of each of us. "Cindy called me. She was worried because she couldn't get a hold of you last night. She told me where she keeps a spare key and told me to check on you. I stayed awake until I heard you come home last night, then I thought you might like breakfast this morning."

If Natasha thinks she can worm her way into my

heart through my stomach, she's absolutely right. It's why she would want to I can't figure out. What difference does it make if I like her or I don't? Oh, God, maybe she has a crush on me.

Rick takes a bite of scrambled eggs. He winces.

"That bad?" I whisper.

"I don't usually eat food. It's not that I can't, it's just that it no longer tastes good to me."

Maybe goulash is the only thing Natasha knows how to cook. I take a bite of my eggs. They're delicious. "Scrape yours onto my plate and I'll eat them, too. I'm starving."

While Natasha makes toast with her back to us, Rick scrapes his food onto my plate. "Can I stay here today?"

I nearly drop my fork. "Why?"

"Didn't get any sleep. Just thought you wouldn't mind since I helped you out last night."

He's saying I owe him, which I guess is true. What happened to my sanctuary? At least Rick already knows what I am. I don't have to hide anything from him. The flip side is, I know what he is, too. "Okay, but you sleep on the couch and no biting anyone around here, understand?"

"Got it," he says. "Are you going to the hospital to check on your friend this morning??"

"What friend?" Natasha slides in next to us.

"Terry. He's a detective with the city. He had a mishap last night and is in the hospital. He was completely out of it last night. The doctor on duty told me to come back this morning."

"Is he hurt bad?" Natasha asks, chomping on a piece of bacon.

"Just a concussion. I'd better get ready and get down there."

"I'll clean up the mess," Natasha offers. "I have a shoot later today."

"I'm going to crash. Thanks for breakfast, Natasha."

She nods and Rick goes to the other room to sleep on my couch. "I want to thank you for breakfast, too," I say. "It was really good."

"I like to cook," she says with a shrug. "Makes me feel like I have family again."

Now she's pushing her luck. "I have to clean up. Show yourself out when you're done, okay? Don't disturb Rick. We were out . . . partying late last night."

"Okay," Natasha chirps. She slides off her stool and starts cleaning up the breakfast mess.

An hour later, I'm showered, changed, and ready to visit Terry at the hospital. I wear a turtleneck. I still have bite marks on my neck from that creep who wanted to kill me last night. They should heal quickly and I hope Rick was right when he said a bite can't turn an unnatural into a vampire. That's all I need. Natasha has gone and Rick is asleep on the couch. I let myself out.

• • •

Terry in a hospital gown is not anything that will give me horny dreams. He looks a little pale, has a bandage on his head, but seems okay all things considered. When I walked in, nurses were buzzing around him checking vitals. I can tell he can't wait for them to leave to start asking questions.

I tried to think of a plausible explanation as to why I just happened to be in a neighborhood he warned me away from. There isn't one. I must fall back on my nonexistent psychic abilities.

"Dr. Anderson said you could be released today," one of the nurses says to Terry. "You should have someone drive you home. Maybe this nice young woman." She nods toward me. "You'll get a list of instructions upon release. Any questions will be answered at that time."

· The nurses file out and I'm left alone with Terry. I start the conversation. "How are you feeling?"

"Okay, but confused," he answers. "I can't really remember what happened last night. I heard a noise and went to investigate. Everything beyond that is blank."

"I found you unconscious," I provide. "Someone had obviously clubbed you over the head."

Terry sits up and stares at me. "How did you find me, Lou? And why were you there when I told you that neighborhood is dangerous?"

Acting and lying aren't the same thing, right? "I had one of my visions," I tell him. "I saw you lying unconscious. You told me what area you would be in. I found your car parked and went looking for you."

He shakes his head, then winces as if the motion hurts. "I'm surprised you didn't get attacked or worse. And how did you manage to get me in the car? I out-weigh you by at least a hundred and fifty pounds."

I shrug. "That freakish upper-body strength I have, I guess. That and the adrenaline rush of knowing I needed to get you to a hospital. Instead of riding my ass about it, maybe you should just thank me for saving yours."

He glances away. This is a hard pill for him to swallow. Being rescued by a woman. A model who only worries about shoes and clothes and makeup. I enjoy watching him squirm.

"You probably saved my life," he admits. "That doesn't mean I'm happy you risked yours to do it. I can't figure out what whoever bashed me over the head wanted. They didn't take my wallet or anything."

"Did you have your badge?" I ask.

"I always carry my badge."

"Maybe they saw it and thought better of robbing a cop."

"Maybe," he agrees.

"Do you want me to drive you home? I can call a cab from your place."

Terry reaches for a cup of ice water and flashes

me with a glimpse of bare ass. I reconsider that a hospital gown can't be sexy on a man. "Some of the guys came by this morning before shifts started. A couple offered to give me a ride if I got released today. But, sure, if you don't mind."

A nurse comes back in. "I have your release forms ready," she says to Terry. "And your instructions. Your doctor was on the ball this morning. Looks like you can go as soon as we're finished."

She hands him his personal items, all sealed up neatly in an envelope. Terry takes out his keys and tosses them to me. "Good thing you know where I'm parked."

"He'll have to be taken down in a wheelchair," the nurse tells me. "If you'll pull up at the hospital entrance he can just get in the vehicle."

I rise from the only chair in the room. "Okay, I'll go down and get the car."

Nothing is fast moving at a hospital. Two hours later I settle Terry back into his apartment. He's hungry and we order Chinese to be delivered. I wait on the delivery person while Terry showers. While I wait I check my messages.

The first message is from Stefan. He wants to know if I want to ride to Vermont with him for the shoot. The second call is from Karen. She wants to know if I want to ride with her. The third message is from Cindy. She's glad I'm all right since she couldn't get a hold of me last night, but wants to know what's going on with me.

She has a meeting with her dad today and she's nervous. The fourth message is from Morgan Kane. He has information and needs to talk to me in person. He says he'll be in the office all day. Morgan's call gets top priority.

As soon as the food arrives and I scarf mine down, I plan to call a cab and make a beeline for Morgan's run-down building. I wonder if Rick is still napping on my couch. I wonder if he can still be a bloodsucker with ground-down fangs. I wonder if I'll go home to find everyone in my building drained.

"No food yet I take it from the lack of smell." Terry walks through the apartment in a towel and nothing else. He goes into the kitchen, opens the fridge, and takes out a soda. He lifts it up. "You want one?"

"No, no food yet and yes, I want one." I want more than a soda. Terry is built. I forgot how good he's built. I also know what's beneath the towel.

Terry pauses in all his glory to hand me a soda. He's got great legs. Long and muscular. He's got great abs, too. A nice little eight-pack. He also has a tent thing going on in the front of his towel.

I glance up and lift a brow. "Is that a gun under your towel or are you just happy to see me?"

He grins at me. "Happy to see you."

I'd be flattered but I'm fairly certain Terry should

not be considering having rough sex on his first hour home from the hospital. Maybe I can concentrate on not being rough. What am I doing? This is the same man who thinks I spend all my paychecks on shoes.

Reaching out, I take the soda. "Thanks. And you can tell Mr. Happy, or whatever his name is, it's not happening."

He shrugs. "You can't blame a guy for trying." Terry leaves the room.

I assume he went to get dressed. Or at least I hope so. My willpower is very weak. It's the beast in me, I guess. Horny bitch. She may be horny, but at least now I know she isn't a murderer for the sake of being a murderer. I killed last night, but it was in self-defense and my mind was my own, although my body did a complete transformation. I haven't had much time to dwell on last night and what it means for me.

It means I don't have to be afraid of myself. I still must be afraid for myself, but not of what I might do. I am not a beast without human thought to guide me—to tell me wrong from right. I don't like killing. I'm not an animal except in appearance. I allow myself a moment of joy. A moment of relief. A moment to let it all sink in.

After seven years of being afraid, no, terrified, over making another transformation and killing again, I now have at least that answer.

So my life isn't so good . . . it isn't so bad, either.

The speaker buzzer sounds. "I'll get it," Terry

says, moving through the living area in baggy jeans and a T-shirt. He talks to the delivery person then buzzes them in.

He fishes money from his wallet and a few minutes later a knock sounds on the door. I rise and take the food while he pays. It smells delicious and I'm hungry even though I pigged out at breakfast. I take our food boxes to his small two-top table and set them down, then retrieve my soda from the coaster on the sofa table in the living room.

Terry comes into the kitchen, digs out silverware and napkins, and we sit down to eat. I learn Terry isn't much for conversation while he eats, but that's okay, my mind has already galloped ahead to my meeting with Morgan Kane, and what information he has for me.

CONFESSION NO. 24

There's one consolation for girls who
beat up men in bed. Some like it rough.

Kane has failed to make any improvements to his
building. I'm guessing the rock-star business
doesn't pay that well for him, or I was misin-
formed and he's not that good at private investigating. Which makes me a little nervous about forking
over the other fifteen grand I drew out of the bank on
the way over.

The money is his first concern. "You bring the
other half?"

I dig in my beauty bag and stack the cash on his
desk. A certified check would have been better, but I
don't want anyone tracing my activities. "What information do you have?"

He reaches out and scoops the money into his top drawer. I guess he doesn't want me taking it back if I fail to be impressed with whatever he's turned up for me.

"That information you gave me on your adoptive mother's maiden name paid off." Kane leans forward in his chair. "Just so happens a Norma Ford was once employed at Hawkins Research Facility in Grandbury, Nevada. She worked there as a secretary from 1977 through 1980. In 1979 she married Clive Billington. You were born in 1980."

I'm shocked by Kane's discovery. This is too much of a coincidence.

"I did some research on Hawkins Research Facility. What they basically do is test experimental drugs for pharmaceutical companies. Here's what I'm thinking might be going on. A lot of drugs need testing to see if there are any harmful side effects to a fetus. Wendy Underwood works for them, she finds herself in a family way, the guy runs out on her, she wants to put the baby up for adoption. Instead, the laboratory talks her into taking money to test these drugs, probably assuring her they believe no harm will come to the fetus. Turns out they were wrong and there is some type of abnormality that shows up when the mother and fetus are tested. You have any odd medical conditions?"

Do I ever. "Not that I'm aware of," I answer.

Kane continues. "Now the lab has a problem. They have a mother carrying a baby with some type of birth defect. Norma Billington works for the company. She's newly married and maybe she already knows she can't have kids for whatever reason. The laboratory offers a baby to her. Wendy Underwood's baby. The details are handled through a legit adoption agency so everything looks normal. Wendy Underwood takes her payoff and disappears. Norma Billington takes her defective child and moves away to raise the child in a small town in Texas."

What type of drug could they have been testing that would make me a werewolf? I think drug testing for the market is a stretch and then some to explain what has happened to me. But *something* happened in Nevada.

"You need to let me go to Nevada," Kane stresses again. "Something fishy is going on at that lab."

He might find too many answers. "No, I told you, this is something I want to do together. I want a sense of place where my biological mother lived. I also think you need me to help you get information. The lab owes it to me to tell me if I have some type of defect I'm not aware of. I'll threaten them with legal ramifications if they don't. You just need to sit tight until I get back from a modeling shoot I have in Vermont this weekend."

Kane sits back in his seat with a sigh. He runs a hand through his hair to get it out of his face. "Okay, you're calling the shots. I just thought you'd be anxious to find out what's going on."

"I am," I assure him, which is the truth. "But first I have to honor my work obligations. I leave in two days. I'll be back in five. We can wait."

"Contact me the minute you get back so we can make arrangements to fly out."

"My dime, I'm assuming," I say sarcastically.

He shrugs. "Your problem. Your dime."

What Kane doesn't know is that he's not going. I'll call him from Nevada and tell him I decided to snoop around on my own. He'll be mad as hell, but like he said, I'm the one calling the shots. I don't dare tell him now because he's just the type to go without me while I'm in Vermont.

"So what's happening in Vermont, cupcake?"

I've figured out bitching at him about his pet name for me does no good. I won't waste my breath. "Just a normal shoot. Skiwear."

"Taking your boyfriend?"

"Not that it's any of your business, but no, and for the record, he's not my boyfriend."

"Your decision or his? On the boyfriend part?"

Gathering my beauty bag, I rise and head toward the door. Kane hurries from behind his desk and meets me at the door.

"You know, you don't strike me as the turtleneck type."

Before it registers what Kane is about to do, he pulls my turtleneck down. I swat his hand away.

"Wow, that's some hickey," he says. "Got a little rough, didn't he?"

I knew the day would come when Kane pushed me too far. Today is the day. I slam him up against the wall. "Keep your hands and your comments to yourself!"

He gives me that shit-eating grin. "Nothing wrong with the rough stuff. If you like it, that's fine. I'll tell you a secret. I like it, too."

He's not just saying that. We're pressed up against each other and he has a boner to beat the band. Pun intended. I shove away from him, grab the door, and storm out. "Pervert," I mutter on my way to the elevator. I don't have to turn around to know Kane stands in the hall; I'm sure he's staring at my ass as I walk away. He can stare all he wants but he's never getting a piece of it.

Now I don't feel the least bit guilty about not telling him he's not going to Nevada with me. It's for his own good. I'm sure if I had to spend more than thirty minutes with the man I would end up killing him.

At home, Rick has left me a note. What is it with men and notes? Cops, vampires, they all leave them. At least Rick didn't sign his. It's short and to the point.

"Thanks for letting me crash on your couch. See you around."

In the kitchen, I find another note.

"I left dinner in the refrigerator for you. If you want company later, let me know. Natasha."

What's the deal? I thought the rule was to never feed a stray or they wouldn't leave. Not the other way around. I'm still in a pissy mood because of Morgan. I'm intrigued by what he had to tell me, but the whole cab ride home, I kept thinking about his boner. I gave two men a boner in the same day. I know what's under Terry's towel, and I know it's nice. Morgan felt . . . well, almost twice as nice if you get my meaning. Wonder if he stuffs something down his pants? I hear a lot of rock stars do.

And why am I thinking about this now? I have a ton of other things to think about. One of them is my upcoming travel plans. I've decided to go with Karen, and probably against my better judgment, I'm asking her if Natasha can tag along with us. If Karen says no, I'll tell her Natasha will bake us goodies for the road. That should seal the deal.

Stefan sounds disappointed when I tell him I'm going with Karen. I ask what's bothering him and he says his dad isn't doing well. His dad lives in Ireland, so Stefan can't just rush over to see what's wrong with the guy. He says he thought we could "talk" on the ride. I'm thinking about two boners today; adding a third would make me a real slut. I suggest we "talk" later, maybe while we're relaxing at the inn. Maybe by the time I get to the shoot location, I'll have figured out what to say to him, or where I want our relationship to go, or not go.

Because of my pissy mood, I don't invite Natasha over. I feel guilty about this because I'm scarfing down her goulash. Terry calls at seven, asks me where exactly in Vermont I'm staying. Natasha left the information for me along with her note. I give it to Terry and ask how he feels. He says okay, he's working on the possible connection between murders and missing girls in other states during his time off. I think he's lonely, but he doesn't ask me to come over. We hang up after a strained silence.

My freakin' phone rings again. I glance at the caller ID. It's Cindy. "Hey, stranger," I say when I pick up.

"Hey, stranger yourself," she says back. "What's going on with you? You never go out at night and I haven't been able to reach you for the past two."

Because I love Cindy and figure she has enough to deal with in the real world, I don't tell her about vampires who bite nice and vampires who bite mean and girls who take being wolfy to the extreme. "Just hanging out," I say. "Coffee with Terry." Which isn't a lie.

"Have you gotten him in bed again yet?"

"No, but I gave him a hard-on today," I offer.

"I guess that's something."

I move to the couch and plop down. "Tell me what's happening on your end. Did you talk to your dad today?"

"What a nightmare," she says glumly.

My heart sinks. I'd hoped that her meeting with her dad went well. "Don't tell me he was an ass."

"He was an ass and then some," she says. "He not only yelled at me, said I was going to hell, but he yelled at Mom for asking me to come home and visit. The only bright spot of the day was that she yelled back at him."

"Your mom?" I'm shocked.

"Yeah," Cindy says with a laugh, and the fact she can laugh makes me feel better. "She got right in his red face. She said he wasn't going to tell her what kind of a relationship she could have with their only child. She ended up telling him to go to hell."

"Where is she now?"

"Downstairs in the hotel lobby, having a drink."

I sit up straight. "A drink drink or a soda or something?"

"Apple martini, per my suggestion. I've got to get down there in a minute and make sure she's not getting looped and hitting on the lounge singer."

The picture of that makes me laugh. Cindy laughs along with me. "Hey," she says, sobering. "You're being okay to Natasha, right? I'd hate to think telling her you were really a nice person was a mistake."

"You could have let me know you told her she could camp out at your place," I scold her. "But yeah, I'm being all right to her. I'm even letting her cook for me. She's pretty good."

"Okay, I really have to go check on Mom. I can't wait to see you in a couple of days. I miss you, kid."

My eyes get misty. I sniff. "I miss you, too. See you in Vermont."

As soon as I hang up, the phone rings again. Sheesh. "What?" I snap upon answering.

Nothing. Then heavy breathing. "Kane, is this you?"

No answer.

More heavy breathing.

"Very funny. Real mature." I start to hang up, then the laughter begins. Chills race up my spine. I slam the phone down. How the hell does everyone get my unlisted number? I'm off the couch in two seconds, out the door, and pounding on the one next to mine. Natasha answers.

"I thought we were going to hang out."

She practically beams. "I made brownies just in case."

"Brownies! I love brownies!" My enthusiasm is a little too much. I push past her, shut the door and lock it, then head toward Cindy's kitchen. If I'm lucky, Natasha knows how to make happy brownies. Two days can't get here fast enough for me.

CONFESSION NO. 25

*Beware of photographers asking
you to bare your gifts.*

The little inn nestled away near Mount Snow is fabulous. It has Colonial charm and all the furniture inside is antique. Karen and I take in our surroundings while Natasha hugs and laughs with the owners. The car trip wasn't too bad. We mostly pigged out on the baked goodies Natasha brought. The rest of the time we sang songs none of us knew the words to and enjoyed the beautiful scenery.

Stefan comes inside, stomping snow from his boots and looking very handsome in a black stocking cap. The man really needs to grow some hair. He smiles at us, walks over, and hugs each of us in turn. He hugs me the longest so I know I'm still his favorite model.

"I've been scouting around for a good location," he says. "The snow is marvelous. I can't wait to get started."

"Can we unpack first?" Karen asks sarcastically.

About that time what sounds like a herd of horses comes down the stairs. Cindy materializes a minute later.

She squeals when she sees me. What the hell, I squeal, too. I drop my bags and we hug. "I've missed you so much!" she exclaims. "And you," she says, hugging Karen. "And you!" she shouts toward Natasha and rushes over to give her a hug.

Cindy looks great. There's a bloom in her cheeks and a sparkle in her eyes. Going home has done her good, even if things didn't turn out so great with her dad.

"The inn is busy," Stefan says. "Ski season and all. Afraid you girls are going to have to double up, so pick your roommates."

Karen loops her arm in mine. "I get Lou."

This is odd. I normally thought if anyone had to pair up, I'd be with Cindy. Cindy knows it's close to my PMS time and won't be shocked if I walk out of the bathroom with hair sprouting from my chin.

"Guess Natasha and I will room together," Cindy says, casting me an apologetic glance.

I can't make a scene without hurting Karen's feelings. She doesn't know Natasha that well and asking her to room with her would be awkward. Rooming with Karen is awkward for me. But what else can I do?

"Great," I say, putting an enthusiastic face forward.

"Why don't you ladies take your luggage up. Meet me in the restaurant in thirty minutes and I'll buy you lunch. We need to talk about the shoot and what I expect."

Karen groans. "Work work work," she mutters. "He's such a spoilsport."

We grab our luggage and head for the stairs. As rustic as the inn looks, each room has its own bathroom and fireplace. Karen and I have two double beds and a view that I'm sure I've seen on Christmas cards. "This is something," I say, staring out the window. "I don't like snow, and I hate snow in the city, but it's really beautiful when spread like a blanket over the countryside."

"I'm catching a power nap," Karen declares. She throws her luggage in a corner and claims a bed. "Wake me up when it's time for lunch."

"Sure." I place my luggage on the unclaimed bed and start to unpack. There's an antique wardrobe complete with cloth hangers. The wardrobe has two drawers at the bottom. I'll claim one for the dozen or so turtlenecks I brought along with my underwear and leave the other for Karen.

Deciding to scope out the bathroom, I take my beauty bag and toiletries into the small area. Shower only, but that's okay. I seldom take baths. I close the door and take a look at my neck. The bite marks have almost healed, but they're still noticeable.

Hope Karen doesn't find it odd for me to wear a turtleneck beneath my favorite flannel pajamas.

When I exit the bathroom, Karen's already asleep. I go next door to Cindy and Natasha's room and knock. They don't answer for a moment and I wonder if they've already gone downstairs to the restaurant. I move away and the door opens. Cindy looks even more flushed than she did downstairs.

"Hey, Lou, what's up?"

I motion her out to the hallway. She glances behind her, says something, and comes out and closes the door.

"Where's the stuff you brought me?"

"I packed it in a suitcase. Maybe I should hold on to it if you don't want Karen snooping in it."

"Who says Natasha won't snoop in it?" I ask.

"Because my luggage was already here. Karen knows what you brought. She might think an extra suitcase showing up out of the blue is suspicious."

Cindy's right. I'm itching to get my hands on that suitcase. It's been so long since I had anything from my life before I ran away. I also want to see the note the Billingtons left me. "Okay," I agree. "You hold on to it, but make sure Natasha doesn't snoop around in it."

"Why would she snoop around in my stuff? Don't worry about that."

"I'm bummed we're not rooming together," I tell her. "I wanted to catch up on everything that happened to you while you were visiting your mom."

"Yeah, me too," she says. "I guess we just have to make the best of it. We're only here for a few days."

"Want to go down and have coffee before everyone shows up for lunch?"

Cindy glances at the door behind her. "What about Natasha? She might feel left out."

I blink back at her. "So?"

She sighs. "So. It's rude."

"Since when have we ever cared about being rude? Everyone knows we're best friends. She shouldn't find it odd that after being separated we'd want to get together and catch up."

Biting her lip, Cindy glances at the door behind her again. "I guess," she says. "At least let me tell her I'm cutting out on her and we'll see her at lunch in a few."

"Oh, tell her to wake up Karen before she comes down."

"Okay." Cindy disappears for a few minutes and then comes back out of the room. "Let's go. We only have fifteen minutes before everyone else joins us."

I link my arm with hers and we walk down the hallway toward the stairs. "You look great, Cindy. Whatever you're doing, keep doing it."

She smiles. "I plan to."

Once downstairs, we enter the restaurant/coffee house/bar. That's what the sign says. The inn isn't that big and the restaurant area isn't that crowded. A few people dressed for skiing dot the tables. Cindy and I sit at a two-top in one corner near a crackling fireplace.

"It's really pretty here," I say. "Karen doesn't seem to appreciate the scenery, but since I don't ski, I've never been to a place like this."

"It is pretty," Cindy agrees. "But I'm really missing home and my apartment. Living in a hotel for a few days has made me appreciate the comforts of home."

"Prepare to find it more comfortable than when you left," I warn her. "I think Natasha bought you dishes. You know, the kind you don't throw away once you've eaten off them?"

Cindy's cheeks bloom brighter. "Probably just a thank-you for letting her stay at my place."

"She's made your apartment quite homey," I go on. "I guess she brought some of her stuff over because I've noticed added touches here and there. Your apartment is starting to look like a grandma lives there."

"Natasha has old-fashioned tastes," Cindy says. "I wouldn't call her taste 'grandma style.' She told me she likes antiques and things."

"I've been nice to her." The waitress pauses before us and Cindy and I order coffee, letting her know we'll be joining a group for lunch in a few minutes. I turn back to the conversation. "But I can't say I won't be glad when we get home that she's gone and you're back. I've missed you horribly."

Cindy reaches out and pats my hand. "I've missed you, too. Lou, I need to talk to you about that."

My gaze naturally scans the room. I'm not surprised to see people glance in my direction. I have a familiar face, and if people don't recognize me as a model, they're usually trying to figure out where they've seen me before. A lone man sits at a table in the back. He's really into the ski thing. He wears a ski cap, dark goggles, and is bundled up like he's still on the slopes. I wrinkle my nose. People must sweat beneath all their ski gear. BO hangs heavy on the air.

"About what?" My attention returns to Cindy.

"About when we get home," she clarifies. "Natasha won't be leaving."

I'm confused by her statement. "Surely her apartment has been fumigated by now."

Cindy takes a sip of her coffee. "Her apartment was never being fumigated, Lou. She moved in with me."

I'm still confused. "So, you're roommates now?"

Cindy rolls her eyes. "No, dimwit. We're lovers."

For a moment I think Cindy is being sarcastic. When I realize she isn't, it hits me. "She's the new friend you've been seeing? She went home with you?"

"I didn't want to say anything until I saw how we did together out of town. I guess until I saw what my mother thought of her, but yes, Lou, she's who I've been seeing."

Confusion sets in again. "She said she didn't like girls. She slept with Stefan. Is she bi or what?"

Sighing, Cindy leans back in her chair. "It's hard to explain, but no, she's not bi. She thought no one liked her and the only way to be accepted into the group was to sleep with Stefan. She thought it would win her popularity points, not alienate her further. She was really down when she told me all this. I asked her point-blank if she was gay and she said yes, but she thought admitting as much would hurt her career."

"Do I have gaydar or what? I told you she was gay."

"You think everyone is gay, Lou. When you think everyone is gay you're bound to be right once in a while."

Now that I know the truth about Natasha, and her relationship with my best friend, I have to ask myself if I'm happy for Cindy or not. Countless times I've said to her and to myself that all I want is for Cindy to meet a nice girl and settle down. All I want is for her to be happy.

Our whole relationship is about to change. I'm not going to be number one with Cindy anymore. She won't be available for me at the drop of a hat. I'm not sure how I feel. Honestly, I am sure. I don't like it.

"Give me time to adjust to the idea," I say. "It's hard when one friend moves on and the other one doesn't."

"But you are moving on, Lou," Cindy says quietly. "You're making new friends. Sheesh, sleeping with men. Searching for your birth mother, and I guess now your adoptive parents. What's happening to us is normal. It was what our lives were before the changes started that wasn't normal."

Sentimental crap always gets to me. I suddenly feel weepy. Damn PMS is starting up. Great. "Who's going to take care of me?" I ask, on the verge of a sniffle.

Cindy smiles her wise smile. "You are," she answers. "You've been taking care of yourself for seven years, Lou."

I suppose she's right. Cindy is usually right, which is one of the things that annoys the hell out of me about her. "Natasha had better be good to you. She'll get a visit from a werewolf if she isn't."

My friend's laugh has never sounded so genuine. She is happy, I realize, and okay, somewhere deep in the dark pit of my selfish soul, I feel joy for her. I have a new friend, too. And maybe Cindy is better off living in her world than being dragged into mine. Mine is just plain weird.

I'm not sure if I should tell her about the transformation. If I tell her, I'd have to explain what led up to it. She's better off thinking it will never happen to me again. I love Cindy. I want her to be blessed by ignorance.

"Hey, you two, come over and join us."

Stefan calls to us from a few tables over. He has four crew members, Natasha, and Karen sitting with him. They've put three tables together. "Shall we join the party?" Cindy asks, and I know by the soft look in her alien-type eyes, she's not just talking about our shoot buddies.

"Sure," I answer. "Why not."

I thought this was a ski party. No one said anything about beach blanket bingo in the snow. At least not until Stefan dropped that surprise on me during lunch. I'm mad as hell about it, too. I gave him the cold shoulder through the rest of lunch.

Once we're back in our room, Karen asks, "So we're modeling bikinis in the snow instead of ski-wear? What's the big deal, Lou? It's not like we haven't modeled underwear during a blizzard, re-member?"

The big deal is the big hickey on my neck I thought I would get away with hiding. And my PMS makes me unreasonable and bitchy. "I don't like to freeze my ass off for the sake of prosperity and Ste-fan knows it. He purposely led me to believe we would be modeling skiwear for this shoot."

"He wanted you to come," Karen says, wiggling her eyebrows. "You have to admit the setting is pretty romantic. Picture this. You and him, a king-sized bed, and a cozy fire. If that doesn't warm you up, there's something seriously wrong with you, girl."

Stefan knew by the look I gave him at lunch there would be no cuddling between us. At least not until I cool off. I guess as far as our relationship goes, I can't put him off forever. I'm just not sure how to handle it. Or him.

I'm confused about my feelings. Can I really be in love with Stefan and be in lust with Terry? Can I be in love with anyone until I figure out what's going on with me? I know in order to love, a person must trust. I don't trust any man to love me for who and what I am.

I guess I just answered my own question.

"Us girls are going scouting around before dinner. Want to come with us?" Karen asks.

Normally I would be game, but I'm feeling a little blue. Natasha and Cindy made their new relationship known to all when they held hands and whispered in each other's ears all through lunch. Karen thinks it's great. I'm trying to, but I'm not there yet. Besides, if the girls are gone, I can sneak into Cindy's room and look through the suitcase. I'll have her leave me the key.

"I'm tired. I think I'll nap before dinner. You guys go and have fun."

"There's lots of shops and stuff," Karen says, trying to tempt me. "We even talked about grabbing dinner in town if they have a place that looks decent."

"I may just order something brought up," I say. "I'm sure they have room service. Really, I'm tired and wouldn't be good company. Freakin' PMS."

"Oh." Karen nods her understanding. "I'm horrible during PMS. I lock myself in my apartment and don't go out in case I kill someone."

Ironic. I laugh. "Yeah, me too."

Karen glances at herself in a mirror that's hung over an antique basin and sink. She pats her hair, grabs her purse, and heads for the door.

"Hey, would you ask Cindy to step in here for a minute before you all leave? I need to ask her something."

"Sure," Karen answers. She pauses to glance at me with concern. "You're okay about this thing between her and Natasha, right?"

"'Course I'm okay with it," I answer. "Why wouldn't I be?"

She shrugs. "Well, broad shoulders sleeps with your man, then she sleeps with your best friend. Next she'll be hopping into bed with me."

Maybe my gaydar isn't that good. "And you would feel how about that?"

"Not receptive," Karen assures me. She grins. "Your man, well, that's another matter. I swear if you don't jump him soon I'm going to. There is a statue of limitations on that sort of thing, and I think seven years is long enough, Lou."

"I have been warned," I say sarcastically. "If you jump him, just don't tell me about it, okay?"

"Deal," she says a little too cheerfully. I wonder if I've just given her permission. Does she need my permission? Yes, I think according to the friend's handbook she does. Karen leaves and Cindy comes in a few minutes later.

"Karen says you aren't going with us. Lou, if

you're upset about Natasha and me, maybe I should stay and we should talk more about it."

"Conceited much?" I ask. "I want to stay because I want to look at the stuff you brought and I want privacy. Give me your room key so I can go in there and get the suitcase while you're gone."

Cindy frowns at my sarcasm. She fishes the key from her pocket and hands it to me. "It's the blue suitcase in the corner behind the red suitcase."

"Thanks. And have fun."

She pauses at the door. "After I gathered what I thought you would want, I thought about something. I looked at those photos and I said, that's not my friend. Not the friend I know and love now. Maybe you need to bury Sherry Billington for good, Lou. You're not her anymore."

The door closes. Do I really want to take a stroll down a memory lane that was for the most part a painful walk for me? Do I want to revisit that plain girl who was so unhappy most of the time? I've always been a glutton for punishment. I go get the suitcase.

CONFESSION NO. 26

A walk down memory lane can be painful. Like
mourning the loss of someone you once loved.
Or even someone you realize you once hated. But
sometimes while you're searching for answers that
hide within hazy images of who you once were,
the truth jumps up and bites you on the ass.

I sit on my bed, the blue suitcase open and pictures
from my past scattered around me. A sad-faced little girl with stringy hair and too-prominent buckteeth sits on a tricycle in front of a house where the
lawn needs mowing. A woman stands behind her,
straight and stern looking, no smile on her face.
Christmas. A tree. Presents. Still no sign of joy. A
skinny girl with big eyes and a skinned knee stands
with her arm thrown around a taller girl with dark
hair and haunted eyes.

Grabbing a Kleenex, I wipe my wet cheeks and
blow my runny nose. I knew my past was painful,
but somehow I had managed to make it into something it wasn't. After I ran away, I needed a place to

visit in my mind where there were no fangs or fur or claws. No bloody corpses of a boy I had killed on prom night. A place where I suffered the illusion I was happy and normal. Pictures don't lie. I was never happy and normal. This is what Cindy saw. This is what she wants me to bury.

I reach for the note the Billingtons left me. Follow the signs. What signs? I put the note aside and stare at my high school yearbook. I'm hesitant to walk down that particular part of memory lane. It was the worst time of my life. At least the kid on the tricycle hadn't yet learned how cruel other children can be.

Before I talk myself out of it, I flip open a page in the yearbook. Junior class. All one page of it. There are two pages of seniors. With trembling fingers, I turn to the next page. Being a *B*, I'm right there at the top. Me with a stupid bow in my hair. I laugh when I see Cindy's picture. She didn't even bother to comb her hair. My gaze lands on Tom Dawson. He was good-looking, smiling that wolf smile of his. No one would guess by looking at him that his soul was so dark, his hatred so deep. I can't look at him.

I flip backward, but there he is again. The football team, grinning like the idiots they all were—jerseys off, posing to show off their tattoos. Wolverines. A flash goes off in my head. The man walking away at Freddie Z's. The only letters I could see. *INES*. WOLVERINES.

"Oh, my God," I whisper. The pages flip through my fingers. On the inside page of the yearbook, where usually good wishes from classmates are written, I see Cindy's note to me . . . and one that was not there before.

> *You are not the only one. Tom was adopted, too. We don't know what happened. Why he is gone, and you are gone, but you were never like him. His parents were afraid of him. They told us he was always cruel. He tortured animals. He hid his dark nature behind a sweet smile. He is a wolf in sheep's clothing. We pray you have not become one of his victims. Know there are others like you, Sherry. Some can help you, some can hurt you. We pray you are safe. We pray you are still normal. If you have changed, you will have questions. Some things are better left alone. But we know you too well. Start in Nevada. And trust no one.*

My hands shaking, I drop the yearbook and grab my cell. I have to warn Terry about Tom Dawson. When I flip my phone open, I get nothing. There's no signal. I crawl across the bed and grab the phone on the nightstand. After reading the instructions for an outside line and punching in the number, I hear Terry's phone ring. His answering machine picks up.

"Terry, if you're there pick up." I wait for a few seconds. "Terry, the werewolf killer's name is Tom Dawson. I went to high school with him. Plug him into the system and see if you can pull anything up. Call me."

After I hang up, I'm too nervous to sit still. I pace back and forth, glancing at the relics of my past. Cindy is right. I am not Sherry Billington anymore, nor will I ever be. If the past were even a nice place to visit, I would keep the items she brought me. It's time to let them go.

Cindy had crammed the items in a large envelope. I tear out the senior picture page with Tom leering back at me, then shove everything else in the envelope. I'm going to burn it. The fireplace in the room isn't lit. I imagine someone comes in and does that in the evening. There is a bar downstairs. I'm guessing they have matches.

I grab my coat and put it on, shove the envelope and my cell phone in my beauty bag, and go downstairs. Although smoking isn't allowed in bars these days, for some reason, they always have a heaping bowl of matches on the bar, I guess to rub it in for those who do smoke. I grab a handful of matches, turn around, and run into Stefan.

"Lou? I thought you went with the other girls."

"Hi, ah, no, had some other stuff to do in my room."

He slides his arm through mine. "Good. I hoped we could find time alone to talk. How about I buy you a drink?"

Stefan obviously thinks an answer isn't required. He steers me toward the same cozy two-top Cindy and I shared coffee at earlier. "I still have some stuff to do," I say.

Running a hand over his bald head, he sighs.

"Look, I know you're mad about the swimsuit thing. I didn't tell you because I knew you wouldn't come, and Lou, I want to talk to you. Ignoring me will not make me go away. I have feelings for you. I think you have feelings for me, too."

Burying my past for good will have to wait. It's time I resolve this issue with Stefan. I'm no longer confused. I know what I must do. "All right," I say, taking a seat.

"What do you want from the bar and I'll run and get it for us. Apple martini?"

"Shot of Wild Turkey."

He takes a step back. "Since when do you drink rotgut?"

"Since I need it," I answer.

Shrugging, Stefan leaves to get our drinks. My hands still shake and I shove them into my pockets. I get that prickly sensation at the back of my neck, like someone is watching me. The bar is deserted except for me and Stefan and the guy making drinks behind the bar. Why is Tom Dawson still alive? I was sure I killed him on prom night. I woke naked and shivering, blood beneath my nails and a mound of dirt beside me that assured me I had buried him.

"One shot of Wild Turkey." Stefan sets my drink in front of me. He settles across from me. I down the shot quickly.

"Damn," he says. "Let me at least catch up." Stefan drinks Crown and Coke. He downs his drink then motions the bartender for two more.

"Surely what you have to say to me doesn't call for both of us being drunk," he teases.

"I'm not sure what to say to you," I admit. I'm sure, just not sure how to say it without hurting his feelings.

He studies me over the rim of his empty glass. "It's not going to happen, is it? Me and you? You're hooked up with someone else. With that cop."

"I'm not hooked up with him," I correct him. "I have a relationship with him, but it's not serious. At least not at the moment."

"Then why do you keep shutting me out? I never worried about the men in your past. You always left them before anything got started. But since I know you're spending time with someone now, it spurred me into action. I guess I'm afraid of losing you."

I suppose jealousy tactics do work, if that was what I was trying to do with Terry. But it wasn't. I reach across the table and place my hand on top of his. "You're never going to lose me. At least not as a friend. Someday, things might be different for us. Right now, I like them the way they are."

His big puppy-dog eyes actually turn misty for a minute. He blinks and sets his empty glass on the table. "You're the only woman I can't have, Lou."

I squeeze his hand. "Maybe that's why you want me. Maybe you need to examine the reasons you suddenly want a relationship beyond what we've had all these years."

He glances up at me. "I know the reason. I love you. I've loved you from the first moment I saw you."

I choke on my own saliva. Thankfully the bartender puts my whiskey in front of me and I grab the glass and take a drink. Hearing Stefan say those words causes all kinds of emotions to explode inside of me. None of which I have the time to examine at the moment. We were immediately drawn to each other. I do know that.

After what I had experienced with Tom Dawson, it surprised me to feel that connection with Stefan the minute he walked into the café where I worked. And if we had that connection, why did we both refuse to act upon it? Why wasn't Stefan the first man I made love to? Instead I had chosen someone I hardly knew simply because I wanted to wipe away the memory of Tom's attack.

Who would have been better than Stefan to teach me about sex? And yet I put up a wall between us from the start. I'm still doing it, and I don't know why. No, I do know why. I've known why from the beginning. He's given me too much to deceive him the way I would have to deceive him if our relationship were more than what I've let it be. I do love him, but I have to learn to love and trust myself before I can ever fully give my heart to a man. I'm going to work on that. Just as soon as I bury my past.

He's waiting for a response, and it's not going to be the one he wants. "I love you, too, Stefan, but I'm not in love with you. I'm not ready for that type of commitment with a man. When I am, I hope you're still in my life, but if you're not, I'll always treasure the friendship we've shared these past six and a half years. When I fall in love, I want to fall all the way. I want to give it everything I have. I can't do that right now."

Stefan pulls his hand from beneath mine. "Thank you for being honest. That's one thing I've always loved about you. Your honesty."

Then he can't be in love with me. I've basically been lying to him since we met. Lying because I can't tell him the truth. Somehow, I think if I loved someone the way I should, I could be honest. About everything.

Stefan finishes his drink and rises. "I'm off now to drown my sorrows in the privacy of my room."

I don't believe him for a moment. He's off to find a replacement . . . if only for the night. I still don't like that. Maybe because he's selling himself short. He always has. Deep down, I don't believe he's just a playboy out to sleep with every woman he meets. He's missing something, I don't know what, but this is the way he compensates. I watch him leave, grab my matches and my ugly past, and head outside.

I have never smelled air so crisp and cold and clean. The snow crunches beneath my boots as I make my way along a path cleared behind the inn. The path leads to a woodpile stacked high, and beyond that, to a thick forest of leafless aspens. The mountains make a beautiful backdrop, pristine white with a blue sky darkening as evening approaches.

Maybe I'm wrong to dislike snow. The only time I've really seen it is when it mucks up the city and makes getting around difficult. Out here, it looks as if it belongs. As if it's showing off, and with good reason. Glitter shimmers, catching the sinking sun. It takes my breath away. So does trudging around in it at high altitude in boots that are more for show than snow. I don't plan to go far, just far enough so that no one sees smoke from my burning past and comes to investigate.

The woodpile is stacked so high I use it as a barrier between me and whoever might be glancing out a back window at the inn. Smoky Bear would not be happy about me doing this. I move a little farther from the woodpile. Bending, I scoop snow so that I have a pit of sorts. My hands are freezing and I blow on them to thaw my fingers. I lay the envelope in the pit and dig in my beauty bag for the matches.

It takes several attempts to set the envelope on fire. I finally have to douse it with a little hairspray to get it going. Sitting back on my haunches, I watch it burn. Once my past is nothing but ashes, I'll cover it with snow to make sure I don't cause a fire. I hold my hands over it, letting the warmth spread to my fingers.

"What's this obsession you have with setting things on fire?"

The voice startles me. I glance up. A man leans against an aspen. The sinking sun casts him in shadow. It doesn't matter that I can't see his face. I know who he is.

"You're supposed to be dead, Tom."

He shrugs away from the tree and approaches me. "Sometimes your past just won't stay buried. Sooner or later, it always catches up to you."

I rise from my crouched position next to the burning envelope. "Why are you stalking me?"

Tom laughs and it has that garbled sound to it. "You know why. You took away my life. I had scholarships. I had a future, and one skinny, ugly little girl, a nobody, took that away from me. You made me a monster."

He doesn't know, I realize. He's unaware that he was already a monster. I suppose when he triggered me, I triggered him. The small flame from the burning envelope casts light across his face. It isn't a face I expect to see. The wolf in him is hidden. Tom was a good-looking boy in high school; now, he's short of magnificent. No wonder he so easily lured women to their deaths.

"You're surprised," he says, as if reading my response. "And you were so bright in high school. Look at yourself, Sherry. If changing can do that for you, you should have imagined what it would do for someone good-looking to begin with."

I never considered it because for all those years, Tom was dead in my mind. Why does the change include a transformation to beauty? To lure, I realize. To attract. Something built in to assure survival of the species?

"It took me a while to find you," he says. "I knew you'd be better looking than you were in high school, but I didn't expect you to be a fucking supermodel. Of course as you know, I did eventually figure it out. Something in your eyes as you stared back from all those photos plastered everywhere. The haunted look you had even when you were ugly. You can't hide that."

And so I am living a false sense of security to believe no one will ever associate me with Sherry Billington. Tom just proved that to me. "All those women you've killed. Did you kill them because you thought they were me?"

He laughs. That horrible soft laugh that sends shivers up my spine. "No. I killed them because it felt good. They were nobodies, too, wanting to be somebody. So grateful that a man who looks like me would be interested in girls who weren't the prettiest, or the brightest, or anything at all. I've tracked you from Texas to New York, but I was in no hurry. I had my fun along the way."

Rage churns bile in my stomach. All those poor women. Women who, like me at one time, could never see past the outer surface of a person. If ever there was a perfect example of beauty being only skin deep, Tom is it.

"I didn't make you a werewolf," I tell him. "You were already one, just like me. We triggered each other on prom night when you attacked me."

He cocks his head to one side, very much like a dog does at times, as if trying to understand human words. "That's a load of shit. You made me a monster. It's your fault!"

Like most murderers, Tom needs someone to blame for his psychosis. I doubt that I can convince him of the truth. I'm not even sure what the truth is. He steps closer and I back up. My little fire still burns, the photos holding up the process.

"I figure killing you might end this for me," he says. "But first, I wanted to show you how it feels to see your life slipping away. I knew something about me made you change. Predator sensing predator. I wanted you to suffer what I've suffered before I kill you."

I wonder why the changes haven't already started for me. Tom must be standing downwind. I can't smell him. I'll have to get closer. That could be deadly. He hasn't started the changing process, either. Why?

"What triggers you?"

He smiles. "Rage, fear, sex. My rage, a woman's fear, sex of any kind."

This man, this THING, has terrified me in dreams for seven years. He'd like for me to be afraid now. "You don't scare me," I let him know. "I'm not helpless. I can fight you."

Tom grins. "Then I guess it'll have to be sex with you. You should have just given it to me on prom night. We could have avoided all of this."

My rage builds. I remember the beating, the humiliation, the near-rape. "I thought you got the message that I didn't want to have sex with you when I ripped your face off."

He winks. "You were just playing hard to get. All women want to have sex with me."

I've often heard that in the mind of a rapist, this is a common belief. The woman wanted him to. The woman was asking for it. It's always the woman's fault in their delusional way of thinking. Darkness is close to falling, and so is the temperature. There's only one way to kill Tom Dawson again. Egg him on.

"You want it, come get it," I challenge.

He does.

Tom lunges across the flimsy fire and knocks me to the ground. His breath above me is like I remember. Fetid despite the white toothpaste smile. I'm fairly certain he eats raw meat. I'm more than certain he is not going to rape me. I bring my knee up between his legs. A grunt of pain explodes from his mouth.

"Bitch," he growls, then takes a handful of my hair and bangs my head against the ground. The snow softens the blow. I smell him now. His foul odor. The scent begins the transformation. I use my upper body strength to switch our positions.

"What do you do when a woman isn't afraid, and when she's stronger than you?"

He proves I'm not stronger by knocking me aside. I roll in the snow. He rises up from the ground, and I swear he's taller than he was.

"Then I just get pissed off!" he growls at me.

His eyes glow red in the near-dark. If I'm going to survive, I need to get just as pissed off as he is. Remembering I was once at the mercy of this monster helps. Remembering the way he hit me when I resisted—the way he made me feel like a nobody. I lift my hand, relieved to see claws. My skin itches. I welcome the unpleasant sensation.

Tom stumbles toward me, nearly trips over my beauty bag and kicks it aside. It lands on top of my flimsy fire. That really enrages me. All my makeup is in there. He's probably broken something. I lunge at him and scratch his face with my claws.

His pretty face isn't so pretty by the time he manages to shove me away. I fly backward and hit a tree. It knocks the breath from me again. While I gasp, he marches toward me. His nose lengthens into a snout. The transformation comes quicker for him. He's done it more often than I have. The seams of my clothes burst. At least I know I'm on my way. When Tom lunges at me again, I move and he hits the tree. He stumbles back a step. His own clumsiness fuels his anger. He tilts back his head and howls.

The sound sends a chill down my spine. In the silence that follows, I hear my clothes rip. I'm not cold anymore. I think I've grown a fur coat. Tom now has hair on his face and hands. Sharp ugly teeth protrude from his gums.

I might need an equalizer. I know I'm stronger than an average man. I don't think I'm stronger than an average male werewolf. My gaze darts from left to right. The woodpile isn't far. A good sturdy log should help even things out. I take off. Tom jumps into my path. I run into him and knock him back, but he scrambles forward, blocking my way. I need a distraction.

"Stop or I'll shoot!"

Terry stands a few feet away, his gun leveled at Tom. I can't believe my eyes, and if Terry sees as well in the dark as I do, I don't imagine he can, either. But I don't think Terry can see as well. He's squinting. It's nearly dark. The problem is rectified a moment later. A big fiery blast explodes from the fire pit I dug. Tom Dawson stands too close to the pit. He goes up in a big ball of flame. The howl that sounds from him this time is one of pain.

In a macabre dance, he stumbles toward me. Terry fires his gun and drops him. Tom makes a big fire, and I know any minute, Terry will take his eyes off his target and glance toward me. I know what he will see. I have no choice but to run.

"Lou!" Terry shouts. "Lou, come back. He can't hurt you now!"

I keep moving. I still have my clothes on, although they're ripped in several places. Since I can't feel the cold, I must assume I'm still wearing the fur coat. I run deeper into the trees. When I glance back, I still see Tom's burning body. I don't see Terry, though. I assume he's coming after me.

There are advantages to being a werewolf. I see in the dark, and I run faster than the average person.

That isn't saying that Terry is average, only that he's not up to speed. I keep moving.

"Lou!"

His voice echoes around me. He's frantic. I'd rather have him frantic than scared to death of me. I wonder if werewolves can climb trees. I hook my claws into a sturdy aspen and give it a shot. I shimmy up that thing with a speed that would make a monkey jealous. Then I wait.

Terry passes beneath me a few minutes later. Fool. He's going to get himself lost if he keeps looking for me. Frozen, too. From my vantage point, I look back toward the inn. Tom Dawson's body is still on fire. He's toast. I don't think he can come back from the dead this time. While Terry searches for me, Tom is being cremated.

I notice the cold. Lifting one hand, I see that my claws have retracted. I touch my face. Still hair, but as I rub it falls away. Running my tongue over my teeth, I don't snag on any fangs. I'm nearly back to normal. That's a good thing. And that's a bad thing. I look down. It's a hell of a drop.

CONFESSION NO. 27

There are worse things than being a werewolf
supermodel. Being dead tops the list.

Terry appears below me again. He cups his hands to his mouth. "Lou!"

There's no way I can get out of this tree by myself. Climbing up it seemed like such a good idea at the time. That must be what cats think. Hey, there's a big-ass tree. I think I'll climb it and worry about getting down later.

"Terry."

He looks around. "Lou?"

"Up here."

His head swivels back. "Lou? How the hell did you get up there?"

"I, ah, climbed. Now I can't get down."

"Are you all right?"

"I have a branch up my ass."

"Stay there. I'll run to the inn and see if they have a ladder."

"If I could go somewhere I would," I point out.

Terry takes off.

"Hey, bring back a blanket. I'm freezing up here!" I call after him.

I'm not that cold. My clothes are fur lined even if my body no longer is. But I figure the blanket will hide that fact when and if I ever set foot on solid ground again. In the distance, Tom still burns, although not as brightly. Is the nightmare really over? I keep expecting him to get up and come after me. Real life is thankfully not a B movie and he doesn't.

What seems like an eternity later, I hear the sound of feet crunching through the snow. Terry and my crew race toward me with a long ladder. Natasha's Russian inn owner friends pause in front of Tom's smoldering body and spray him with fire extinguishers. The smell of his burned flesh hangs on the air.

"Lou!" Cindy appears beneath me. "Oh, my God, Lou. Are you all right?"

"I'm okay," I call down to her. "Be sure to have that blanket ready for me."

She knows what I mean and why I'm asking. Terry appears. Stefan has one end of the ladder and he has the other. Natasha shows up, and last, huffing like she's going to die, is Karen.

I've got a lot of explaining to do. I'm glad I'm alive to explain. The ladder is extended toward me.

It's tall enough to reach. Terry comes up while the others steady it. When he reaches me, he looks like he's aged about ten years.

"You okay?"

I can't be too okay. Terry still expects me to be a woman. "I think," I say in a shaky voice. "I was so scared I didn't know what I was doing. I just knew I had to get away."

"Do you think you can climb down?"

"I think so," I say in the same shaky voice. What I'm thinking is, get out of my way. He starts to move down.

"I'll be right beneath you so if you start to fall, I can help you."

Reaching out, I place my hand over his on the ladder rung. "How did you know? How did you get here in time?"

He sighs. "Cocky bastard slipped a note under my door this morning. I assume he thought I was at work and wouldn't see it until tonight. Until it was too late."

I squeeze his hand. "My hero."

"Yeah, right." He laughs. "Just what the hell do you carry in that beauty bag? I assume that's what caused the explosion."

"A woman never reveals her secrets," I say dryly. "I guess he just couldn't handle a day of beauty."

Terry shakes his head. "Can we get down from here now? I don't know about you, but I could use a drink."

In the distance, sirens sound. I'm assuming some-one called 911. I hope there isn't press coverage of this.

"Yes, let's hurry."

The hot shower spray feels wonderful. Terry is downstairs seeing to the removal of Tom Daw-son's body. The shoot has been called off. Un-der the cover of darkness, we will slip away and head back to New York before the press gets wind of what's happened and swarm the place. Karen's in our room packing us up. Cindy and Natasha do the same next door. My clothes are ruined and I stuff them in a trash bag. I still had hair all over me when I took them off. I'm glad I'll be gone when they try to unclog the shower drain. Wrapping a towel around my hair, I dry off and slip into a pair of jogging pants and a turtleneck.

I enter our room. "Almost done," Karen says. "You sure you're all right?"

"I'm fine," I tell her.

She shivers. "You should have told us you were being stalked, Lou. We would have all watched out for you."

"I didn't want my friends involved. Terry was handling it."

"He wants to talk to you." Karen zips the last suit-case. "He's waiting in the hall. We'll get the car loaded up."

"Thanks."

She opens the door. Terry stands leaning against the wall. He has a beer in one hand and what appears to be a shot of Wild Turkey in the other. Cindy and Natasha come in and help Karen drag all of the suitcases into the hall, then Terry comes in. He hands me my drink and goes back to close the door. Now I have some 'splaining to do. I do the shot first.

"What is the connection between you and Tom Dawson? I got your message when I was almost here, but I couldn't get a signal to call you back. I tried calling to warn you when I took off this morning. When you wouldn't answer your cell I went crazy."

He must have tried to call when we had the music blaring, singing songs we didn't know the words to.

"Do you know every cop in this area is working an avalanche?" He shakes his head. "I couldn't catch a break."

Now I know why he looks ten years older. "You should have had the Wild Turkey instead of me," I say. "Calm down. Everything turned out all right."

Terry sits on the bed and runs a hand through his hair. "It could have just as easily turned out bad. Real bad."

I sit beside him. "I went to high school with Tom Dawson. He beat me up and tried to rape me on prom night. That's when I ran away from home. I never went back."

His eyes are tired and bloodshot when he looks at me, but his jaw is clenched and I know he's pissed.

"I'm sorry that happened to you. So why did he come after you seven years later?"

I don't think Terry can't handle the truth. At least not yet. "I guess he thought I might tell on him at some point. He had football scholarships and his life was looking pretty good until he attacked me. Maybe he thought I'd wait until he was a football star then blow the whistle on him or try to blackmail him. I don't know. He's crazy. Or he was. He waited because it took him this long to find me. I've changed a lot since high school."

"Why didn't you know it was him before now? You saw him in visions."

"I never saw his human face in my visions. You saw him tonight, didn't you? In the light of the fire?"

Terry glances away from me. "I'm trying like hell to tell myself that was some kind of trick."

"It wasn't a trick." I figure Terry can handle more than I give him credit for. "He was a werewolf. That's how he came to me in my visions. That's why I didn't know who he was."

"I've seen some weird shit in my life, but I've never seen anything like that. It's easier to tell myself I didn't see it."

Reaching out, I turn his face toward me. "Maybe this is your wake-up call. The chance for you to accept things that you've previously discounted as being real."

He runs a hand through his hair, then gives me the half-smile. "Like psychics and things that go bump in the night?"

"Exactly," I answer.

While I have his face turned toward me, he leans forward and gives me a kiss. Just a short one. "I need to take your statement, and then we all need to get the hell out of here. I'll try to keep your name out of it, but a serial killer caught and killed, that's going to make the headlines."

"I don't need the publicity," I agree.

"I'd offer you a lift back, but there are still things I have to take care of here before I can leave."

Rising from the bed, I say, "That's all right. I'll go back with Karen and the other girls. They're a little freaked out by all of this. I need to assure them everything is okay."

Terry also rises. "Your photographer buddy downstairs needs assurances, too," he says. "He's been pacing the floor ever since we got back."

It's time to go home. I'm tired and figure the girls are just as anxious to get out of Vermont as I am. "Take my statement. The girls are waiting and it's going to be very late by the time we get back."

He whips out his pen and notepad.

An hour later, Karen, Natasha, Cindy, and yours truly are back on the road. The atmosphere isn't nearly as festive as it was on the drive up. You'd think I would keep reliving the confrontation with Tom; instead, I keep thinking about my goodbye with Stefan. He was hurt and angry that I didn't confide in him. That my life was in danger and he didn't even know about it. He said he might never forgive me. He also said he was leaving.

He'd gotten a call and his father had taken a turn for the worse. Stefan planned on going from New York straight to the airport when he arrives home. He's going to Ireland.

Regardless of what I said to him in the bar before I went out to burn my past, I feel a hollow spot in my heart. I said I wasn't ready for a committed relationship. I never said I wanted him out of my life. And is Terry now out of my life? Tom has only added to the questions about who I am and why I am what I am. Why he was a werewolf, too. The Billingtons told me to start looking for answers in Nevada.

I made my travel arrangements before I left New York. I leave on Tuesday because I didn't know I'd be coming home the same day I left for Vermont. Maybe I can bump the arrangements up. I've decided to tell Cindy I'm going to Vegas to get away. She probably won't buy that, but I prefer her to concentrate on her new relationship rather than worry about what I'm up to. She insisted on sitting in the backseat with me. Now I feel her hand slide into mine. I squeeze and that's all we need. We're best friends. Werewolf, lesbian, whatever, we'll always be best friends.

I close my eyes and sleep when Natasha and Karen break the silence and discuss work. When I wake up, Cindy is helping me from the car in front of our building. Ralph rushes out with a luggage carrier.

"Didn't expect you back so soon," he says. "Lou, that young man named Rick told me that you said it was all right if he stayed in your apartment while you were gone. I couldn't get a hold of you to verify the information, but I know you let him stay there one other time, so I said okay."

I glance at the doorman's neck. No bite marks.

"Who's Rick?" Cindy asks.

"He's this really nice friend of Lou's," Natasha provides.

He's a freakin' vampire, I want to add, but don't.

"Where did you meet him?"

"It's a long story," I tell her. "Come on, let's say good night to Karen, she looks like she's about to drop."

We all give Karen a hug and send her on her way. Ralph brings the bags and we ride up to the tenth floor. I have no idea if Rick is having a vampire party in my apartment, so I knock. He answers, looking pale since he's not wearing makeup.

"Lou, what are you doing back?"

"Shoot got canceled." I take suitcases off the luggage carrier and shove them inside the door.

"Hi, Natasha," Rick says pleasantly, sipping wine from one of my crystal goblets.

"Hello, Rick," she responds. "This is Cindy, my partner."

"Hi, Rick," Cindy pipes up.

I close the door before the party spills into my apartment. "What are you doing here?"

Rick shrugs. "You said you'd be gone. I live on the streets, Lou. This is much nicer."

Out of habit, I move to small entry table where I usually set my beauty bag. I don't have it. Poof. It's gone. I feel naked. "I let you sleep here once. That was not an open invitation."

Rick walks over and pulls one of my bags farther into the living room. "I have problems now. I need sanctuary."

"What kind of problems?"

He opens his mouth and points to his ground-down fangs. "I can't eat the way I used to. My fangs aren't long enough to get penetration. Maria was very frustrated."

I'm relieved that Rick isn't capable of biting anyone at the moment. It makes me less nervous about him being here. "So, what are you going to do? You have to have blood to survive, right?"

"Right," he answers. "I only had one choice. I robbed a blood bank."

I blink at him. "And the blood is where?"

He smiles. "In your refrigerator."

Glancing at his glass, my lip curls. "And I suppose that is not wine."

"You can pretend it is if it makes you feel better."

"Out!" I point to the door.

"Come on, Lou. That's like declawing a cat and throwing it outside to fend for itself. I know you're not that cruel."

I'd like to be, but he's right, I'm not that cruel. "Okay, here's the deal. I'm leaving as soon as I get my flight changed. I'll be gone for a while. You can be the caretaker here, but no wild parties and no biting anyone, especially the next-door neighbors."

"I can't bite them," he reminds me. "I've been fixed."

He looks so pathetic about it that my heart softens. He did come to my rescue that night Terry was attacked by vampires, and he did lose two of his friends because of that. "Okay, help me with these suitcases."

After Rick helps me unpack; we both sit on the couch watching *Court TV*. It's not the same as having Cindy, but Cindy has a love life now. I guess Rick will be my new Egore for a while. Someone knocks on my door. I'm wearing my favorite pajamas and I suspect curiosity has finally got the better of Cindy.

When I open the door, it isn't Cindy standing there. It's Terry. He holds a stack of files.

"What are you doing here?"

"I know it's late." His gaze moves over me. "I guess your cell is out of commission. I tried to call first."

"My cell was in my beauty bag," I say. Nodding toward the files, I ask, "What's that?"

He shoves them toward me. "On the drive home, I got to thinking about what you said. You're right. I saw what I saw. It made me think about a few unsolved cases we have that seemed pretty weird at the time. I thought you might take a look at them and tell me if you get anything from them."

Lifting a brow, I ask, "You mean like that psychic crap?"

He smiles. "Yeah, like that psychic crap."

"Lou, I'm getting something to drink. Want anything?"

Rick's voice echoes behind me. Terry's smile fades. "Sorry. I didn't know you had company."

"Just have a friend over," I say.

Terry suddenly looks very coplike. "I'd better get home. Lots to do tomorrow. You might want to lay low for a while. I'm not sure I can keep your name out of this."

"I'm leaving town again as soon as possible," I assure him. "I have business in Nevada. I'll take the files with me, though, and look over them while I'm gone."

"Fine."

He starts to turn away. I feel more needs to be said between us. "Thanks for saving my life and stuff."

Facing me again, he shrugs. "Thanks for saving mine. I guess we're even."

I don't like being even. It sounds more like being over. "Well, technically, Dawson might have been dead before you shot him. I'm sure he would have been dead even if you hadn't shot him, so maybe you still owe me."

My teasing fails to get the expected smile from Terry. I suppose Terry's tired. I know I am. "Give me a call when you get back," he says, and turns and walks away.

I watch him move down the hall. I step out, thinking he'll turn and say something else. Like maybe now that the case is over, he'd like to get beat up again. He does turn. He does say something. Just not what I expect.

"Nice hickey."

He turns and keeps walking. I slap a hand to my neck. Rick knows what happened and how I got the marks on my neck. I didn't think hiding the hickey with a turtleneck beneath my pajamas was necessary with him. I haven't got a clue how to explain the hickey to Terry. I'm about lied out at the moment, and although he's becoming more receptive to the possibility that the world is not exactly as he thought it was, I think telling Terry a vampire bit me after I turned into a werewolf and got involved in a gang fight is a little too much too soon.

I go back inside, past Rick who sips another glass of "wine," and head for my bedroom. "Sheets and pillows are in the linen closet. I've had a long day. I'm turning in."

"Pleasant dreams," he calls.

For the first time in seven years, I think that might be possible. I think a lot of things are possible. My life isn't so bad. I have good friends, a new one who is a vampire but everyone has their problems. I'm still a supermodel and love my job. I have peace of mind now to know that even if I do turn into a werewolf, I won't kill someone just for the hell of it. I'm still working with a hot cop who will probably get over the fang hickey at some point, and at least now I have a clue where to begin looking for answers about my condition.

There are others like me. There are others who aren't like me, but I'm not alone. I'm not the only one, and somehow, that makes me feel better. Since Tom is dead, does that mean I can't be triggered again? But there are others, so perhaps I can't make that assumption just yet. The thing is, I didn't mind being a wolf so much. There are possibilities there that I haven't even begun to explore. What about the underworld? Can Rick get me in if I need to go searching for answers there, as well?

When I crawl beneath the covers, I admit that not everything in my life is rosy. Stefan's mad because I didn't tell him that I was in danger and is now on a plane traveling thousands of miles away from me. Terry is mad because I have a vampire hickey. And boy, is Morgan going to be pissed when he finds out I went to Nevada without him. I smile at the thought of his face when he realizes I've ditched him.

I see his face a few hours later in my dreams. Morgan doesn't turn into a monster. He doesn't try to kill me or anyone else. Oddly enough, we're making love.

Okay, we're not making love. We're having sex. Hot, sweaty, nasty, rough, fabulous sex. I can only view it as another nightmare. I'm just not one hundred percent certain that if I wake up screaming, it will be for the right reason. And I really, really, really hope that I am not psychic.